MW01275290

The Hidden Adventures of Sherlock Holmes

by

Bill Paxton

Illustrations by

Kerstin Paxton

Best Wishes Bill Paxton 1-14-2003

Published by
Omnibus Enterprises, LTD.
12907 East 36th Street Terrace
Independence, Missouri 64055
United States of America

Printed by
Community Press, Inc.
Chillicothe, Missouri 64601

Bill and Kerstin Paxton

DEDICATION

I sincerely dedicate this book to the memory of Sir Arthur Conan Doyle whose literary talents have given so much pleasure to so many of us.

I gratefully acknowledge the help of my wife Kerstin. I thank her for all of her efforts in editing the stories and furnishing illustrations. Most important has been her encouragement and loving friendship which has been my inspiration.

What a happy time I have had reviewing all Doyle's works and writing these stories. I hope that you, the reader, will enjoy them as much as I have.

Bill Paxton

Bill Paxton

INTRODUCTION

I have known Bill Paxton all of his life as he grew up in my neighborhood. Throughout his life, he has had a profound interest in world history, its events, its people, religion, contemporary and ancient philosophies, the occult and the supernatural. He successfully practiced law for 34 years in the city where he was born and retired in 1994. He received his Juris Doctorate from the University of Missouri in 1959 and as a member of the Association of Trial Lawyers of America attended their National College of Advocacy annually for eight years prior to retirement.

Bill has had many interests including his community where he took an active part in its improvement. As a young man he was very active in the Junior Chamber of Commerce (Jaycees) and served in many offices including National Director from the State of Missouri and First State Vice President. He received their local and state Distinguished Service Award in 1954. He served as first, second and third Vice President of the Independence Chamber of Commerce and declined to run for President. He served as Chairman and member of the Ethics Committee of the City of Independence for 3 years.

One of his interests is handwriting analysis and he graduated from the International Society of Graphoanalysists Advanced Course in Graphoanalysis in 1955 and published a booklet "Jury Selection by Graphoanalysis" by American Legal Tech, Inc., which was a forms company which he founded and served as president of. American Legal Tech, Inc. under his leadership published

Bill Paxton

forms as detailed worksheets in 58 areas of law to be utilized by paralegals which standardized information recall by the firm. He is credited by some as establishing the format for law clinics in the United States.

He was a member of the Independence and later the Eastern Jackson County Bar Association and served as their president and received their Distinguished Service Award in 1971.

Prior to graduation from law school, Bill was President and controlling stockholder of the Retail Merchants Credit Bureau in Independence and purchased the Kansas Credit Association and Credit Bureau of Clay County. Prior to that time he served as an investigator for Retail Credit Company now known as Equifax and managed the Independence, Missouri office which conducted the security investigations on prospective employees at the Lake City Arsenal. He also served three years in the Army Counter-intelligence Reserve as an agent.

All of his adolescent life he has enjoyed the Sherlock Holmes adventures as written by Sir Arthur Conan Doyle and one of his goals at retirement was to re-read all of his 56 stories and four books and use the well-known, highly regarded fictional characters Sherlock Holmes and Dr. Watson when taking off on his literary journey where he can combine his experience of legal deduction and his desire to explore the mysteries of the world.

I sincerely hope that you may enjoy these three stories and a novel as much as I have.

Respectfully

Susannah Gentry
Retired Editor of the Independence Examiner,
   now the Eastern Jackson County Examiner

Table of Contents

All That Glitters...

A Sherlock Holmes Adventure

by Paxton Franklin Watson

You knew my uncle John well, John H. Watson, MD, from Sherlock Holmes fame. I am his great nephew, Paxton Franklin Watson. Uncle John died on April 13, 1923. Sadly, he had no children and his last wife had predeceased him. His death was normal and his life had been a good one. Sherlock Holmes had died a normal death, two years before, at his bee-keeping villa in the country. Retirement which had been the goal for both of them had been a letdown from the adventurous life they were fortunate to have led. Mr. Holmes had his bee-keeping, violin and writing. Uncle John had his books and, of course, both had their pipes.

My grandfather, Thomas Alan Watson, uncle John's younger brother by seven years, was born on September 17, 1859, to loving parents in England. Grandfather came to the United States to study under a scholarship which he received from the Virginia Military Institute in Lexington, Virginia. He graduated with honors in 1878 while Uncle John was serving in Afghanistan in the Army Medical Department. Although they were very fond of each other as children growing up, their lives became separate as each grew into their own lives and professions. They were to see each other only once again when grandfather made a visit to the family home in England.

Grandfather took a job tutoring the 16 children of Andrew Jackson Paxton on a cotton plantation in Arcola, Mississippi, from the summer of 1882 until the fall of 1883. His employer encouraged him to go to law school and, to make this possible, made him a loan. Grandfather was graduated from Washington and Lee University with his L.L.B. degree. He set out for Missouri to practice law. Independence, Missouri, was the last outpost of civilization before the prairie and it was there that he set up his practice. It was from Independence that the Mormons started their trek for the Promised Land which they found in Utah. It was coincidence that uncle John's first case with Mr. Holmes involved this journey in "A Study In Scarlet".

It was in Independence, Missouri, that the Prophet of the Mormons, Joseph Smith, visioned that God would set his temple on judgement day and there is a lot here, the Temple Lot, where the temple is to be set down. As a very young man walking by this lot, I was careful to keep at least one eye to the sky just in case it was the time.

Grandfather married in 1885 to an Independence girl and they had one son, my father Jonathan Frazier Watson, born March 13, 1893. When uncle John died, grandfather inherited his estate which included the notes and papers located in dispatch boxes in the vaults of Cox's Bank at Charing Cross, London. With these papers passed the Holmes papers and, more particularly, his files. These were transferred to the United States and placed by grandfather in the Bank of Independence vaults. The papers passed to my father upon grandfather's death, and upon his death in 1937, passed to me. They were held by father's law partner in trust for me to be delivered at age twenty-one. I have always longed to get to those notes and have wondered about the untold but often mentioned stories. I have had no idea of what I might be able to make of them or whether I have the ability to tell them in an interesting, yet factual manner. Now at age sixty-six and retired after thirty-four years of law practice, I dived into Pandora's Box and what interesting mysteries I found. Please let me share this one with you.

I make my apologies up front. No one can tell of these great adventures as well as uncle John, but if they are going to be told, I had best be about it. We are invading the inner sanctum of these two colorful legends, which seem to come to life as if they were together still, solving the strange mysteries of mankind.

In reviewing the files, it appears obvious to me why many of these adventures could not be published at that time. But as Holmes would say, "Come, Watson, the game is afoot". So let's travel back to Baker Street to find one of the most baffling cases of Holmes' career, which I have titled, "All That Glitters, Is Not Gold."

We had just finished breakfast at Baker Street and Mrs. Hudson outdid herself with fresh French bread as well as the usual fare when the doorbell rang and a message was brought in to Holmes. Mrs. Hudson had taken it and with its delivery stated that the messenger would wait for a reply.

The letter bore the seal of the great Bank of England. Holmes opened it carefully and unfolded the singular blue sheet. After reading it, he handed it to me.

17 November, 1892

Dear Mr. Holmes:

I request an appointment at your flat at 2:00 P.M. on most urgent business. Please confirm with the messenger. If not convenient, give me your earliest available date and time.

Rodney Grope,
Solicitor General,
Bank of England

"My God, Holmes, the Bank of England needs your help! By all means, we must meet with their Solicitor General as he requests. It must be a serious matter by the tone of his letter. I wonder what kind of a problem that the most prestigious banking system in the world could have?"

"Yes, of course, we must, Mrs. Hudson. Tell the messenger that we shall look for Sir Rodney at 2:00 P.M. today."

"Watson, it is simplicity itself. Someone, somehow, has caused the Bank of England a loss. They have been robbed and they do not know who robbed them. They would not contact me, a criminal detective, if this had not been so. If they knew who did this to them, they would be in contact with Scotland Yard. Hence, they are bringing us a mystery to solve." Holmes' eyes were bright and piercing. What a change from the almost subdued, lethargic Holmes that I was eating breakfast with a few moments before. It had been a slow time for the great detective and, like a bloodhound on a scent, he was more alert than I had seen him for weeks. We adjourned to our rooms and he dressed for an excursion out into the typically British fall climate which was generally miserable.

Holmes returned from some mission, cold and damp, in time for late lunch. We had no sooner finished and retired when we could hear the door open and a small man probably five foot nine inches tall and rather rotund was ushered into the rooms. He promptly introduced himself with a firm handshake. "Rodney Grope, attorney for the Bank of England. We need your services, Mr. Holmes."

What I saw was a man in his early fifties with rat-like facial features and a sharp protruding nose, rather over-sized for his round face. His small, penetrating, intense eyes, bespectacled with gold frames, carefully examined both of us. He was dressed for a funeral in a dark grayish suit with vest and spats. He spoke in a grating voice, but succinctly and rather loudly. I wondered if he had a hearing problem. His speech was abrupt, much like a sergeant of the foot soldiers, and I would  have to say that it was a little offensive, but it may have been his demeanor. He was obviously all business but uneasy.

Holmes took his hand and, returning the grasp, introduced me.

"Mr. Holmes, I wanted this to be very confidential and I do not have authority to discuss this with anyone but you."

"Dr. Watson has been my comrade and aid these many years and he is the most confidential man that I know. I am sure that we will need his help to serve your needs. In fact, I must insist on it. If this problem is of such a magnitude to bring you to our door with this requirement, and a waiting carriage, I know that I will need help to resolve it if I can."

"Very well, Mr. Holmes, upon the accepted condition from both you and Dr. Watson that the matter must be treated with the greatest discretion and confidentiality and be kept in the utmost secrecy. The welfare of our realm depends on that."

"Agreed," said Holmes.

"Certainly," said I.

Holmes by gesture invited Sir Rodney to sit by the fire. Holmes had taken his coat, which was unusually dry considering the heavy rain, and hung it up.

In looking out the window, I confirmed the waiting carriage.

"Please, Sir Rodney, tell me of your problem," said Holmes.

Twisting in his overstuffed chair and, looking directly at Holmes, in his harsh voice he blustered "The Bank of England has been robbed!"

Holmes glanced at me with a wry smile beginning on his lips. Yes, the great detective had told me so. But I could hardly believe my ears. The Bank of England was the pillar of the world financial system. It was totally surrounded by secrecy. Its inner workings were virtually unknown to the outside world. How could this have happened?

Holmes, now the investigator, began. "Please give me the facts in as brief a form as you can and I will take notes. I may need to break in from time to time with some questions for better understanding."

"Two days ago, we had a request for the transfer of 360 gold bars from vault 136. In making the transfer, the stewards inadvertently scratched one of the sides of a bar and to his surprise a silver color showed from the bar. There was an immediate investigation. Governor Lord James Kensington, Deputy Governor Sir Charles Farthingham and the manager of the Note Department, Godfrey St. James, were all present. Each vault has three locks securing the doors when in use. Each of these gentlemen had a key to one of the locks and each is required to be present during the opening and to remain there during all activity that takes place in the vault until the door is again locked. The gold bar bore all of the markings required: it was numbered, hallmarked by the approved melter and assayer, which in this case was the Refinery of China, stating the quality of the gold in parts per thousand and its weight in carats, in this case 375.54 carats."

"How many approved melters and assayers of gold are there?" Holmes directed.

"There are 49 approved melters and assayers in the world located in 14 countries. This approval is necessary for acceptance of the gold in the banking marketplace of the world."

"Thank you, please continue," mumbled Holmes who was absorbed in his note-taking.

"The gold was then returned to the vault, except the bar with the silvered scratch, the locks were replaced and the Governor, Deputy Governor and Manager of the Note Issue Department adjourned. The workers were admonished to say nothing of what had occurred. It was at that point that I was asked to join the group in the conference room. It was decided that the bank's own metallurgist, William McBeth, make a complete investigation of the contents of Vault 136 and report back to the group as soon as possible.

McBeth was locked in the vault to make his investigation and after 5 hours was able to report back to our committee that 140 of the bars, all with proper markings coinciding with our inventory were lead bars with gold plate and 220 of the bars were authentic."

"What test did he make to determine this?", Holmes inquired.

"He used a jeweler's solvent," Sir Rodney's raspy voice replied.

"How much does a bar of gold weigh?"

"A gold bar to meet the 'good delivery' standards of the London market must be at least 995 parts per thousand pure gold, containing between 350 and 430 troy ounces of fine gold."

"How many ounces of gold is the bank missing, Sir Rodney?"

"Exactly 56,095.116 ounces, Mr. Holmes."

"What's its value?"

"Today's market 238,276.9 pounds."

"Good grief," said I, who was living mostly on a disability pension. I hardly believed that there was that much real money in the world.

"How do you know that there is not a greater theft?"

Sir Rodney's raspy voice continued, "Our metallurgist has begun the checking of all gold bars in the bank and has completed the west wing where this theft occurred under the same procedures that I have outlined."

"Were all of the lead bars from the same melter and assayer?", the investigator queried.

"No, there was no pattern. They were from all over the world."

"Do you have any idea when this exchange occurred?"

"No, Mr. Holmes," grated a dejected and desperate Sir Rodney, "that is why I am here. Will you help us?"

"Yes, it is an intriguing and puzzling state of affairs. We'll do it, hey Watson?"

"Yes", said I.

"What will you need from us, Mr. Holmes?"

"We will need to meet with the Governor, Deputy Governor and Note Department Manager tomorrow. Oh, yes, we should require a retainer of 3,000 pounds."

Holmes stood up abruptly, putting out his hand and said, "We will see you at 9:00 A.M." Sir Rodney put on his coat and descended the steps to his waiting carriage.

No sooner had the door loudly closed, when I addressed the great detective "what about all of this 'art for art's sake'. It is not like you Holmes." I was referring to his standard line when the subject of money and fee comes up with a client.

Holmes smiled wryly, "Who can better afford it? This case will take far more time that you can imagine and much by way of expenses. We have a real mystery here, Watson. Now, it's time for a little culture. I'll be at the library and should I be late, I'll see you in the morning." With that he put on his coat and famous two-bill cap, grabbed his pipe and disappeared into the rain.

When I descended the stairs refreshed, there Holmes was reading over some notes.

"Good morning, Watson," retorted Holmes, and went back to his reading.

"What have you learned?", I eagerly inquired.

"Too complex as yet to know much about anything. I have just learned a great deal about the building of the Bank of England. Not sure what part it will play, but it is part of our groundwork. Interested?"

"Yes", I said as I began my breakfast. Breakfast was not a handicap for Holmes as he had already finished.

Holmes leaned back in his chair with pipe in hand, heavy aromatic smoke swirling around his head, and he began a most interesting narrative: The Bank of England was formed by Parliament in 1694 to fund the national debt of England and to raise funds to allow the English government and William III to wage war in the Low Countries. A Royal Charter allowed the bank to operate as a joint-stock company. A loan to the government was the origin of its establishment. The loan which was 1,200,000 pounds was subscribed in little more than ten days between Thursday June 21 and Monday July 2, 1694. On Tuesday July 10th, the subscribers appointed Sir John Houblon Governor . The first 24 Directors were elected on July 11, 1694. In a nutshell, Watson, the Bank of England was, and is, a private company authorized to issue notes to the extent of the government debt and issue notes for the value of the bullion that it possesses. The stockholders elect the Directors, Governor and Deputy Governor. The theft of this gold means that there are 237,872.88 pounds in notes, paper money, issued by the Bank of England which is not supported by gold. The amount is insignificant compared to the assets of the bank, but the principle is unmistakable. The bank is in violation of the Act of 1844 which established the bank as we know it now."

Holmes continued with a brief summary of its operation sites: "It began business at Mercer Hall in Cheapside on July 27, 1694; moved to Grocer's Hall in Poultry in 1694; then began a building on Threadneedle Street at the present location on August 3, 1732. After its completion, the bank began business there on June 5, 1734. The bank had purchased the town house and garden of its first Governor, Sir John Houblon. The chosen architect was George Sampson, who oversaw the building of the central part of the structure as we now know it. His past is interesting in that he had held the post of Clerk of Works at both the Tower of London and Sommerset House. Very little else is known about him.

On June 5, 1734, they began business. The first major expansion was to the east and the architect for the bank was Sir Robert Taylor. The building to the west of the original structure was occupied by the St. Christopher-le-Stocks church which overlooked the bank.

In 1780, the Goden Riots occurred during which the bank had been besieged by the mob. This poised an obvious threat to the security of the bank should there be future disturbances. An Act of Parliament approved the acquisition of the church and thus begins the last acquisition of the premises now occupied by the Bank of England. In 1782, the Church was acquired and demolished. Architect Taylor began this new construction of the west wing and it was nearly completed at the time of his death in 1788. Sir John Soane became the architect and continued in that capacity until 1833. I rather doubt that the bank has an architect on its staff as the building has been completed for over fifty years. I believe that the bank has a consultant architectural firm. It is imperative that we secure these plans and drawings. We must have them and the architect's notes and perhaps photos if we are going to understand this mystery."

"Well", said I, "I have certainly had my history lesson and I doubt if my eggs and sausage will ever digest. I'm impressed, but I can't understand how this will help us in the case of the lead bars."

"Time to get ready for our adventure", said Holmes, bolting from his chair. The electricity in his manner was almost child-like and infectious.

At 9:00 A.M. promptly, we were ushered into the Court room where the Directors meet. It would befit a palace. A huge room with a long, highly polished, rectangular oak table, surrounded by 37 red leather, upholstered chairs, positioned beside it . The chair at the head of the table had a higher, commanding back. The brads which held the leather to the chairs appeared to be made of gold. Three large beautiful chandeliers adorned the ceiling. The walls were paneled and appeared to be made of cherry wood. It was located in the center part of the building behind the main hall. Three distinguished appearing gentlemen were there with Sir Rodney and he promptly made the introductions.

"Mr. Holmes, this is our Bank Governor, Lord James Kensington, and this is his Deputy, Sir Charles Farthington, and the manager of the Note Department, Mr. Godfrey St. James, and bank notes totalling 3000 pounds as you requested."

I looked at Holmes as he accepted the notes and had the urge to shake my head or pointed finger, but the dignity of our hosts quickly put that feeling to rest.

The Governor and his Deputy were dressed in formal wear: black tuxedo, white tie and embroidered cummerbund. Mr. St. James was fitted in a brown Scottish tweed business suit. The formal dress surprised me for a moment, but then I realized that these gentlemen met during their working day with the heads of state, including kings and queens. It was indeed a proper attire. All of them were stern and perplexed, but Mr. James was so nervous that he exhibited a twitch in his upper lip and his eyes reflected great strain.

Lord Kensington was a man close to 70, well fed and rounded and his fat face carried red glowing checks. His hair and full beard were gray and well manicured. He reminded me of an aging Prince Albert. His manner was extremely gracious, but he was embarrassed that this situation has occurred while he was Governor. He probably had six feet of height in his youth, but was now stooped forward and his shoulders were some- what slouched. He spoke slowly and distinctly in a deep mellow voice.

Sir Charles was a slender man in his mid fifties, his hair was strikingly black, his face clean and well shaven, and his features were intent, but not otherwise remarkable except for his large big brown eyes that seemed to never blink. They appeared to come from the 16th century where the royal figures were dominated by large eyes.

Mr. St. James appeared to be a nervous type of man. Perhaps abrupt would describe him, a little like Sir Rodney. He was trim and athletic, closer to the height of Lord Kensington. Mustached with brown, unmanageable hair which was very full. His nose was rather flat, like that of a boxer. He had thin lips which exhibited a slight twitch.

Lord Kensington bade us to be seated at the table and he took his high place at its head. "Gentlemen, this is a grave day for the Bank of England. This loss of gold makes our Note Department balance in violation of the Act of 1844. To put it simply, we have over 200,000 pounds in notes without the gold bullion to back them up. We have decided not to bring the matter to the Directors until we know what has happened to our gold.

I have personally transferred securities and notes to the bank as a loan to bring the account in balance. None of us have any idea of how or when this could have happened. We are utterly shocked and compromised," said the Governor, shaking his head in despair.

"Have you contacted Scotland Yard?", asked Holmes, obviously knowing what that answer would be.

"No, Mr. Holmes, we have not and do not intend to do so at this point. The Bank of England, because of its place in world economy, cannot afford even a hint of this type of scandal. We have come to you, who we believe to be the world's greatest detective to sort this thing out. We will follow your advice and will make ourselves available for any help we can give you," stated Lord Kensington.

"Does the bank have an architect on its staff?"

"No, it has not been required as the principal building occurred during the time that Sir John Soane was our architect. That has been over 50 years ago."

"Do you have the building plans used in the building of this building?"

"Yes, we have all of the plans, drawings and specifications of our architects through Sir John. They are kept in the archives."

"It will be imperative that I have immediate access to those records."

"Of course. Sir Rodney will make them available to you any time you want. We do ask that they not be removed from this building and that no notes or drawings of any kind concerning our operation be transferred from the bank.

You can understand why this security measure is required. Further, only you are to have this access. You are asked not to discuss any elements of these plans or the bank's problems with anyone outside of this room. Is that understood, Mr. Holmes?"

"Yes, of course, I quite understand, Lord Kensington."

I nodded affirmance.

"What is the most recent report from your metallurgist? I believe his name was William McBeth."

Sir Rodney gratedly replied "The same! We are now half finished and no other lead bars have been found. It appears that vault 136 is the only place where this substitution has occurred. We have discretely checked with the major banks doing business in London to see if any of these bars have been presented to them for credit and none of them have been. The banks record any transfer by melter, assayer and number. We had them check back to the time that the gold was moved into vault 136 after the inventory of 1844."

"Gentlemen, I can tell you with certainty, based upon my preliminary research, that the gold has been removed and melted down by one of the 49 authorized melters and assayers. I believe that they have been recast as tola bars weighing 3.75 ounces or pocket size kilo bars so popular in Switzerland, France, Beirut and Kuwait, all certified. These bars were melted and assayed by the Thompson Motherhead Group by our thief."

"How can you possibly know that, Mr Holmes?", Sir Rodney sarcastically quipped.

"Simplicity itself, Sir Rodney. A bar of gold weighs some 33 pounds, give or take a few ounces and by simple mathematics we are talking of 5,280 pounds of gold. These bars are simply too heavy to transport far and are immediately traceable in that form. They are as absolutely identifiable as if a person had his name tattooed upon his forehead. As these bars were not surrendered to any of the major gold trading banks in London and because of their traceability, it is most probable that they were not surrendered to the banks on the continent for the same reason. As the thief did not know when this theft would be discovered, he or she did not want to transfer an identified gold bar. Gold would be of no value if not converted into currency so it could be used. In order to convert this gold into currency it would have to have been certified by one of the 49 approved melters and assayers when it was reduced to a small size for its negotiation. The Thompson Motherhead Group represents six of these approved assayers and they are the only one who has a refinery in the London market. This gentlemen is where your gold has gone. The question is who, how and when?"

"Of course," exclaimed the Governor. "I have heard of your powers of logic and deduction as chronicled by Dr. Watson, but I am amazed at its simplistic and swift result. I can see that we have secured the right man to help us."

"I will need to have access to the personnel files and smelting records of the Thompson Motherhead Group. Can you help me do this?"

Sir Charles first entered the conversation, "My brother-in-law is the superintendent of this facility which is located on Hatton Garden. Our relationship has been exceptionally good and, even though there is confidentiality involved here, I believe that he would look the other way and accept my explanation that we must have access to these records for the sake of our realm. It is also true that, if we went to Scotland Yard, they would make him produce them."

"Splendid!", said Holmes. "Please set up this appointment for as early a time as you can. Now, gentlemen, let's take a look at vault 136 and the lead bars."

Sir Rodney excused himself as an unnecessary party, delivering a list of the lead bars, fully described and identified, to Holmes.

I couldn't believe my eyes. Gold everywhere! Stacks of gold! The gold cellar is what they call it and what a huge place it was. The outer walls were all made up of cells approximately 10 ft by 10 ft with a little extra for the separation between the concrete tiles which made up the floor, and in the center of the room there was a repeat of this with two cells back to back with 10 feet in between to allow for the movement of bullion carts from Bartholomew Lane. One-inch wrought iron rods, approximately 1 1/2 inches apart, enclosed each of these cells with a large door, probably five feet wide, and hinged by three large wrought iron hinges. The locking hinges controlled a large iron bar which went into the metal door frame of the other side and was held in place by the locking device. There were three of these devices, each with their own large lock.

The vault number was on the front of the door with a complete list of the inventory of its contents. Out of curiosity, I looked at the inventory which simply referred to the 160 bars separately without further identification other than "special bars".

Vault 136 was well lighted, but you could see where the Murdock gas lights had been previously installed and the brass pipes with perforated tips were still in place.

The floor was made of concrete, one-foot square tiles concreted together. St. James explained to me that, because of the great weight of the stacked gold bars, the concrete needed to be able to shift at the tile seams.

When we arrived at vault 136, our hosts took out their keys and the door was opened. Immediately, Holmes began by inspecting the lead bars, and then the gold bars. This cell, or vault if you will, was located in the west corner of the gold cellar so that wrought iron bars were only on two sides. I should add that the wrought iron bars were set in concrete. The gold had been stored in the center of the room in 12 piles as they were stacked one on the other like children's blocks with about one foot or one block separating them. Each contained 30 bars of gold except for the lead bars. The twelve piles were three across and four deep as you entered the vault. There was a six-inch drain in the southwest corner covered by a cast iron cover.

Holmes went to the entrance log which clearly showed that, since the original inventory in 1844, except for cleaning each four months, there had been no withdrawals or handling of the gold bars until this discovery entry. He confirmed from this log that there had been no repair of any kind in this vault, except for running the electric wire through the cell and the installation of an electric light near the old gas jet on the south wall. He then took out his pen knife and went to all fours, eyeglass in hand, and began scrapping concrete between the concrete tiles and examining the drain. He asked for and received 100 envelopes and then he proceeded to take scrapings from around each block which he numbered, beginning on the northwest corner, from one to one hundred. He scraped and inserted bits of concrete into numbered envelopes. He carefully examined the mortar, block and seam, mumbling to himself as he methodically inspected this flooring. He looked much like a small child who could only crawl. Then, after about an hour of this exhibition, he abruptly rose to his feet and said, "That will do."

Thereafter, Holmes took one of the opened locks and knocked on each of the concrete blocks. There was no resonant hollow sound. He requested and received a small step ladder.

He then examined the two solid walls by knocking the lock against the stone wall with the same result. How his eyes sparkled in their intent concentration! Holmes moved as if he were a young man in love. His attention turned to the wrought iron bars concreted into the floors and ceiling. He examined each point carefully.

Holmes then inquired of the three bank officers as to security procedures as it existed in 1844 to now. It was St. John who responded. "Our guards patrol in pairs. They make their rounds every hour and make their report to the officer of the watch. Any personnel seen in the gold cellar were reported and it was the officer's duty to check out the reason for their presence. It is mainly for fire but they visually inspect as they walk through the corridors. Our real fear is from without."

"Thank you, gentlemen," said Holmes obviously in his deep inner search. "I would like to be directed to the archives and you, my dear doctor, can return to your practice."

St. James quickly retorted that he would escort Mr. Holmes to the archives and give the necessary instructions to the custodian and I was escorted out. I thought to myself, what a fascinating adventure this had been. It was absolutely inconceivable that this had occurred. And yet, there we were in the gold cellar of the Bank of England with 160 gold plated lead bars.

It was dinner time when Holmes returned to Baker Street. He had a wry little smile of self-fulfillment on his face and I knew that he had had a good day.

"My God, Holmes, you look like the cat who just ate the canary! Is there something that you want to share with me?", I quipped.

As we began to enjoy our beef Wellington, Holmes smilingly said, "How is your history of London, Watson?"

"Good," said I, and then I asked him to continue with his game. It was obvious that his game was afoot.

"Did you ever hear of the New River aqueduct?"

"Holmes, the only aqueduct that I am familiar with was the River Leet Aqueduct built for Plymouth by Sir Francis Drake around 1500."

"The New River aqueduct was built in 1609 to bring water some 38 miles into London. It has, of course, long since been abandoned. In reviewing the drawings and file of Architect George Sampson who built the first Bank of England, I found that the sewer plans were drawn in great detail. This was probably because of his past employment as Clerk of the Works for the Tower of London which is not far from Threadneedle Street. These plans clearly show this aqueduct passing by the west side of the present site of the bank building and then veering east to the Tower of London. This aqueduct at that point was three feet by three feet and was covered by earth more than four feet below Princes Street. It had been abandoned for over 100 years, at the time of the construction of the last wing of the bank. It was cheaper to lay the pipe rather than dig into this stone aqueduct. Hey, what we have, my dear Watson, is a tunnel just outside the west wall of the bank which goes for some 38 miles. It is clear to me that this was used to remove the bars."

"But how?", I exclaimed.

"If you recall from your history lesson on the building of the Bank of England, Watson, the last construction site was the St. Christopher-le-Stocks church after the Goden riots in 1782. Except for the riots that occurred there, not much is known about the church. The bank architect, Sir Robert Taylor, built this west wing and it was near completion at the time of his death in 1788. Sir John Soane finished it. Taylor's records give us some layout of the old church and, surprisingly enough, there was a wine cellar located just below good old vault 136. This cellar was below the basement level of the church and secreted by a hinged door in the floor with steps descending down into it. It is my bet that it was a small room used for the storage of wine and food for the priests who lived in the rectory. I need to complete some experiments to confirm this. But if

I am right, Watson, this wine cellar was sealed off at the time of the last construction, a connecting passageway was made to the aqueduct and, at some time after the gold was transferred to vault 136, the theft began. The superintendent of the construction was a man by the name of Reginald Thorpe. Strangely enough, the assistant super, Thomas Harcore, died in an accident that occurred during the latter days of construction. Something about a stone falling on his head from above. It takes one back in time to the pirate lore, 'dead men tell no tales'. I cannot conceive of this being hidden without the knowledge and authority of Thorpe as well as Harcore. I want to confirm this theory further after dinner Watson."

"Holmes, you never cease to amaze me. I do not know how you are able to dig up all of these facts and then put them together in such a logical form. Amazing, sir, absolutely amazing!"

"Elementary, my dear Watson. When you have a problem without a solution, it is because you do not have the facts or because you have not applied practical logic to the facts you have."

The beef Wellington having been completely annihilated, we lighted our pipes and adjourned to our rooms where Holmes immediately went to his little laboratory in the corner of our sitting room and started through the envelopes that he had taken from the bank, filled with his scrapings. After about two hours, Holmes let out a cry in excitement. "I have it! My theory is correct."

With that, Holmes came and sat beside the fire where I was reading my medical journal.

"How ingenious! I believe that Thorpe and Harcore covered this old wine seller whose steps ascended to the level of the gold cellar after first tunneling to the old aqueduct. The aqueduct at this point was three feet by three feet so that a man could easily crawl through it. They then found a place, probably along Princess Street, to make entry so that they would have access to this room. The floor was braced at the top of the stairs, probably with iron plate, and then covered with dirt and rock for the concrete tile. Between these tiles, in the south west corner of vault 136, is where the drain is located. Between blocks 91 and 92 precisely. This drain is covered by a perforated round cast iron cover, held in place by gravity, which fits into the opening for the drain. When this cover is pushed up from below from the old wine cellar, it would give our thief access to the sounds of the room and with a periscope of small mirrors, our thief could see and study the movement and times of the security patrol. Having removed the plate and dirt from beneath the tiles from the old wine cellar, specifically two of them, blocks 91 and 92, the thief would be able to raise up blocks 91 and 92 from below, sliding them to the side, enter into the vault and remove the gold bars. First he would make tracings of their respective indicia, then mold the replacement bars and then exchange the gold plated lead bars with the originals. The two tiles would give a two-foot square to enter into the vault. The tiles would have been braced from below so that they could be replaced after each visit with some sort of lipping. The thief replaced the seam around the blocks on each entry, but probably made only a few entries: one to get the tracings and another to exchange the bars. The thief would then remove the gold bars to the safety of the cellar for later transfer and smelting. The drain was removed from below and replaced after the mission was accomplished on each visit. The drain pipes were larger on one end and easily fit into the section of lead pipe below it. A twelve-inch pipe was common for this stacking and it could easily be taken apart and reassembled to function properly. Actually, gravity would hold them together. Thorpe and Harcore were familiar with the storage practices of the bank and were safe to choose the corner. The first problem was that Harcore knew of the plan and had to be eliminated, and the second one was that vault was not used until 1844. Considering the years, I believe that Reginald Thorpe is dead, but that he left this secret and plan with someone who has completed the plot. This might well be a son. I should not be the least surprised to find that someone by the name of Thorpe was in supervision at the Thompson Motherhead Group in 1844. I believe we will find that Thorpe was a qualified assayer by profession."

"How can you possibly come to that conclusion?", I exclaimed.

"Elementary, my dear Watson. The concrete used to replace the seam on slabs 91 and 92 was Portland Cement. The entrance records confirmed that there has been no construction in Vault 136, except for the installation of electric lights. This building was completed in 1788. Portland Cement was invented by Joseph Aspdin, a builder in Leeds, who obtained a patent for it in 1824. This is usually made from a calcareous material such as limestone or chalk and from alumina-and silica-bearing material such as clay or shale, and it is easily identifiable under the microscope. The manufacturing process essentially consists of grinding the raw materials, mixing them intimately in specified proportions and burning them in a large rotary kiln, where the material sinters and partially fuses into balls known as clinker. The clinker is cooled and ground to a fine powder and gypsum is added to control the speed of setting when the cement is mixed with water. Simply put, when the thief was finished with the theft, he concreted the space around 91 and 92 using a cement that appears like the other cement but has exquisite characteristics and which was not invented until 1824. We know that the theft occurred after 1844 when the first bars were placed in vault 136 and there had been no construction, except for the installation of electricity. It is below blocks 91 and 92 that the stairway is located and it probably has been filed in."

"How in the world could they concrete the surface and get out of that vault?", I exclaimed.

"Watson, if you will recall, the drain entered the vault between slabs 91 and 92. The drain was made of lead and had a lip which held it up. It is undoubtedly in sections. The top section could be pushed up from below and, when replaced, would be held in place by gravity. Probably the lipped section was not longer than three to four inches. When the thief had completed the removal of the 160 gold bars, he moved one of the blocks carefully into place from below. From the open space of the other block, he cemented the replaced block on three sides. He then placed a strip of concrete around the opening which he had been working from and then, reaching out of his hole, raised up the last block and lowered it into place. The thief reached up through the six-inch drain cavity and smoothed out the seams of the last slab and the joining area between the two. He cleaned up his mess with rags and water from the drain and replaced the drain pipe into its hole. At that point, he replaced the wrought iron drain cover. The pipe sections were assembled in sections until it was functional. The pipe was tapered so that the smaller end would fit into the mouth of the next pipe below it. That basically has to be the way it was accomplished. We must fall back upon the old axiom that, when all other contingencies fail, whatever remains, however improbable, must be the truth. Here we had to have an entrance into vault 136 other than by the door."

"You never cease to amaze me, Holmes. I just don't know how you do it. You make it so simple and yet everything has escaped me."

"In fairness, my dear Watson, you did not have access to the building records and without them I would not have arrived at these conclusions."

"Let's celebrate with a glass of sherry before bed, hey Watson." With that, Holmes headed for the decanter containing my favorite beverage.

We were having breakfast when there was a knock on the door and Mrs. Hudson came with a message from Sir Charles. It was the same Bank of England envelope and blue paper confirming an appointment at 2:00 P.M. with Charlton Thomas, Superintendent of the London Branch of the Thompson Motherhead Group. Sir Charles had suggested a meeting at the bank at 1:45 P.M. He further requested confirmation by the messenger.

Holmes turned the letter over and scribbled "Imperative that I meet with you, Lord Kensington, Godfrey St. James and Sir Rodney an hour before leaving for the meeting with your brother-in-law. Unless I hear otherwise, we will see you at 12:45 P.M. at the bank. Sherlock Holmes."

He then passed the letter, back in its original envelope, to Mrs. Hudson for return to the messenger.

After breakfast, Holmes put on his hat and coat and left instructions for an early lunch and off he went on his errands, one of which, I was sure, was a visit to his own bank.

Luncheon over, carriage waiting, off we went to the Bank of England. We were promptly ushered into the Court Room much as before. We took our same seats at the grand table and Holmes began to relate his findings and conclusions. St. James, with the Governor's consent, would exhume this wine cellar. Then Holmes related what he anticipated finding at the Thompson Motherhead Group. He began his evaluation and his conclusions:

"This morning I found where Reginald Thorpe had lived and it was on Princess Street about four blocks from the bank. I have found an older address and then the latest one in the records of Sir Robert Taylor. During the six years of construction, Thorpe had changed his address to Princess Street. He lost his first wife early on and had taken on a younger Scottish woman to wed. Around 1800, give or take a few years, a son, Macdonald Thorpe, was born to them. Macdonald was raised in the goldsmithing trade working first for one and then another of the five major goldsmiths of London. He then went to work for the Thompson Motherhead Group where he rose in responsibility. Reginald Thorpe died sometime around 1820 and his wife ten years later. Macdonald was living in the Princess Street home until about 40 years ago, sometime around

1852. The house had mysteriously been destroyed by fire and Macdonald was never seen again. Interesting that he did not marry here and he absolutely disappeared. I believe that we will find that he was night manager of the melter. He brought the gold bars to his home, then to the refinery, causing the gold to be made into a reduced and popular size and negotiated them from his employer to the other banks with branch offices in London and specifically the Riksbank of Sweden, Bank of Hamburg, Bank of Amsterdam, Bank of Venice, Bank of France and Bank of Germany. These large banks dealt heavily with gold bullion and would convert the gold into any currency of the world. The gold could be deposited using a false identification in London and with the receipt and other identification could be collected in Stockholm, Paris, or wherever the bank had offices. I believe that we will find that the gold was transferred by the Thompson Motherhead Group to these banks to the deposit of a fictitious client by Macdonald and that all traces of these numbered bars are gone. Macdonald collected these receipts for this fictitious client, paid the melters' fee and went to the home bank to collect his money, either in gold or currency of any country. I believe that this occurred during a ten-year period. The lead bars had been fabricated with the exact numbers of your gold bars which would be easy for a person with Macdonald's qualifications to do. We will find 160 of such instances and I believe that Macdonald used the same fictitious names from time to time. I believe that we will find that Macdonald has been gone from his employer since about 1854. If he were alive, he would be about 90 years old. I do not think we will ever find a trace of him or his whereabouts. He could be anywhere. Now the reason for this depressing story. I feel that the Thompson Motherhead Group is responsible for what has happened to you. Rather than being secretive with your brother-in-law, Sir Charles, I feel that we should make him aware of what has occurred. Their own records will verify the facts that I have stated. This would not have occurred if their security were efficient. It is my feeling that they should pay your loss in kind, 56,095.116 ounces of gold plus the fee that you have paid to me. They cannot survive a scandal. Their business consists of 12.2% of all of the certified melters and assayers in the world. You should make demand for this sum."

The Governor rose and asked my friend and me to step from the room for a few minutes and, of course, we obliged.

In about 15 minutes, we were summoned back to the Court Room.

"Mr. Holmes," said the Governor, "we want to thank you for your help and you also, Dr. Watson. You are right, this really becomes a family matter and one that Sir Charles will take up with Charlton Thomas, and we will relay your story. We want to keep this matter to ourselves as much as we can. We will let you know if we need you further. "

The four gentlemen stood and warmly shook our hands. Their appreciation and gratitude was so obvious. We then returned to Baker Street.

Two days later, a message arrived from the bank. It was addressed to Holmes with the same indicia as the first letter and with it came a large bar of gold-plated lead with all indicia and hallmarks removed.

Mr. Holmes,

You were absolutely correct. We have found the wine cellar and the tunnel to the aqueduct. They had been partially destroyed but appeared exactly as you described. Macdonald Thorpe had left his employer in 1854 and has not been seen nor heard of since. And, by the way, all of the gold has been replaced. I cannot tell you how pleased we are with your prompt resolution of our problem. They even paid your fee. The lead bar is your souvenir.

Your humble servant,

Rodney Grope,
Solicitor General,
Bank of England

"Watson, alchemists have been trying to make lead into gold since the beginning of time. Looks like Macdonald Thorpe did it! We would have a hard time ever convincing Macdonald that 'crime doesn't pay', hey Watson."

Paxton Franklin Watson

The Macabre Affair

A Sherlock Holmes Adventure

by Paxton Franklin Watson

Chapter I

THE QUEST

It is my pleasure to relate to you another great adventure of Sherlock Holmes and my great Uncle John, Dr. Watson, reconstructed from the notes from Sherlock Holmes and the papers from the vaults of Cox's bank at Charing Cross which I have inherited.

A cheery, crackling fire warmly burned in the rooms on Baker Street occupied by Holmes and me for these many years. It was late in February, 1896. Winter was beginning to contemplate its demise and spring was too bashful to make its appearance. Mrs. Hudson's dinner settled comfortably in my innards and I was at home sitting with Holmes by the friendly fire in my favorite chair, engaged in my favorite pastime, reading a medical journal.

Holmes was intensely devouring a journal of some kind. Pipe in hand, smoke swirling about his head, he seemed to be talking to the author. "Hmm, good," I heard him utter. "Right, I have always thought so." Finally, out of a distracted curiosity, I inquired, "Holmes, what in the world are you reading?"

"Watson, this is an English translation of a publication called L' Année Psychologiqué, which translates into 'The Psychological Year' and is published by Alfred Binet who founded the first psychological laboratory. I really should say that he is the Director of this laboratory and uses this paper to publish the results of their studies. A most intriguing gentleman. He first studied law, then medicine and then psychology which apparently is where his love is. He is working on a testing system to evaluate the intelligence of children. He has always been interested in graphology and is convinced that graphology has potentialities as a technique for personality testing. As you have chronicled in your notes, I have been very interested in this subject and it has been useful to me in my deduction. I believe that certain character traits can be determined by strokes of handwriting. This is why I have kept all of my notes, correspondence and data and I have catalogued them by the similarity of crime and the handwriting of the culprit. I feel confident that I can tell certain character traits by observing a person's handwriting. It is the only waking manifestation that we exhibit that is not controlled to some extent by our mind. We do it without thinking or covering up our real personality. Dr. Binet has just conducted an experiment with seven graphologists at his laboratory at Sorbonne. He secured thirty-six one-page samples of handwriting from 18 successful men and let these graphologists tell him which were which. All seven were more than 50% correct. One of these graphologists had a score of 92 percent correct. Two of these graphologists came from Italy, one from Germany, two from Switzerland, one from Austria and one from France. It was the German who stole the show. A man by the name of Karl Knoepker who teaches graphology at the University of Leipzig. He holds a

doctorate degree in graphology which is rather uncommon. In England we really do not recognize it as a profession."

"Balderdash," said I. "You would be better off with a gypsy fortune teller or tea leaf reader. I think both you and Dr. Binet have lost your senses if you believe this."

"Well, Watson," retorted Holmes with a wry smile on one side of his mouth, "I will save my conclusion and demonstration until after we have met with Drs. Binet and Knoepker. What about a trip to Paris and Leipzig?"

"A trip, demonstration or papal decree will not change my mind, but a holiday sounds good. My associate can handle my practice. Maybe it will hurry spring or at least fill its indecision."

"Good, I will make arrangements. I will send telegrams off tomorrow to both of these gentlemen and inquire whether they will see us."

After a toast to our adventure with my favorite sherry, we retired.

Two days later, Holmes received telegrams back confirming our visit to Paris and Leipzig. He had scheduled two days in Paris and three days in Leipzig. He had inquired whether an interpreter would be required and, to his pleasure and mine as well, both of these gentlemen were very proficient in English.

The following Monday, fully packed, we left by train for Dover, then by boat to Calais, France, and then by train to Paris. What a gorgeous day! It was as if the goddess of spring were teasing us. It was as if she were saying, "Now that you are leaving, I will show you what you will miss." We left London at 8:00 A.M. The sun was in command of the cloudless sky, but the briskness of the air reminded us of this tease.

Holmes was in a cheerful, condescending mood and extremely alert as we boarded the train. He had brought a briefcase full of papers to occupy his time. Frankly, I was looking forward to enjoying the scenery and view. Holmes had thoughtfully booked a private compartment so we sat there together facing each other. The hissing steam and the clank clank of the track resounding on the iron wheels of our carriage told us of our movement. It would easily put anyone to sleep and, having qualified, I fell almost immediately into a deep slumber. I awoke just as we were pulling into the station. Holmes' papers were scattered over the seat and he continued to have the same aura of blissfulness.

"Good nap?", he asked.

"Extremely good," said I.

"Ready to go to sea?"

"More of an infantryman myself, Holmes. I have to admit that I do not enjoy any journey by sea and particularly across this treacherous English Channel. But with steam ships this crossing will only take a short time, so I guess I will be jolly all right."

"We should be in Paris by late afternoon. I have billeted us at the Hotel d'Alsace. It is an exquisite setting and it is on the right bank, close to the Sorbonne. It is quite a contrast from our bachelor quarters in Baker Street, but the change will do us good and it is a holiday...right, Watson?"

"By all means, Holmes."

We transferred with ease to the docks and boarded the "Prince of Wales" bound for Calais, France. The trip was uneventful and we found ourselves on a fast train for Paris. Customs was quite informal and we had no difficulty locating our luggage and transporting ourselves to the Paris-bound steam engine. The countryside moving past us had a mesmerizing effect and the next thing I was aware of was passing Amiens which was about half-way to Paris, then St. Denis just outside Paris.

"Watson, it will be quite an experience to see the Eiffel Tower. I was here while it was being built in 1887, but have not seen its completion. It was finished the last of March of 1889 for the Paris Universal Exhibition as a memorial to the French Revolution. Gustave Eiffel, the engineer who designed and built it, really made it a monument to engineering, but there is no reason that it cannot serve two purposes. Did you know that there were 12,000 parts? It is called the 300 Meter Tower and is 984 feet high."

"It has been the talk of Europe. What an engineering achievement! I am looking forward to viewing it."

Then we were in the streets of Paris. There is not only a sound of Paris, but a distinct flavor which is a combination of odors, colors and energy. It almost takes your breath away! Spring was a little closer in Paris than in London, except for our parting day. People were in a hurry and had little time to display what we in England would define as social graces. In fact, they seemed a little rude, or at the least, preoccupied.

Then we were off by cabby to 13 Rue des Beaux-Arts where we would spend two days at the Hotel d'Alsace, which I knew was one of the most fashionable hotels in Paris or, in fact, the world. It was a small hotel with each room furnished individually with a period furniture and velvet wall covering. We had adjoining rooms and each had his own sitting room.

We unpacked and freshened up in preparation for dinner and it was close to 8:00 P.M. when we returned to the lobby. Such grandeur! Furnished lavishly as for a king! Tapestry, golden carriage lights, a great chandelier with dazzling crystal throwing dancing images across the walls. The whole room came to life with elegance. I had seen photographs of it back in 1894 when Sarah Bernhardt performed Oscar Wilde's play "Salome" which was a serious drama about obsessive passion.

I mentioned this to Holmes who promptly retorted, "That was before the sodomy trial involving Lord Alfred Douglas. Wilde is serving the two-year sentence at this moment. Fine Irish poet and playwright, but very strange in his ways. I am going to give us a treat tonight, Watson. What is Paris without Maxim's?"

I was flabbergasted. What a treat indeed! I was not sure that we two conservative gentlemen could handle the racy reputation of this boisterous meeting place. Truly a meeting place of royalty.

We were ushered into the dark, paneled main room of the restaurant. Shadow tones of leaded glass adorned and separated the open area. Lights in the shape of large flower buds extended out from the walls and ceiling, supported by gold-colored ornate fixtures. The lights gave off a subdued tone of elegance giving a mystery to the patrons seated at tables around the room. Large Victorian gilded mirrors hung on the walls enlarging the perspective of the huge dining area. Entries to private dining rooms ran off the main room. A piano played light classical music suited for a pleasant dining experience. Maxim's was the first restaurant in Paris to introduce piano music for dining. Maxim's would never think of distracting its guests from the delights of conversation and gastronomy with a show. And then of course the food and what fine food it was through five courses! I will spare you the details, but it is enough to say that I had pheasant under glass as my main course and Holmes in all of his conservative tastes simply had Beef Wellington. I wonder if he was reminding the French of our great Duke who sent the French Emperor to Elba.

After dinner we returned by carriage to our hotel and then to bed. Our appointment with Dr. Binet was for 9:00 A.M. at Sorbonne. It had been a full day with all of the traveling. I was very tired even though I had a nap. Holmes continued in the pleasant, patient manner which was unusual to say the least.

I was aroused by a knock on my door by a fully dressed Holmes at 7:00 A.M. He had thoughtfully ordered coffee and rolls to my room, knowing my early morning energies were low or, depending on the day, non-existent. Holmes left me to my struggle to review his papers and prepare for our visit with Dr.Binet.

By 8:00 A.M. we had hired a carriage and were on our way to the Psychological Research Laboratory at Sorbonne. We could see the top of the Eiffel Tower dominating the skyline of Paris. Its cold steel bound together in a harmony of simple beauty, awesome in its emotional impact. Vive La France!

We passed over Pont Alexandre III, which was a recently completed bridge which crosses the Seine with a single 350-foot-long span. The foundation stone of the bridge was recently laid by Tsar Nicholas II, although it was named after his father, Alexander III. I remember reading that the functional purpose of the metal girders is effectively concealed beneath the lavish ornamentation, whose splendor seemed to me to ring a little hollow. I could see the pylons at each corner of the bridge which were crowned by gilded forms of an allegorical figure, and at the bottom there were groups of cupids and lions which were as gratuitous as the decoration of a Bavarian rococo church. We passed the huge glass dome of the Grand Palais which reminded me of the Crystal Palace designed by Sir Joseph Paxton at the Great Exhibition in London around 1850 and was moved and reconstructed on the outskirts of London. The cab had stopped before an imposing Greek-style building and Holmes and I entered the front door to the reception. Holmes was able to communicate to the nice lady that we were there to see Dr. Binet. Holmes never ceased to amaze me and his knowledge and use of the French language was effective, although I must admit that I would be no judge of that.

We were escorted down the hall to a large doorway which entered into a reception area, much like a large sitting room, with overstuffed chairs and settees located in clusters. We were immediately approached by a short man of about five feet, nine inches in height, dark black hair closely trimmed and with an intense manner. His small black eyes penetratingly engaged your stare. His clean-shaven face showed a rather long face, thin lips and a plain friendly nose. He was in a dark gray suit with vest, white shirt and cravat. He gave a well-groomed professional appearance. His complexion matched the darkness of his features. His smile was broad and his manner friendly when he came up to us with his hand outstretched to Holmes.

"Mr. Holmes, welcome to Paris. How you honor us by your visit! What a treat it is for me to visit with the world's greatest detective of such world-wide fame. I have read all of your documented adventures. Your use of extreme detailed observation, reasoning and deduction are not dissimilar to my discipline. I had no idea that our paths would ever cross. Of course, this must be your chronicler, Dr. Watson. What a pleasure it is to meet you both, please be seated. Let me take your coats and hats."

We were then ushered to a group of five chairs surrounding a small table and asked to be seated. Then our host sat down as well. "What can I do for you?", he asked of Holmes.

"I know of your interest in graphology. I have read your psychological journal L 'Année Psychologiqué where you addressed the test with seven graphologists from around Europe. I was amazed to find that Dr. Karl Knoepker did so well on identifying the successful from the unsuccessful. I know also that you believe that graphology has potentialities as a technique for personality testing. I, too, believe that handwriting reveals a person's character as we do write without any conscious control of how we write. It is perhaps the only uninhibited thing that we do. Where have your studies and experiments taken you in this quest?"

"Let me state, Mr. Holmes, that I do not have the ability to read character traits from handwriting. Knowing you, through your chronicled adventures, you already know that I have studied law, medicine and now psychology with a special interest in children's intelligence and testing for it. So what I am doing is trying to find the credibility factor in what we call graphology and, if credible, then how it may be used and by whom. This took me to a study of graphology and, with your indulgence, I will happily share with you what I have learned. Graphology is the study and analysis of handwriting to assess the writer's traits or personality. Aristotle was the first known scholar who became interested in handwriting and its differences from writer to writer. It was he who first questioned what this meant. Julius Caesar turned the village known to him as 'Lutetia Parisiorum' into a Roman Town. Paris began as city at that time. I tell you this as Julius Caesar also believed that handwriting revealed personality, traits but he was unable to read them. Interesting, too, is that Julius Caesar as a young man studied in Athens at the school of Aristotle.

Throughout history, artists, historians, philosophers and scientists have been interested in the relation between handwriting and writer. The first treatise on the subject appeared as early as 1622, and efforts at graphological systematization began in 1872 with the work of the French abbe Hypolite Michon who died in 1881. Both Michon and his compatriot Jules Crepiux-Jamin developed the so-called School of Isolated Signs, which attempted to relate specific handwriting elements to specific human traits. Michon is regarded as the father of graphology but was never able to really make it work.

A German philosopher, Ludwig Klages, has advanced the hypothesis that handwriting is an expressive movement, similar to gesture, gait and facial expression. His theory postulated a unifying principle called rhythm, exhibited in expressive movements that is a measure of normality in the personality. It is my feeling that his system at this stage provides no adequate procedure for distinguishing between various degrees of rhythm, so that evaluation depends ultimately on subjective judgement. Others attempt to interpret decorative flourishes in handwriting without any substantial conclusion.

Handwriting consists of measurable elements, such as slant and size, and of descriptive elements, such as letter form and tendencies to the right and left. A basic problem of graphology is establishing a common denominator for both types of elements to permit comparable objective evaluation. Other problems concern the validity of the interpretations; validation of graphology is complicated by the same difficulties that confront other techniques of psychological testing.

Attempts to determine the validity of detailed handwriting analysis include experiments in which graphologists answer specific questions concerning the writer's feelings, behavior and attitudes on the basis of examination of handwriting specimens. Clinical investigations of the relationship between handwriting and various mental diseases are in progress toward similar objectives. Although the results of handwriting analysis sometimes correspond impressively with experimental evidence, graphology has still not been fully accepted as a branch of psychology.

Now we come to Dr. Knoepker of Leipzig. He participated in our clinical study and was given credit for being 92 percent correct in his evaluation. Gentlemen, that is a very impressive figure. He has studied over 10,000 specimens of handwriting. He has conducted follow-up investigations and interviews and has reached some very startling conclusions. He has developed a character identification system to establish known character traits and this vocabulary of tested signs is growing. As a result of my testing, I feel that Dr. Knoepker can evaluate 92 percent of the character traits of the writer from the examination of the writer's handwriting. I have come to the conclusion that graphology, when developed, will be an indispensable tool in the practice of psychology and psychiatry. That really is all that I can tell you of my knowledge on the subject. When Siegmund Freud was here at the University of Paris back in 1886, we discussed this subject at length, but with the same conclusions."

"Thank you, Dr. Binet," reflected Holmes. "Most interesting analysis. I have compared my papers and handwriting samples to try to determine some conclusions with some revealing results. Unfortunately, mine are more a study of criminal traits which would be of little use in general personality testing. We have taken enough of your valuable time. I would like to look over the samples of handwriting used in your testing and the results found by the graphologists. I would like to study those today and tomorrow. We leave for Leipzig by train tomorrow afternoon."

"I have already anticipated that request and have them set out in the conference room to the right of the door. There is one price I will want you to pay, Mr. Holmes. Will you and Dr. Watson join us for dinner tonight?"

"Delighted," retorted Holmes.

"My pleasure," said I.

It was established that a cab would be sent to pick us up at the hotel at 7:00 P.M. and with that we were ushered into the conference room filled with all of those interesting papers. It was agreed that I would return to the hotel and meet Holmes there at dinner time. This would give me time to see some of the sights and walk the streets of Paris. I was impressed with Dr. Binet and his candor. I have always felt that small men seem to be active and aggressive. He was impressive indeed.

Holmes and I arrived at our hotel at the same time about 5:00 P.M. and went to our rooms. Holmes had ordered tea and cakes a little late in the day, but it offered some energy to prepare for our evening.

"How was your study, Holmes?", asked I.

"Good, Watson. This Knoepker is indeed on the right trail. I have a little more study to complete. It takes a little longer because of my notetaking. It is slow work but very gratifying. What of your day?"

"Holmes, I have had a delightful day. I played the role of the British tourist. I visited the Cathedral of Notre Dame, the Louvre and the Invalides which houses Napoleon's tomb. That is enough culture for any man. I was most affected by the painting of Mona Lisa and of course the Venus de Milo, but clearly Leonardo Da Vinci's work took the day. I am actually fatigued. I need a hot bath to get going again."

"Good for you. The tea should help give you a lift. I have a feeling that this will be an interesting evening. It looks like Dr. Binet has had an opportunity to plan this. I feel that we will meet some of his friends. Are you ready for it, Watson?"

"I look forward to it, Holmes. I will undertake my body renovation and meet you here shortly before 7:00 P.M."

We were seated in the beautiful lobby when a cabby announced our carriage and off we went to the Sorbonne faculty quarters.

"Good evening, Mr. Holmes and Dr. Watson, good of you to come. Please come in. This is my wife Anne."

After taking our coats and hats, we were invited into the sitting room where a delightful couple was standing for an introduction.

I would be remiss if I did not tell you about Anne. Such a petite beauty I have never seen. Such delicate features! She had long curled brown hair which danced like angel springs from her head. She was small in stature and exquisitely formed in the ways of a woman. Such charm! Such a friendly smile and firm and warm handshake but feminine in every way.

Our host continued with his introductions. "These two are our love birds. They have been married now about a year and they are fascinated by each other. But they have wanted to meet the world's greatest detective and are ardent fans of your chronicles, Dr. Watson. Please meet Marie and Pierre Curie. Pierre is a professor at the School of Physics and Chemistry. Pierre and his brother have been interested in studying the electric potential which is produced when pressure is exerted on a quartz crystal. They named this phenomenon Piezoelectricity and Pierre discovered about 2 years ago a certain temperature which we now call the Curie Point at which magnetic substances lose their magnetism. In fairness, I should say that Marie has been interested in the recent discoveries of radiation. Wilhelm Roentgen discovered X-rays in 1895 and, in 1896, Antoine Henri Becquerel discovered that the element uranium gives off similar invisible radiations. Marie began studying uranium radiations and, using Piezoelectric techniques devised by Pierre, carefully measured the radiation in pitchblende, an ore containing uranium. She is the first to use the term radioactive. Enough of this puffing but I thought that you should know your surprise additional hosts. Please, let's use first names here. There are too many doctors and it would be fun to use the name Sherlock."

What I saw before me was a bright pretty young lady of about 30 years of age. She, too, was short in stature, but with a high forehead. Her brown hair was course and full. It was closely cut, but bushed out on the side and top. She had a very determined mouth, long neck, little ears and a sculptured bob of a nose. Her lips were larger than normal but somewhat sculptured, almost Roman. I knew of her because of her work with X-rays and have read several papers on the radioactive rays which she was working with. My recollection was that she was Polish by birth and came here to study. Yes, she changed her name, I remember.

Pierre was eight or nine years her senior. He was average height, slim and very French. His hair was full and black with a full beard, neatly trimmed to match. His eyes were sparkling black and his nose was small for his face. He was smiling and pleasant, giving off a warm, friendly presence.

"Very pleased to meet you all," said I. As a medical man, I have been most interested in the X-ray discovery and I am familiar with Marie's work on radioactivity. There have been several papers translated into English which our medical board has circulated. My name is John. Thank you for inviting us."

Holmes, obviously fascinated by his stimulating hosts entered the conversation. "It will be interesting to see how 'John' chronicles this meeting as we never use first names between us or, in fact, I use the term doctor only when I am in the presence of others and usually to stress his medical background. Never have I met such charming hosts. I am familiar with Pierre's discovery of the Curie Point which is an important point to know in my line of work. I have also been fascinated by the study of X-rays and radioactive material which will prove revolutionary in the medical profession and even in mine."

We all found our overstuffed chairs in the comfortably and tastefully furnished room. Our host offered us whiskey or wine and we began to talk about the cases of Sherlock Holmes and his faithful companion. How much fun it was to talk about our adventures. We discussed many of our unchronicled cases, but discretely withholding names or events which would identify the parties. Moriarty was worth at least 2 glasses of whatever we were drinking at the time. We adjourned to the dining room where the first course was laid out. Herring on potatoes, served with schnapps. We drank wine with our leg of lamb Provencal which melted in our mouths. After a desert of French pastries, we were back to the sitting room and whiskey. It was around 10:00 P.M. when the cab picked us up to return to our hotel. I must admit that I was just a little inebriated from all of the drink. I am not sure whether this form of drinking was for us the French way or a little of the Polish way for Marie. But, what fun we had! Sherlock was in rare form. Adventure after adventure was tastefully revisited. Our hosts were charmed by his manner and succinct recollection. I had never heard him be such a story teller. We gave our thanks to our amiable hosts and bid our farewell. Holmes had made arrangements to continue his studies in the morning with Alfred.

The morning came and, by the time I had gathered my senses, I noted that Holmes was gone. I continued my sight-seeing in the morning after having fully packed. Holmes had completed his packing and his suitcase was by the door.

By early afternoon we were on our way to Frankfurt where we would spend the night and then continue by train the shorter part of our trip to Leipzig. We had arrived late in Frankfurt and were up early to continue our journey. I really have little memory of this trip. Holmes continued to work with his papers and I must admit that I got a lot of sleep.

In Leipzig we had taken quarters close to the university and there was nothing special about them. Functioning and adjoining rooms. We had arrived in mid afternoon and our meeting with Dr. Knoepker was to be in the following morning at 8:00 A.M. After a heavy German dinner we took our tired traveled bodies to bed to meet this uncivilized appointed hour.

Leipzig had acquired the sobriquet Kline Paris or "Little Paris" in the late 18th century when it became a center of a classical literary movement under the leadership of the German scholar and writer Johann Christoph Gottsched. Many prominent Germans had studied there including von Goethe, Bach and Mendelssohn. Robert Wagner was born there. I did not feel that this was Little Paris. The architecture was old and worn. It is the printing capital of Germany with all of its dirt and sounds that shroud those endeavors.

We arrived at the Administration Building of the university and with the directions furnished by Dr. Knoepker found our way to his room. His private office was off to the right of the room as you entered it. The door was open and Holmes stuck his head in and called out, "Dr. Knoepker?"

"Sherlock Holmes?"

Then the German, probably 6 foot six inches tall, began to emerge from the chair and, it seemed to me, continued to emerge like a great crane coming from the water in flight. Here was a graying man, clean shaven and bespeckled. His features were distinct. His large piercing eyes were bright and gray in color, enhanced by the thick lenses of his glasses. His nose was rather sharp and prominent. His lips were thin but well sculptured and his smile was boyish...all teeth.

He shook our hands firmly. "Gentlemen," he

said resolutely. "How honored I am that you would make this long journey for a visit with me. I know that you have just come from Dr. Binet in Paris and you want to know about graphology, which is my love. I teach afternoon classes and will be able to assist you in the mornings. I have many papers which I have written but, of course, they are in German."

"Dr. Knoepker, I know that you have been trying to establish a common denominator to permit comparable objective evaluation. I have been studying this for years but primarily in relationship to my occupation. I have been studying the criminal personality. I have been working on my own analysis traveling through Europe and at the Sorbonne and thought that we might be able to compare some of these traits and the handwriting strokes and see what we can make of it. This is asking you to make a sacrifice of time and knowledge, but perhaps it can be rewarding in results for both of us. I am not trying to enter your field, but rather I am trying to evaluate the state of this art or science. I plan to spend several mornings with you. Although my German is not good, I think that I would be able to review your notes on this search for a common denominator. Will you help me?"

"Certainly, Mr. Holmes, let us begin."

"I will be taking notes and sometimes will interrupt to better understand what you are telling me. You are the professional and I am but the student. I say this so you will understand. Also, I am so excited about this subject which has puzzled me for these many years that I may appear impetuous. So, I humbly ask your indulgence."

"Agreed. Where shall we begin?"

"Have you established a common denominator in handwriting analysis?"

"Yes, to some extent. There are certain characters in handwriting that have a proven meaning to me at least and I have checked them against the histories and data and feel that the conclusions that I can draw on these characteristics are correct. Let the discourse begin."

"I feel certain that you can tell whether or not a person is emotionally expressive by the slant of his or her handwriting. The slant is determined by drawing a straight line from the base of the letter to the top of it. It is more obvious in the 'T', 'L' and 'D'. In fact, the slant of a handwriting can be determined from any of the

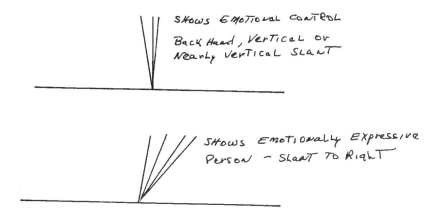

letters. I will discuss the difference when we get to it. Let us look at this key of crossed lines which I have placed on the chalkboard.

"The writing that is back hand, vertical or nearly vertical shows a person with a controlled emotional response. This person does not readily show his or her emotional feelings. In fact, the opposite is true. That person shows only what he or she wants to show you about their feeling on a subject. You never know what that writer really feels. The more the slant to the right of the center perpendicular line, the more emotional expression the person has. That means that if you will study the behavior of an emotionally expressive person and their emotional expression, you will always know what they feel. Simply put, when they are happy, they will show it; when they are sad or angry, they will show it. If they are uncomfortable, they will show it. This allows you to understand the real emotions of the subject. But with a backhand slant or vertical writing, straight up and down, or nearly so, you will only know what emotion the subject wants you to know...I say, their head rules their emotions, not their heart."

"If a person is emotionally expressive, I find that, if the 'O','A' or lower loop of the 'D' is not closed, this indicates that the subject will verbally express their emotions...if closed, it means that the person will show emotions but not verbalize them. This pertains only to the handwriting that is slanted to the right. I will illustrate on the blackboard what I mean. First the closed letters:

then the open loops of the same letters."

"Dr. Knoepker, what if a person is right- or left-handed?"

"My studies have confirmed that it makes no difference at all. These signs are the same. It would be the same in any language. There have been studies made of people who have no arms and who write by holding a writing instrument between their teeth and the slants are there. In several of those cases the subjects had learned to write by holding the writing instrument with their feet and the slants are there. In fact, the same is true with all of the traits that we will discuss. Shall we look at another character trait which you can determine from observing handwriting?"

"Please continue, Doctor," mumbled Holmes, now engrossed in note-taking and observing the blackboard.

Dr. Knoepker picked up my pad of note paper. "I can tell you, Doctor, from your handwriting, that you are very emotionally expressive, both in action and word. You, Dr. Watson, have an inferiority complex."

"Ridiculous," said I. "How could you possibly know that?"

"Elementary, my dear Watson. I think that is what Mr. Holmes says to you when he makes a deduction and I want to point out that this is a study of deduction using a different medium. Look at the second loop of your 'N' or the third loop of your 'M'. If the last loop of either sticks up above the loop of its predecessor, this sticks up like a sore thumb and indicates that the subject has an inferiority complex and the more it sticks up, the more of a complex the subject has. See how simple it really is. The more characters exhibiting this trait, the more dominant the trait is. If there are only a few of them and most of the time they are normal, it means that you only have this trait some of the time as to certain activities. Let me illustrate it for you on the board.

While we are looking at the 'N' and the 'M', let me share other confirmed data about those letters that I have learned. If the loops of the 'M' are rounded, not pointed, it indicates a slower moving mind. This subject thinks about action some time before taking it. This person has more patience and has more creative abilities of working with his or her hands. Let me illustrate:

The more pointed the loops, the quicker the mind.

The valley between the loops indicates ability to analyze. The sharper the 'V' between the loops or lines that form the 'M' or 'N', the greater analytical ability. See:

The lack of these valleys shows the lack of analytical ability.

If these letters have a straight line angling downward at the beginning of the letter, it indicates temper. The stronger the line and the more frequently it is used, the greater the capacity for temper. It also appears in the letters 'B' and 'F', but anytime you have this straight line starting a letter, it indicates temper. Let me illustrate:

"Can we determine the depth of one's emotion? Yes, we can. How deeply does the subject feel? The deeper the feeling, the longer lasting the feeling becomes and the more extreme it could be. The harder that the writer presses on the paper with his writing instrument, the deeper the writer's feeling. You do have to judge the writing instrument, as some pens write in broad strokes when easily used and some hard pencils would have an opposite result. You must test the writing instrument before you can evaluate this trait. When you have a person with deep, long-lasting emotions, you have a person who over-indulges where the senses are concerned. This subject feels that if a little bit is good, a lot is better. This writer tends to never forget, like an elephant. This subject can react with extreme emotion. The lighter writer on the other hand doesn't carry emotions over to the next day or even the next hour. This writer is a 'forgive and forget' kind of person. Moderate in habits, gentle in nature. Really doesn't have strong emotions about anything. I really can't demonstrate this trait with chalk, but I hope that I have described it to you as it will affect your evaluation of a written specimen."

"Fascinating," muttered Holmes. "Just as I expected."

"One of the most reliable common denominators involves the letter 'T'. It consist of two parts: the stem and the bar which crosses it. It can tell us much about our subject. The stem is the part that comes up from the base line and is usually retraced to descend. It sometimes contains a loop, which I will discuss later in this session. The bar is the line set out to execute a crossing, but does not always cross it. First let's look at the stem. A tall 'D' stem indicates vanity. The height of it in relationship to the other letters around it...the 'O', 'A','U', the lower loop of the 'D' or the top of the 'G'. The higher it is in that relationship, more than twice the height, the greater dependent this person is. Dependent upon others. This dependency is usually emotional dependency, the need for stroking, hence vanity. If this stem is very short near the other characters mentioned, it shows a very independent person. Let me illustrate. I will need to remove my other illustrations, so if you need to copy them, let me know.

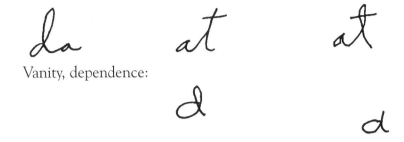

Vanity, dependence:

Independent nature. The subjects will do what they want to do when they want to do it.

If this stem has air in it - a loop which you could also find it in a 'D' loop - it shows sensitivity, and the more air, the greater the sensitivity. If there is a lot of air in it, the person will be offended very easily.

If there is no air in this loop, really a straight retraced line, then the person has no sensitivity. You would have trouble offending them.

So when you have a short stem, with no air in it, you have a person who is very independent and if they offend you with their independent action, they really do not care. Here let me place an example of this.

On the other hand, if the short stem does have a lot of air in its loop, that person will be sensitive and will be bothered if they offend you, but, because of their independent nature, would likely repeat the same offensive act again under the same circumstances.

Now let us examine the bar. It has so much to tell us about the subject. Let us first look at where it crosses the stem. The higher the place where it crosses the stem in relation to the bottom of the stem, regardless of the stem's height, the higher the goals the writer sets for himself or herself. This will show you the effort a subject will put forth towards his or her goals. You must realize that even though a brilliant person with a sharp mind can quickly and almost effortlessly master a situation and produce productively, they might not have to set their goals for themselves very high because of their great capacity. The higher people set their goals, the greater the accomplishments they will have in relationship to their ability.

You will have several heights of goals in one page of a subject's writing. All this means is that, in those areas of interest, the subject will set his or her goals higher and the lower goals would probably be in something the subject would rather not do, such as gardening or cleaning the house.

If the bar crosses the stem above the upper limits of the stem, it shows a person who sets unrealistic goals for himself or herself, but there are other factors which we will consider which could give this person a chance of reaching the impossible. Don Quixote probably crossed the 'T' in this manner:

This person is seldom, if ever, satisfied with his or her efforts towards personal goals. The same is true of the person whose bar crosses close to the top of the stem. This person does not give himself or herself satisfaction of a job well done. There always seems to this individual to be something else that he or she could have done to improve the results which, by all normal standards, would be considered outstanding.

Look at this bar again. Let's look at the darkness of the bar in relationship to the rest of the writing. The darker this bar is, in that relationship, the stronger the writer's will. This tells us of the will-power of the writer. If all of the writing is written in dark heavy strokes, it would mean that the will-power, even if of equal darkness, would be excessive. The weaker this bar, the less will-power the writer possesses. If it is stronger at the beginning but tapers, we have a person who exhibits strong will-power but it vanishes when engaged. It doesn't last. Likewise, if it is light in the beginning and gets stronger as it goes, we have a person who does not exhibit strong will, but if you push this person, the strong will appears and the harder you push, the stronger the will-power will be."

Strong Will-Power

Weak Will-Power

Tapered Will-Power

"How do you show procrastination in a person's handwriting?"

"When the bar does not pass through the stem from the left of the stem, it shows tendencies to procrastinate, to put off until tomorrow what you should be doing today. The more of these incompleted 'T' bars in the specimen, the stronger the trait."

"Dr. Knoepker, are their certain handwriting characteristics that demonstrate criminal tendencies?", Holmes inquired, showing total absorption in the theme.

"No, Mr. Holmes, because each crime is different. We would try to fit the personality traits, which by deduction and reason, your tools Mr. Holmes, would be required to commit the crime, to our suspect. For example, let's take a crime of passion. We would have deep emotional feelings. Very dark handwriting which almost seems to bleed. The writing would not have clear lines. This person would probably have a temper, depending on how the crime was committed. The instrument used might give us an idea of the intelligence of the person and so might the mode of entry. We would try to create a profile of the criminal and then review our suspects and see if we could fit that profile to our criminal. I have found one characteristic which indicates that the writer has a secret, a deep secret. In one case, an attractive young lady admitted to me that she was a lesbian and, in another, a middle-aged negro woman admitted that her father had sexually abused her when she was a child. If we were dealing with a crime of deceit, I feel certain that that sign would be present. It consists of a clear loop or even a distinct retracing within the 'O', 'A', bottom loop of the 'D' or the 'G' loop above the line. Let me illustrate:

Within the letter loop which is fully closed, there is secreted a form which is either a small loop, tick or check. There is the secret. In summary, Mr. Holmes, we must study the crime as it was committed to determine what the character traits of the criminal would be. We then would try to find a suspect with those traits through graphology."

Frankly, I was a little too old to go back to school. The chairs were wooden and I was tired of sitting, listening to this tea leaf reader talk to me, a medical doctor, as if this graphology were a profession. The mind can only absorb when one's rear end is comfortable and mine was certainly not! I was pleased when he told us that he would finish up with the 'T' and then allow Holmes to review his notes and start again tomorrow.

"Sarcasm is shown by the 'T' bar, tapering to a sharp point.

When the 'T' bar is slanted upward, it shows that the writer is optimistic and when slanted downward, it shows pessimism.

When the 'T' bar begins on the right of the stem, this illustrates a domineering trait and when slanted downward, an abusive trait.

If pointed at the tapered end and rather dark, you have a caustic trait. This might well be a sign that you would be looking for in a crime of passion.

Also you might look for words ending in a heavy blunt line, slanting down to the right below the base line This is another indication of this domineering trait.

Enthusiasm is demonstrated by the length of the 'T' bar. The longer the bar that crosses the 'T', the more enthusiasm the writer will have. This can be an important factor when combined with a strong will. In the case of persons who set their goals for themselves beyond reality, the Don Quixote type. If their will-power is strong and their enthusiasm is great, they might just reach that unreachable dream.

Gentlemen, that should do it for today. I will meet with Mr. Holmes to furnish him with the data he requires and we will get back at it tomorrow at the same time."

I went outside to smoke my pipe while they interchanged. What a pleasant chap this large German was. His broad smile and friendly nature made me like myself. I have to admit that I will review my notes and check my own handwriting for these traits. This is heavy dialogue. Holmes joined me shortly and explained that Dr. Knoepker had made certain of his papers available and that he would stay, using a colleague's room to study them. He would join me for dinner but would be working in the evening reviewing Dr. Knoepker's papers. How excited he was! He acted like Lancelot of King Arthur's time, about to locate the Holy Grail. I knew that he had been studying handwriting for years and now, with Dr. Knoepker, he could see this study as developing a new and wondrous tool.

It was dinner time and Holmes knocked on my door. "Hey, Watson," he said, "it's time for dinner." He continued to maintain that blissful manner, so unlike my companion. His eyes were visibly tired but, the twinkle was still there.

"Right," said I.

We ate at the hotel restaurant. Food was good and definitely German. We discussed our day and I shared with him my visit to the medical school and had met with some of the faculty. I had been invited to lunch with them and would return tomorrow if our schedule permitted. I had walked through this "Little Paris" most of the afternoon and was bored with it. The Germans seem to me to be a very serious people. I had set aside some time to review my notes and check my own handwriting and the results were enlightening, if not a little intimidating. Well, revealing is probably a better word.

"What do you think of Dr. Knoepker?"

"Pleasant chap. I have to say that he knows his stuff. I really do not have much faith in this graphology, but when I reviewed my notes and my own handwriting, I was in for some shocks. Did you know that I show signs of procrastination? That I do not set my goals very high? Well, this big German will certainly have my attention tomorrow. I would like to look at his handwriting! How was your day?"

"Good, Watson. Knoepker has documented his conclusions. It involves handwriting from all over the world. He is indeed a scholar. Meticulous in detail. Convincing statistics. Did you know that Moriarty's handwriting shows that he has a secret. I'm sure he had plenty of them, but he exhibits this trait. His brilliance flows through the 'M' and 'N's. His analytical ability was the greatest. I could have learned this much earlier and frankly much easier without risking my life had I known what I know today."

With that we retired to our rooms for study and bed. Holmes awoke me again with coffee at 6:00 A.M. and I won't put you through the punishment which I occasioned by this attack. At 8:00 A. M. sharp we were again seated before this huge German. He was smiling broadly and oozing charm.

"Good morning, gentlemen. How was your yesterday?"

"Most invigorating, doctor," responded Holmes. "I have reviewed my cases and my handwriting samples and find that your analysis coincides with mine. I have never been able to so succinctly identify them. You have developed working tools which are a tribute to your profession. I have made you copies of the handwriting from my reported cases with my analysis and documentation. I'm not sure that these will be of much help but they attempt to identify the criminal personality and others. I feel that I owe you this for your taking the time to share your thoughts and studies. I want to complement you on the professional manner of your documentation of proof. There may well be a time that I will want to use your services, Dr. Knoepker. You have given me a different dimension to observation and deduction. Please proceed with your instruction."

"As a medical man, dedicated to the healing of mankind, it is a little compromising to find that, with this method of evaluation, you can see right into a person. You can see a person in a light that the person may not see at all. The person may not admit that he or she has such a trait, not even to himself or herself. It is like being unclothed, stripped in public. Uncanny and embarrassing. I do want you to know that I appreciate your time and your sharing of this study with us. I do not think that I have ever seen Holmes so happy with himself."

"Let the game begin, Watson. Is that your saying, Mr. Holmes?" And with that, Dr. Knoepker began.

"The size of the handwriting tells you of the concentrative nature of the writer. The smaller the handwriting, the more concentrative nature the writer has. Conversely, large writing shows a person who is not concentrative and will not delve into much detail, but will gloss over information. The very small writing will amplify the quality of all other traits shown. Although it is a little out of order, I would like you to know how friendliness is shown.

Friendliness, Mr. Holmes, is indicated by a combination of traits without opposing or contradicting traits. Look for a forward slant with somewhat rounded writing as opposed to angularity. You do not want to find a sharpness of points of the 'M' and "N". Generosity plus broad-mindedness, which is better in this instance if the tops of the 'O' and 'A' are slightly open at the top. The tops of the 'O' and 'A' should not be locked together with hooks, loops or knots. Humor which is shown by a wavy line at the beginning of the letters such as capital 'H' or 'M'. In any event, the following traits must NOT be shown in the writing: Resentment to imposition, vanity and ostentation which is indicated by gaudy, flourished writing. I should point out that resentment to imposition is demonstrated by a short, straight line from the base line to the beginning of the letter.

I should also tell you that generosity is shown by a flowing line after the end of a word, usually extending upward as opposed to a

going   gone never out

straight line, an abrupt end or a line slanted downward. The longer this line, the more generous the person is. You usually find some generosity and some abrupt ends of words. This simply means that the subject is generous in some areas and tight-fisted in others.

Irritability is shown by little birds or straight dashes dotting the 'I' and the 'J'. Loyalty to beliefs and principles and in fact close

Was   giving

attention to detail are shown by an 'I' or 'J' dot well rounded and carefully placed just above the letter."

Thus, our lectures continued through the morning of the second day and third day. We both reviewed our notes in the evening and Holmes continued to review and record his notes and the notes of Dr. Knoepker in the afternoons. I became somewhat of a familiar fixture at the medical school and even addressed a class on the status of medical treatment in England. It has always amazed me how a person can be treated as an expert when he gets more than 50 miles from home. The time passed quickly but, I have to admit that my mind was tired and sore from trying to interlace these different traits to make a composite evaluation. My back-side was still a little uncomfortable. Not sure I ever did it, but many a sherry was used to wash away its insolence.

On the fourth day we left for home. How I wanted to get back. We returned by the same route as we had come. Stopping over night at both Frankfurt and then Paris.

We arrived back in Baker Street late the following day, but in time for dinner. Mrs. Hudson was in rare form. Jolly glad to see us. I was glad to get back to her fine home-cooked meals, soft chairs and the private dining with my companion. After several glasses of sherry, we took our weary bodies to bed.

Chapter II

THE RITUAL MURDER

A fortnight had passed since our return to Baker Street. Holmes had been engaged in a serious affair of state involving the Duke of Austria, which I am not at liberty to discuss, and had returned to the study of the Knoepker notes. We had finished breakfast and I was reading the morning paper when, much to my shock, I saw the headline, "BANK OF ENGLAND MANAGER BRUTALLY MURDERED". Below, the article continued: "The body of Godfrey St. James, the Manager of the Note Department of the Bank of England, was found last night at approximately 9:00 P.M. by a bank security guard. St. James' nude body had been placed on a small conference table with his feet and hands tied to the table legs and a gold dagger was sticking out of his chest near a hole where his heart had been removed. The bloody, dissected organ had been placed between his legs. Lestrade of Scotland Yard, one of their most experienced inspectors, is assigned to the case. His record of public service is exemplary. Superintendent Rathborne gave us a statement that all efforts will be made to bring this heinous murderer to speedy justice.

I remembered our meeting with St. James. He had been a trim, athletic gentleman. Nice appearing, tall, mustached. He had been a little on the nervous side and was somewhat abrupt. What a tragedy this was!

"Holmes, someone has brutally killed St. James. Here, read it for yourself. Dastardly deed!"

Holmes took the paper and scanned the article. He laid the paper down and said, "I think we will be hearing from Lestrade and, unless I miss my guess, that is he at the door."

Mrs. Hudson announced our guests Lestrade and another junior officer, Bradley Macintosh, who were promptly at our door.

"How have you been Mr. Holmes?", Lestrade purred, which was always the case when he wanted Holmes' help.

"Macintosh, this is Mr. Sherlock Holmes and Dr. John Watson, who have given me assistance from time to time. Mr. Holmes and Dr. Watson, this is recently assigned inspector Bradley Macintosh from Edinburgh who will be assisting me."

"The St. James affair?", queried Holmes in his abrupt, get-to-the-point fashion.

"Yes, it is a bizarre tragedy. No real clues as yet. I was hoping that, if you were available, you might accompany us to the scene of this ghastly affair. At my request, the body and premises have been left exactly as they were found by the security guard. I can still feel the sting of your wrath when I removed the evidence before seeking your help. I have to admit that I am lost, except for one theory, but I do not have enough facts to make a solution."

"We will be delighted to give you a hand. Dr. Watson's medical background may be a real asset."

With that, we put on our coats and descended to the waiting coach. Spring had begun her love affair and the birds were singing her praises.

Threadneedle Street and the Bank of England. How my thoughts carried me back to the lead bar case. Now, we had this tragedy and I wondered how our friends at the bank were handling this. We were ushered into the Court Room where we were once again before Lord James Kensington, his Deputy, Sir Charles Farthington and Sir Rodney Grope, Solicitor General. It was the same beautiful room with cherry walls. The large conference table still dominated the room but the mood had shifted from our last meeting to one of abject horror. Terrified grief registered on all of their faces.

Lestrade made the introductions and advised them that he was in charge of the investigation. He showed his ignorance of how the Bank of England was set up and regarded it as another face of the Crown. Holmes did not correct him. Knowing Holmes' feelings towards the constabulary, I was not surprised. He was like the father watching his son learn from his own mistakes.

Sir Rodney returned the introductions and his grating voice said, "We know Mr. Holmes and Dr. Watson and are glad that you have sought their help in this ghastly matter. How can we be of help?"

Lord Kensington was a little older, now closer to his middle seventies, a little more well fed and rounded and his fat face continued to carry his red glowing cheeks. I remembered that he had reminded me of an aging Prince Albert when we first met and now even more so. Sir Charles was beginning to push sixty and his black hair was beginning to show its silver streaks. The lines of aging in his forehead seemed more pronounced if not strained.

It was good to see them again and they returned this same warmth of reunion, though blunted by this grisly drama. The Governor and his Deputy were again dressed in formal wear: black tuxedo, white tie and embroidered cummerbund. This Court Room was the meeting place of kings and queens and heads of state from all over the world.

"Gentlemen, what can you tell us of this tragedy?", asked Lestrade.

Sir Rodney responded in his gruff voice, "St. James was working with the King of Tonga on the issuance of notes to be backed by the Bank of England and I should like to point out that it was one of the Tonga daggers that was found in St. James' chest."

"Holmes," the investigator, began, "I would like to know about this Tonga, if you don't mind, Sir Rodney. Were any of you other gentlemen involved in this negotiation? When did it begin?"

Lestrade reacted to Holmes' questions as if intimidated by his own lack of direction, but I could readily sympathize as it was all new to me as well. I think that Sir Rodney recognized the situation and thus began the history lesson.

"Lord Kensington takes no active part in the day-to-day management of the bank. However he was present with Mr. St. James at a meeting here with King George Tupou II of Tonga and his Prime Minister three days ago. I assisted and had done a lot of background research on this country. The reason for this is obvious as my story unfolds. Let me begin with a background of Tonga. This is a country made up of about 150 islands in the South Pacific Ocean. These islands lie close to New Zealand and Australia and about 4,800 kilometers southwest of Hawaii.

History records that two Dutch navigators, Willem Cornelia Schouten and Jakob le Maire, became the first Europeans we know of to visit Tonga. They landed on some of the northern islands in 1616."

Sir Rodney had seated himself at the great table and was referring, during his dissertation, to papers which he had neatly laid out before him. The rest of us joined him at the table, with Lord Kensington taking the large chair at the table's head. Lestrade, Macintosh and Holmes were conscientiously taking notes.

Sir Rodney's gravel voice continued, "In 1643, Abel Tasman, a Dutch sea captain, visited Tongatapu and some of the other southern islands. The British explorer Captain James Cook, who first visited the Tonga Islands in 1789 called them the 'Friendly Islands'. He later found out that they were not quite as friendly as he first thought. In 1789, Captain William Bligh and 18 crewmen of the British ship Bounty floated through the islands after being cast adrift by mutineers.

The first people to settle in Tonga were Polynesians who probably came from Samoa. Although much of Tonga's early history is based on myths, records of Tongan rulers go back to the AD 900s. The early rulers held the title of Tu'i Tonga. The people believed the Tu'i Tonga were sacred representatives of the Tongan gods. It seems that, in about 1470, the ruling Tu'i Tonga gave some governing powers to a non-sacred leader. Through the years, the Tu'i Tonga became only a figurehead. By 1865, after the death of the last Tu'i Tonga, the non-sacred king held all of the ruling power.

Methodist missionaries from England settled in Tonga during the early part of this century and have converted most of the people to Christianity. Since the turn of this century, civil war spread throughout Tonga. One of the most powerful chiefs, Taufa'ahau, finally united the islands in 1846. He was crowned King George Tupou I and became the first monarch of Tonga.

"Sorry that I have to spell so many of these words," apologized Sir Rodney.

"King Tupou I developed legal codes that became the basis of the Tongan constitution, which was adopted in 1875. King Tupou I died in 1893 and his great-grandson George Tupou II took the throne. It was he and his Prime Minister that we met with just three days ago.

The King really controls the legislation through his appointments and he has a strong control over the nobility. Half of the legislature is elected by Tonga's hereditary nobility and his Privy Council enacts legislation between sessions. The Privy Council is totally dominated by the King's appointees. The Legislative

Assembly could veto a Privy Council action but only by a majority vote. This has never happened, as the nobles stick together. The King owns all of the land and everyone must rent from him but, of course, the nobles get a break in the price. It is a cozy little group.

Now we are down to the reason for his visit. I should also say that the King took the name George in honor of our King George. They are very close to England and have applied for protectorate status which is presently pending. Tonga wants to issue its own currency and wants the Bank of England to guarantee its value. I think that the King wants his image on all the money, so as to remind them that he is the King. This currency would be tied in value to the British Pound Sterling. We do this for many of our colonies and commonwealth countries. Our requirement is that the country issuing the currency have an amount of gold on deposit with the bank in an amount that is at least equal to the value of the currency.

Tonga has always been a poor country. The majority of its people live in small rural villages and farm and fish for food. George Tupou II has brought gold to fund this currency. As the guarantor of this currency, the bank is very careful on the control of printing and issuance of it. King George Tupou II has brought with him 90,000 pounds of gold, not in bullion mind you, but in artifacts, ancient artifacts. This gold has been stored in four vaults in the gold cellar. Our metallurgist, William McBeth, has examined the artifacts and they appear to be pure gold...pure as Russian gold. You probably remember Mr. McBeth from our last encounter, Mr. Holmes?"

"Yes, of course," Holmes retorted, without lifting his head from his note-taking.

"I should tell you that there are a number of emeralds and other precious gems which have been attached to quite a few of the gold objects, some of which are very large indeed and beautifully cut. We have no idea of the value of these. King Tupou II wants to issue notes and coins equal to 5,000,000 pounds sterling and this treasure has been determined to be adequate security. The question that Mr. St. James had been pondering is whether or not all of these artifacts would fetch more than their metal content at auction. It seemed such a shame to melt these beautiful objects back into bars. I do not have the complete inventory, but, from what I have seen, you have vessels, strange idols, weapons, shields, jewelry of all types and tools that appear to be medical instruments. The King has an inventory but it is in Tonganese which certainly isn't much help to us. St. James removed several pieces of the artifacts to see what might be the best course of turning them into cash. One of the artifacts removed was a dagger, bejeweled with rubies and emeralds. I was a beautiful but deadly instrument which, with someone's help, has found its way into the body of Mr. St. James. I do not know how far St. James got with his quest before this happened. We really do not know more than this."

"Where did these Tonganese get all of those golden artifacts?"

"We do not know, Mr Holmes. We do not even know the origin of them."

"Was St. James having any other problems with his Note Department?"

"Not that we know of, Mr. Holmes."

"How many employees does the bank have?"

"About 1700, a little more or a little less. They are scattered all over the world."

"How many are there in the Note Department?"

"Probably 1200."

"Do you know who comes and goes through the bank doors each day?"

"Yes," Mr. Holmes, "we do, and we enter the time of entry and exit. The entrant signs a book logging in the time of entry and his or her destination. When that person leaves, he or she signs out setting down the time of exit. We actually require a signature at both times so we can verify the identity. All employees have identification cards which they must present at the time of entrance and exit. The signing in and out also applies to visitors, who are escorted to their destination and turned over to an employee there. They are also returned by that employee to our main gate at the end of the visit."

"How many employees would have been on the bank premises last evening?"

"The British boast that the sun never sets on the British Empire. Nowhere is that fact brought home more than at the Bank of England, which is servicing countries all over the world. Our local domestic banking is limited to normal banking hours here in London. The rest of the bank, including the foreign domestic department which handles routine banking matters for our branches everywhere, works three eight-hour shifts. I would estimate 300 employees, but the records would exactly reflect the number."

"Holmes," the interrogator continued, "did St. James have an assistant who would act in his absence?"

"His department was divided into two sections. Each had an assistant manager in charge. One section is designated the Domestic Note Department, 'Domestic' for short, and the other the Foreign Note Department, or 'Foreign' for short.

The Manager of the Domestic section is Thomas Kingsley and this position also is the First Assistant Manager of the Note Department.

The Manager of the Foreign section is Percy Fawnsworth and this position also is designated as the Second Assistant Manager of the Note Department."

"Sir Rodney, have you discussed this crisis with either of them?", asked Holmes.

"We are still in shock, Mr. Holmes. The constables have sealed off Mr. St. James' office, so we cannot even determine where he was in his work. St. James was always a good organizer and he religiously made notes to his files. We are in some state of horrified limbo."

Lestrade, somewhat impatient with this dissecting inquiry, blurted out, "Do you have any idea who would want to kill Mr. St. James?"

"No idea, Inspector Lestrade," quickly retorted Sir Rodney. "St. James was a competent manager, well liked by all who knew him. He has been with the Bank some 25 years and has managed the Note Department for at least the last 10 years. He was a family man, happily married, and, to our knowledge, had no enemies. Why anyone would want to do him in is beyond our imagination."

"We should now view the scene of the murder," said Lestrade, rising abruptly from his chair. "Come, Mr. Holmes and Dr. Watson, let us go to the stage of this drama." Lestrade had worked his way up through the ranks. His methods were somewhat unrefined to say the least. Why he tolerated the dissecting of information by Holmes was the fact that Holmes did not care to receive credit for his help. The successes that Lestrade had found, largely by the aid of Holmes, had given him the reputation that he now enjoyed.

We traveled by power lift to the fourth floor and then down the carpeted corridor to room 401. Two constables stood guard at the outside of the only door to the room that was visible from where we were. The constables snapped somewhat to attention, saluted and one, the sergeant, said, "Good morning Inspector." They then opened the door and stood aside for our party to enter.

We found ourselves in a large paneled room with a huge walnut desk at the far end. Behind it was shelving with a counter-height surface giving additional work space to the rear of the desk with shelves above. Some of the shelving was open, where books were stored, and some were closed by hinged doors. There were three large windows, the floor-to-the-ceiling type, to the right of the cabinets behind the desk. There were four upholstered chairs in front of the desk in a semi-circle fashion. There were three suspended brass lamps over the desk and working area. To the right of us was a group of the same type of chairs surrounding an oval walnut table, adorned with ashtrays, a filled water pitcher and crystal glasses. There was a cluster of similar brass lamps suspended over this area. Between the doorway and the desk, on the left, was a small rectangular conference table on which was the strapped nude body of St. James. The golden jeweled dagger stuck out of his chest, next to a hole where his heart had been cut out and placed between his legs. There was very little blood on the table and none that I could see on the floor. Clearly the scene had not been disturbed.

A pile of clothing lay on a chair at the oval walnut table. It seemed to have been thrown there. The coat was on the bottom, then the shoes, then shirt, then trousers, then tie, with the undergarments on top. Holmes and Lestrade were carefully going through each item. St. James' wallet was in his coat pocket, and, according to Lestrade, there were notes totaling thirty pounds. This was set aside on the table as were the contents of his pocket. The piles contained some change, a key ring filed with a number of keys, a handkerchief, a comb, and some kind of native charm. It appeared to be carved from a soft volcanic rock, consisting of a huge head with elongated ears and nose. The clothing was not torn, nor were any buttons out of place. Holmes had carefully examined the shoes. St. James' stockings had been placed in his shoes. Holmes with his eyeglass in hand began looking over the fibers of the coat and trousers of what was St. James' dark blue pin-stripe suit. He seemed very intent in his examination.

Lestrade immediately ordered photographs of the crime scene which Macintosh performed. I should tell you that Macintosh was a charming fellow. He had a typical, friendly Scottish manner. He projected a gentle grace with a warm smile, almost boyish. He was probably in his early thirties. He had a mustache which was a little bushy, but matched his thick brown hair. He was a tall man, very agile and quick in movement. If his wit matched his appearance and manner, Scotland Yard would have a jewel for its crown.

Lestrade ordered an autopsy and one of the constables was dispatched to get the Scotland Yard coroner. He then examined the ties around St. James' extremities. "What do you make of these, Mr. Holmes?"

"They appear to be cut strips of animal hide about one inch wide and about one foot in length, with painted symbols on them," said Holmes, making a close visual examination with his eye glass out. "There is a cactus growing out of a rock and perched on the cactus there is an eagle eating a snake and the design seems to be repeated, at least on the strip attached to St. James' left arm."

"You are certainly correct, Mr. Holmes. Do you have any idea of what they mean?"

"The Aztecs believed in a certain legend that when the priests saw these signs, a cactus growing out of a rock, and, perched on the cactus, an eagle eating a snake, they would establish a great civilization. The priests saw these signs when entering the dismal swamps outside of what we now know as Mexico City. They built a powerful empire within two centuries. It would appear that what someone wants us to believe is that this has been a ceremonial sacrifice in the Aztec fashion. In their sacrificial ritual, the priest would cut out the living heart of the person being sacrificed. The Aztecs regarded being sacrificed as an extreme honor."

"Bloody honor is it," said I. "Cutting out your heart while you are still alive! Barbaric, I say, unnatural and brutal."

Lestrade asked Macintosh to remove the straps. There were no visible fingerprints of any kind. The dagger had been wiped clean. Lestrade removed the golden dagger and handed it to Holmes. "What do you make of this Holmes?"

"I think that you will find that these symbols, on opposite sides of the knife, represent the sun god and the moon goddess. The name given by the Aztecs to their sun god, I believe, was Ultzilopochtli and for the moon goddess, Coyolzauhqui. The Aztec believed that the moon goddess was murdered by her brother, the sun god. The combination seems to indicate death and resurrection. I do not know what the significance is of the emeralds and rubies which adorn this knife."

"You believe that this was an Aztec sacrifice?"

"Lestrade, either that or someone is wanting us to believe that it was."

"Mr. Holmes, do you have any theory on why the heart was placed between St. James' legs?"

"None obvious, unless it could symbolize some special disgrace that I am not aware of. The Aztecs believed that it was a great honor to be chosen for sacrifice in this manner, where the priest would literally cut out the living heart of the victim and hold it up before the crowd from the temple steps. Many times the volunteer victim would be a renowned warrior. This whole thing is puzzling to me."

"You don't think that St. James was Aztec, do you?"

"I don't believe so, but only our investigation will tell us that. Do you mind if I examine the body for any other signs of mischief?"

"No, Mr. Holmes, please continue with your examination."

"Hey, Watson, what is this?", said Holmes as he raised up the head of St. James.

What a contorted expression there was on the face of St. James. His eyes were open and staring into the ceiling. His mouth was grimaced and drawn. I closed his eyes and then went to the back of his head where Holmes had found an abrasion just behind the right ear. It was swollen and reddened with a heavy indentation entering the scalp, deepening in descent. Part of the hair had been torn and was clotted with dried blood. I immediately responded that this man had been hit on the head before he was tied to this table. I would judge from the wound site that he probably died as a result of the blow. This was confirmed by the lack of blood around his body. If this was so, why was this heinous charade carried out? I continued my inspection of the body, but could find no other marks, except at the ankles and wrists, where the victim had been tied to the table.

Holmes scrapped beneath the victim's fingernails and toenails and placed the scrapings in an envelope. Lestrade said nothing of this.

"Lestrade, I would urge you to have his blood examined for any sign of drugs."

"Of course, Mr. Holmes."

I think that we should examine the room closely for any clues. Sir Rodney had indicated that St. James had removed several artifacts from the treasure and we have only found one. There is a locked cabinet behind his desk which I feel will contain the remaining artifacts. We should probably find the key to it on the ring on the table. However, before we start unlocking bank property, we should send one of the constables to fetch Thomas Kingsley who is now in charge of this department. But first I want to complete my examination of the floor."

Holmes disappeared into the hallway from which we had entered. When I looked out into the hall, there was Holmes on all fours, like a bloodhound on a scent, eyeglass in hand, examining the fibers of the brown carpet. It was a tightly sewn carpet with short fibers close together. I could see no signs of trauma in the carpet, but Holmes seemed unusually interested. He suddenly jumped up and came hurriedly back in the room.

"Lestrade, I need very bright lights in the hallway," requested Holmes.

Lestrade beckoned to Inspector Macintosh, "Please get us some bright lights for the hallway, Macintosh. Is there anything else, Mr. Holmes?"

"Please take off your shoes and have your officers do so as well."

We all took off our shoes, which were placed next to the wall near the door in a Swedish manner.

In ten minutes, the hallway was brightly lighted and Holmes had resumed his bloodhound posture. He had crawled some fifty feet towards the elevator, when he suddenly stood with that self-satisfied look on his face and exclaimed, "I've got it Watson!"

"Got what?", said I, not having the foggiest notion of what he was talking about.

"I have found the spot where St. James met his blow. Look at these fibers closely and you can see the black marks made by the heels of St. James' shoes. Here, about six feet further on, is a small smudge of blood which came from his head. Someone has tried to remove it, but bungled the job, probably in haste to vacate the hallway."

Lestrade and Macintosh were with us in an instant. "What have you found, Mr. Holmes?"

"Lestrade, what we have found is the spot where St. James was struck from behind by a man over six feet tall, probably at least six foot three inches."

"Mr. Holmes, how can you know that?"

"Simplicity itself, Lestrade. St. James was struck from behind. St. James is six feet tall. The abrasion behind his right ear has been struck from above him. The wound depends with its entry. This was obvious from the direction of the indentation of his head. I say it was a man who is our murderer, because you don't find many women who are that tall. The blow was so heavily placed that it killed him. Women do not have that strength. An examination of his heels revealed a slight wearing on the back of the heel which could have only been made if the body was dragged to his room. The fibers in his blue trousers will show you the brown fibers of the hallway carpet. He was dragged by his shoulders with his feet dragging on the carpet. Hence, there was only one killer. If there were two, they would have carried him. If you look at the armpit of the sleeve, you can see the stress that sleeve took in this transport. Thanks to your lights, I have found the spot on the carpet where the heel marks begin, so it is reasonable to assume that this spot is where he was struck from behind. We also know that this murderer has a thorough knowledge of the human body and has had some medical training. The incision which was made in St. James' body was exactly where it should have been to reach the heart. The excised organ was in its complete form, with the arteries severed cleanly just above and below the heart muscle. This could have been the work of a surgeon but was definitely done by a man who has dissected cadavers before. I am sure that our killer knew that St. James was dead at the time he undressed him and performed the Aztec ritual."

Holmes had carefully examined the floor around the table to which the body had been bound. There were no foot prints of any kind. The floor of the room was covered with a thick, deep blue carpet. It was so thick that it did not show any impression when walked upon.

Holmes had begun to go though the desk drawers except the lower drawer on the right, which was locked. He opened all of the cabinet doors except the one which was also locked. He then turned to Lestrade and said, "Don't you think that we should check all waste bins close by for any evidence that may have been removed from the scene? Things are a bit too tidy here to suit me. I think that we may find some bloody clothing and rags. Please ask your men to keep their eyes out for anything that appears unusual. Could be a scapula, large metal bar or even gloves." Lestrade turned and dispatched two constables on this chore. At that time, Dr. Mortimer O'Reilly, the Scotland Yard Coroner, arrived.

Inspector Lestrade immediately took charge and made the necessary introductions. "Doctor, we need to know the cause of death as well and whether or not any drugs are found in his blood. We also would like to know if any other signs of trauma are found on the body. Dr. Watson has found that the victim had been hit in the head behind the right ear and feels that this was probably the cause of death. Please check the wound and the excision. We would like to know how it was accomplished. Were any other instruments used? We would like the removed organ saved after it has been carefully examined. Is there anything else you would like to add, Mr. Holmes?"

"Excellent , Lestrade, I would only like to stress that we need to know the time and cause of St. James' death."

Dr. O'Reilly efficiently went about his work. He was carefully recording his findings on a note-pad. He was a man of average height, solid features, pleasant Irish manner and speech, clean shaven, framed in a deep brown mane, in somewhat of a disarray. He had removed his green tweed jacket and donned a long white coat which he had taken from his bag. I noticed also that he was now wearing rubber gloves that came half-way up his arm. It was the sound of these being removed which caught our attention.

"Gentlemen, I have completed my preliminary examination and I will have to continue it at the Scotland Yard Morgue. I will try to answer your queries with the information I have been able to obtain. It is my opinion that Mr. St. James died between 7:30 and 8:00 P.M. last night caused by a blow to the right side of the back of his head, just above the ear. He was struck with a metallic instrument which was tapered to a small edge, but not to a point. It was not a knife. It was more like a flat rod. The incision made into the victim's chest was made with a surgeon's scapula or something very similar. The ribs leading to the chest cavity have been sawed through and then moved aside to reach the heart. The excision of the heart was done with the same scapula-type instrument in a meticulous fashion, with each artery carefully severed and the surrounding flesh cut away. The heart organ had been placed between the legs of the nude body of St. James near the groin area. The dagger had entered the body in the chest area, penetrating the right lung of St. James. There was little or no blood at the point of entry and the stab was singularly inflicted probably with one blow. The killer had turned the blade sideways to allow its passage between the victim's ribs. I found no other evidence of trauma of any kind, except that the ankles and wrists had been tightly tied causing a marking. Inspector Lestrade, if you would be good enough to have the body covered and removed to the morgue, I will continue my autopsy. I have removed the heart organ as requested. I find no evidence of any drug. If I have any further findings, I will get in touch with you. Any questions, gentlemen?"

"Quite agree, O'Reilly. Good job, indeed!," said I.

"Thank you, doctor. I will check later with you at the Yard," acknowledged Lestrade, in quite an official tone.

Lestrade then directed Inspector Macintosh to remove the body which was promptly done.

Holmes had been strangely quiet and was sitting by St. James' clothes, pipe in hand and looking towards the desk and shelving. I had seen him go into such deep thought before. It was almost like he had left this world. It was at that moment that Sir Rodney entered the room, somewhat relieved that the body of St. James had been removed.

"Mr. Holmes, may I have a word with you?", he asked.

"Yes, of course, Sir Rodney," responded Holmes, bounding up from his chair as if he had been startled from his faraway land of thought.

"Could we talk in the hall?"

"Surely."

The two men left the room with Sir Rodney ushering by gesture to Holmes and then following him. When the two men were away from people, Sir Rodney spoke, "Mr. Holmes, Lord Kensington has asked me to employ you to help us understand what has occurred here and what ramifications there may be for the Bank. It is not that we do not have confidence in Scotland Yard, but the Bank has a great stake in making sure that it is properly, promptly and correctly resolved. In this envelope is your retainer of 3000 pounds as before. We will cooperate with you in every way. Will you accept this? Oh, I should say that this employment should not be made public, nor should Scotland Yard know of it. You may, of course, include Dr. Watson in our confidence."

Holmes reached out and took the tendered envelope and responded, "It will indeed be a pleasure to work with you in this most interesting case. I don't know when I have had such a challenge. I must admit that, at this point, I am completely baffled. I will need the help of your staff if I am to understand anything."

"Good. Lord Kensington will be pleased. Of course, we will give you any cooperation that you may need. Please keep me advised of your plans and progress. We would like to have the final approval of any contacts with the staff, except as may be made assisting Inspector Lestrade in the official investigation."

Holmes returned to the crime scene alone.

"What was that all about?", inquired Lestrade, a little irritated by the exclusion.

"Bank business," said Holmes, dismissing the subject.

Inspector Macintosh entered the chamber accompanied by a tall, muscular-appearing man, well groomed in a dark blue suit with conservative accouterment. His features were sculptured and distinct, framed by coal-black hair which was extended by a mustache joining his sideburns, as was the current fashion. His eyes were somewhat smaller than normal, dark in nature matching his hair but very intent. He wore gold-framed spectacles. He reminded me somewhat of how St. James had first appeared to me, without the twitch. He was a man in his middle forties I would guess.

Inspector Macintosh made the introductions. "Inspector, this is Thomas Kingsley, First Assistant Manager of the Note Department. Mr. Kingsley, this is Inspector Lestrade of Scotland Yard who has asked to talk with you about this tragedy."

After introducing Holmes and me, Lestrade began, "What can you tell us about Mr. St. James' death?"

"I was phoned shortly after 9:00 P.M. last evening and advised of the murder. I came to the Bank as soon as I could get here and found Mr. St. James' body strapped to the table with a knife sticking out of his chest. I sealed off the room with security guards and contacted Scotland Yard. I haven't been back in the room since that time."

"Was anything removed or moved in the chamber?"

"No, I did determine that Mr. St. James was dead, but nothing was altered in any manner. I did phone his wife and advised her of what I had found."

"Do you have any idea who would want to kill Mr. St. James?"

"No, I really do not have any idea."

"What was your relationship with Mr. St. James?"

"He was my supervisor and my closest friend. We have worked together for over ten years. Our families would get together for picnics and dinners and our wives were also good friends. We are members of the same club. I would have to say that we were like brothers, or at least I felt that way."

"Did you work closely together?"

"Very. My duties are with the Domestic part of the Note Department, which has to do with the issuance of currency for the government and control of the bullion and notes to back it. On those matters, we worked very closely together. I reported to him on my work, any problems and proposed solutions. We really did not discuss the Foreign Department problems. That is headed up by Percy Fawnsworth. He would keep me abreast of the over-all activities so that I would know what was going on, but he would seldom give me details."

"What projects was he working on these last couple of days?"

"He was working with the King of Tonga to set up the issuance of 5,000,000 pounds Sterling of coin and currency. That would be through the Foreign Department, but we had discussed it. He had made contact with Sotheby's for an auction of the Tongan treasure which the King had brought to us. Mr. St. James felt that it should fetch 4-5 times its gold value. An arrangement had been made with their manager to view to treasure in our vaults today."

"Do you have any history concerning the gold treasure? Where did it come from and how did it get into the hands of the King of Tonga?"

"Mr. St. John felt that it probably came from the Aztec and Inca civilizations. They are the only ones in that part of the world that we know of with that kind of treasure, but we need experts to advise us. How this came to Tonga, I do not know. You will have to get that from the King and his Prime Minister."

Holmes and Macintosh had been intently listening. I guess that I was also, as this Kingsley chap was very eloquent in his speech and delivery. It wasn't like Holmes to take such a back seat in questioning, but then again Lestrade seemed to be doing a good job. Holmes had lit up his pipe and smoke swirled around his head. Lestrade had removed the pile of St. James' clothes and we had taken our seats around the oval table.

"Mr. Kinglsey," queried Holmes, "do you know of any relationship Mr. St. James may have had with Polynesia and, particularly, the Easter Islands?"

"Well, as I am sure that you are aware of, Tonga is part of that island group. Mr. St. James' grandfather, Robert Murdock, served as a cabin boy on one of Captain Cook's voyages to Tonga. He had gone ashore with a landing party which was attacked by a ferocious tribe of Tongans and every member of that party, some twenty as the story goes, was murdered, except for young Robert, who was then about fourteen years of age. Robert was raised by one of the chieftains and literally held prisoner by them for almost twenty years. Murdock then returned to England where he married and had children. I believe that he had two daughters, one of whom was Mr. St. James' mother. Why do you ask, Mr. Holmes?"

Holmes picked up the charm from the contents of St. James' pocket which had been placed on the table.

"We found this charm in Mr. St. James' pocket, depicting a head with very pronounced features, carved out of volcanic rock. It is identical to the megalithic monuments found on Easter Islands which are on burial platforms called ahus. There are some 100 of these statutes on the island overlooking the sea. Some are 40 feet in height. Do you know how Mr. St. James came to have this charm?"

"It was given to him for good luck by his grandfather. He carried it always. I do not know more about it than that. He always carried it."

"Mr. Kingsley, we would like to inspect the contents of the locked cabinet behind Mr. St. James' desk and the locked desk drawer. We think that the keys are here on the table."

"Certainly," replied Kingsley, and Holmes led the way, key in hand, to the cabinet.

"What we saw before us was a collection of glittering gold objects, some of which were bejeweled. Holmes withdrew a beautiful goblet, encrusted with stones which appeared to be emeralds and rubies. There were several idols with the same imaging as we had seen on the dagger. I believe Holmes said that one side was the sun god and the other the moon goddess. They were passed to Lestrade and then placed on the desk for inspection. Then Holmes cackled, "What have we here, Watson?" He then handed me four small knives which appeared to be surgical instruments and indeed they were.

"Holmes, these are scapulas. The finest that I have ever seen. See how they angle. The handles are gold but the blades are carbon iron and honed to razor sharpness. How can they maintain their precision all of these years?"

"I think, Watson, that we will find that they are Incan. They were known for their advanced surgical skills. It is believed that their knowledge of brain surgery a thousand years ago exceeds our knowledge today. I believe that we have found the utensil which the killer used for dissecting."

"I believe that you have, Holmes. There is no doubt that those instruments could have performed the job. I see no signs of blood on the instruments, though. Wiped clean, I guess."

"Exactly, Watson, exactly!"

Holmes then removed a large brown envelope which was labeled in the upper left corner, "TONGA". Holmes then read from the entries on the front, "Here Mr. St. James noted the meeting with the King and his Premier three days ago. Yesterday, he noted that he phoned Sotheby's and set up a meeting here for this afternoon at 3:00 P.M. with their manager Malcolm Hathaway who would bring an appraiser with him. The last entry to the file shows that he met with the King and Premier at 5:00 P.M. yesterday. He gave approval for the note issuance. The coinage and notes were to be created by the Sothis Engraving Company, Ltd. He had been authorized to negotiate with Sotheby's for the auction or sale of the artifacts and the King and Prime Minister would also be present at 3:00 P.M. today. It indicates that the meeting adjourned at 5:45 P.M. yesterday and he had escorted them both back to the check point. That is the last entry on the file. I am impressed with his thoroughness.

'Sothis' is an interesting name Watson. It is the name for the star Sirlus, the Dog Star, given by the ancient Egyptians. Probably not important," mused Holmes.

Holmes then asked Kingsley to open the locked desk drawer. What we saw was an empty drawer. Nothing was inside it, absolutely nothing!

Holmes stated rather matter-of-factly, "It is indeed interesting that our killer would have possession of artifacts worth thousands of pounds and leave them. Yet this drawer is completely empty. I have to assume that it, too, was opened, the contents removed, and re-locked so as to leave it in the same condition as found. But who would lock an empty drawer of a desk? The simple answer is: our murderer! The question is: What did that drawer contain? Do you know, Kingsley?"

"No, Mr. Holmes, I do not. I will inquire around. Perhaps his secretary will know."

"Kingsley, I should like to visit with her, but not at this moment. See what you can find. Anything will help immensely."

Lestrade, who was overwhelmed with our discoveries, blurted out, "Macintosh can question her if you wish, Mr. Holmes. He has a way with women!"

'That would be fine, Lestrade, but these other matters are more pressing at this moment."

"Kingsley, who in the bank knew of this treasure?"

"Mr. Holmes, everyone. It was the talk of the bank. It began with the guards who unloaded it and placed it in the vaults in the gold cellar."

"Who knew of the items that were removed by St. James?"

"To enter a vault in the gold cellar, it requires the presence of the Governor, Deputy Governor and the Manager of the Note Department, Mr. St. James. There are three locks which must be removed for entry and they each have a key to one of them. Guards are also present. There is an entry made on the inventory sheet on the door of what was removed. Practically anyone in the bank could have access to this sheet. Mr. St. James had these items sitting out on this oval table after the first day. I believe that he locked them up only yesterday."

"All of them?"

"To the best of my knowledge, Mr. Holmes."

"Was Mr. St. James having any problems with your Department?"

"None other than normal day-to-day events."

"Do you know of any problems that he was having, other than this Tonga affair?"

"He indicated that he was having some sort of difficulty with the Foreign Department, but had not put his finger on what that quandary really was. He told me that he hesitated to discuss it until he had more facts, but wanted me to be aware of it. As far as I know those were the only things on his mind other than the routine matters."

"Kingsley, I would like you to go through the papers on St. James' desk and see if you can learn anything of the issue. You will want to remove his personal effects for his wife, but we would like to view them before their delivery. I am sure that Lestrade will want to take the dagger and surgical knives into custody and will give you a receipt for them."

"Certainly, Mr. Holmes," responded Lestrade, who had been tranquilized by having Holmes take the laboring oar.

"Lestrade, do you think we should be present with the King and Sotheby's manager?"

"I do, Mr. Holmes, I do."

"Will that be agreeable with you, Kingsley?"

"Of course, Mr. Holmes."

"Kingsley, I know that you will be removing some of St. James' keys. I would appreciate your telling us what each key is for after you have had a chance to examine them."

Holmes turned to our investigative party and suggested, "How about some lunch? Care to join us Kingsley?"

"No, thank you, Mr. Holmes. Things are in a bit of a turmoil and I think that I had better stay in today. Hope that you understand."

"Of course. Oh, Kingsley, we would like to meet with Percy Fawnsworth at 1:00 P.M. Can that be arranged?"

"Yes, Mr. Holmes. I will advise him. He is at the other end of the hall. An usher will show you up."

Lestrade wrote out a receipt for the evidence and directed a constable to take it to the Yard. We left to find our culinary satisfaction.

After lunch, Holmes excused himself to send a telegram and rejoined us at the Bank of England at 1:00 P.M.. He seemed invigorated and when I inquired about the telegram he simply shrugged his shoulders and said, "I am calling in the reserves." I could only think of the young roughnecks that Holmes used to scout London on his errands. I quickly dismissed that thought. So the mystery lingered.

Lestrade had been met by his two officers sent to inspect trash bins.

They were carrying a box.

"Found 'um, sir, in a trash bin in a cleaning closet just down the hall from where the body was. We found bloody rubber gloves, similar to the ones that the coroner used. There was this set of tongs about a foot and a half long. I think that they are used to move gold bars. Looks like a little blood where they come together. Found a small bladed saw. Very narrow blade. Like one a carpenter would use to saw a small hole. I think they are called key-hole saws. Blood all over it. There were four rags, two of them were still damp and all red. Looks like blood to me," reported the sergeant.

Holmes had arrived just as Lestrade was reviewing the find and they both inspected it together.

"What do you make of these, Mr. Holmes?"

"It is as I expected, Lestrade, except I did not think that the murder weapon would be so long. With a foot and a half fulcrum and with the jaws extending downward from the end of the instrument, it would lower the required height of the murderer. One thing is certain and that is that our killer has planned this affair very thoughtfully."

Macintosh, who had been like a shadow to Lestrade picked up the tongs and swung them, like a person who was going to strike an imaginary tall person in the head. Holmes' conclusion was obvious.

This time our entrance was more formal. We signed in the registry and then we were assigned an usher to deliver us to Percy Fawnsworth. We exited the lift on the fourth floor and went down the same hallway but in the opposite direction. We followed our guide into a reception room which was tastefully paneled in a dark walnut. The couch and chairs were leather covered and the room gave a manly warmth. The receptionist excused herself and announced us.

"Good afternoon, gentlemen. You wanted to see me. I am Percy Fawnsworth. Ghastly business! Poor Mr. St. James. We are all in a kind of shock, you know. Just does not seem possible. Right here on the same floor. You might say just outside my chambers."

Lestrade stepped forward and made our introductions. Percy Fawnsworth was a tall, rounded man. Not fat, but a little plump. He was balding in the forehead. He combed his thinning brown hair forward much in the manner of Julius Caesar. His hair was shortly cut. His facial features like his body were somewhat rounded and cleanly shaven. His manner was somewhat nervous. He obviously had a keen mind that was busy all the time. His hands were large and it seemed to me that he had at one time been a person who used his hands to make a living like in the building trades. He also wore small,square, gold-framed glasses that perched on the end of his nose. I suppose for close reading because when he looked at you, in talking, he peered over the tops. He looked like a character out of Charles Dickens' stories. His clothes were well tailored, dark gray, with a vest, which he filled. His tie seemed to match the suit, neither adding nor taking away from its formality. He was probably a man in his mid forties.

Fawnsworth lead us into his conference room through his office which was occupied by a large desk at one end, encircled by chairs like we had seen in the reception room. Here, I found a large rectangular walnut table that would seat twelve, with extra chairs along the side of one wall. We were then joined by his secretary, who was introduced as Miss Philpot and they immediately took the chairs by the door with Fawnsworth sitting at the head. We just found ourselves seats with Lestrade and Holmes close to where our host was sitting.

"Miss Philpot will take the notes of our meeting. The Governor has requested it. You are welcome to review or copy them after they have been typed. Where do you wish to begin, Inspector?"

"Tell us what you know of Mr. St. James' death."

I thought to myself, Lestrade never changes his dull ways.

"Inspector, I first learned about this when I was called at my home shortly after 9:00 P.M. last evening. I came down as quickly as I could and met Mr. Kingsley, our first assistant Manager. He had advised Scotland Yard and we visited the scene of the horror. Dear me, poor Mr. St. James! A big hole in his chest and that dagger sticking straight up. I shall never forget it. And his grimmaced face with his eyes staring straight up at the ceiling. I don't feel that I slept at all last night.

Mr. Kinglsey then sealed the room by locking the door and assigned two of our security guards to prevent entry. They have rotating shifts. I returned home and returned here in the morning at the usual time. Our guards were replaced by constables. I did see them remove the body. That is about it."

"Mr. Fawnsworth, what do you know about the Tonga matter?", queried Holmes.

"Last evening, before I went home, I was advised by Mr. St. James that the currency had been approved and that the Bank would guarantee the issuance of coin and currency in the amount of 5,000,000 pounds. I was instructed to set up an appointment with the Prime Minister of Tonga, Robert An'aga, to meet with Pa'uba Tu'ma who would work out the details. This meeting was set for 7:00 P.M. last night. Mr. Tu'ma is in charge of our South Pacific operations. Nice chap. I advised him that the pa'anga, which is the Tongan dollar would be equivalent to the British pound Sterling and that the coinage would be based on 100 seniti's being worth one pa'anga. Other than that, I did not give him further instructions. I knew that Mr. St. James was meeting with a representative of Sotheby's to look into the possibility of an auction of the treasure. I did see the artifacts on the oval table in Mr. St. James' office. Exquisite artifacts they are! We do not have any idea of the value of the stones. That just is not our cup of tea. I did view the treasure stored in the vaults, as its safekeeping is my department's responsibility. I have their inventory, in Tonganese, which has been of little help. We thought that the inventory could be made by Sotheby's with representatives of Tonga present. Kill two birds with one stone, so to speak. Sorry about that, my timing is bad today. Yes, I think that about does it. Any questions, gentlemen?"

"Does Mr. Tu'ma speak Tonganese?", asked Lestrade.

"Not necessary, Inspector. The King and Prime Minister both speak the King's English, and very well, I am told. It seems that the nobles of Tonga have been taught English by the Methodist missionaries since the turn of this century. It is required."

"What was your relationship with Mr. St. James?", continued Lestrade.

"I have worked very closely with him for the past ten years, since he became Manager of the Note Department. Before that, for about the same period, we both headed sub-departments within the Note Department. Nice man. He was a nice man, very nice. He was my supervisor and we seemed to work well together. I was never very close socially to him. He was very much business, you know. If he had a sense of humor, I was not privy to it."

It was at this point that Holmes entered in. "Was St. James having any problems with your department?"

"Well, I guess that you could say so. He did not really confide in me what he was about. Seemed like he was interested in our African Department. He requested a number of documents concerning currency guarantees in that sector and their reserves. He was also looking into the Asian Department. It seems that after Disraeli led Parliament into proclaiming Queen Victoria Empress of India all devil has broken loose with the financial markets there. This strong nationalistic movement grows daily."

"Who heads up those departments: African and Asian?"

"The African Department is headed by Said Karnak and the Asian Department by Bahadus Meerut."

"How long have they been with the Bank?"

"Karnak has been in charge of the Department less than a year, but has worked for us for probably 5 years. Meerut was managing his department when I took over the Foreign Department. Probably been here 20 years."

"How do you regard their work?"

"Meerut's work is sterling. Karnak is too new in his present position to be properly evaluated, but he seems to be doing a good job."

"Have you personally had any problems with their Departments recently?"

"No, Mr. Holmes, I have not. I can only reiterate that Mr. St. James was concerned about something."

"Have the files requested by Mr. St. James been returned to your Department?"

"He has direct access to our files. Funny that you should ask. He wanted to get the files himself. The documents we furnished, but not the files. He or one of his assistants would remove and replace the files. So I would have no knowledge of the movement of those files."

Lestrade, re-entered the game. "Do you have any idea of who might want to kill Mr. St. James?"

"No, sir, I do not. Can't think of anyone who would want to kill that nice man."

"Who was Mr. St. James' secretary?', Holmes asked.

"Daisy Talcan. Her office is just this side of his."

"Lestrade, shall we pay her a visit? We have some time before our meeting with the King."

"Of course, if you think it necessary, Mr. Holmes. Thank you very much for meeting with us, Mr. Fawnsworth."

With that and our individual "Thank Yous" we were in the hallway heading for the office of Daisy Talcan, and what I might as well say, Miss Daisy Talcan, which she quickly proudly emphasized, was a charming, attractive lady of near 40 years of age. She was small in size, well formed and dressed conservatively, but in good taste. Her blond hair was long and gathered with a bow tied behind her head, with the golden strands falling to the middle of her back. She wore horn-rimmed glasses, which gave her the scholarly appearance. Her teeth were beautifully glistening through her smile. Her large blue eyes showed from beneath the sorrow of the moment and the apprehension that she surely felt.

Lestrade had entered first, followed by Macintosh, Holmes and me. Lestrade made the introductions and asked if he might talk to her about her work. Because her office was small, she invited us back into the scene of the crime and we were again seated at the oval table. St. James' clothing had been removed.

Lestrade began, "Miss Talcan, what can you tell us of the death of Mr. St. James?"

"Really nothing, nothing at all. I read about it in the papers. I still cannot believe it. I expect him to enter at any moment." She was starting to break into tears as her face grimaced and then she recaptured her composure.

"Do you know of anyone who would want to kill Mr. St. James?"

"No, Inspector, no one. I have worked with him some four years and honestly say that I have never known a more pleasant man. He was all business, of course, expected a lot, but appreciated what you did to assist him."

"Did he discuss the work with you?"

"Not as he would with one of his Managers. I would say that, though I was his personal secretary, I was not his confidential secretary. Sure, I reminded him of family birthdays and engagements, but our exchanges were primarily about business. He had a formal, but gentle manner about him. He was well liked by his staff."

"Did he ever indicate a sense of danger or threat of harm?" Holmes joined in the examination.

"No, Mr. Holmes, he did not."

"Did he indicate any problems with the Department?"

"Yes, Mr. Holmes, he did. He was worried that authorized currency guaranteed by the Bank had been intentionally issued in excess of the reserves."

"Any suspects?"

"Not by name. He was concerned about the African and Asian Departments. He had me pull a lot of files. He was reviewing them last night. He did not tell me more than that. He would not want to create any suspicion that was not justified. That is the kind of man he was."

"Were you working with him last night?"

"No, Mr. Holmes, my job ended at 5:00 P.M. I can say that there has never been an occasion that kept me after hours. I have worked some Saturday mornings, but only a few."

"Did you assist Mr. Kingsley in going through the papers located on Mr. St. James' desk?"

"Yes, but I found none of the files that Mr. St. James had asked me to pull yesterday. He could have put them back himself, but that is not likely."

"Miss Talcan, do you recall any specifics about the files that you had pulled the day before?", queried Holmes.

"He had asked me to pull all current transactional files from both the Asian and African Departments, which I did."

"Have these files been returned to their respective departments?"

"Yes, Mr. Holmes, I checked this morning, and they appear to have been refiled."

"Thank you, Miss Talcan," said Holmes as he rose from his chair surrounded by pipe smoke.

Lestrade thanked our charming hostess as the hour was approaching for our meeting with the Tongans and auctioneers. What a full day this had been.

Thomas Kingsley returned to his new office shortly before 3:00 P.M. He had firmly stepped into his new role. His black eyes were surrounded with the strain of his office. "Good afternoon gentlemen. I have completed the review of the papers at Mr. St. James' desk and found nothing but the usual reports and correspondence. I engaged the help of Miss Talcan, whom I understand you have met and we both searched the desk and documents. She told me that he had been reviewing files from the African and Asian Departments, but none of the files were there. I have reviewed the keys; the two you are familiar with and a third which unlocks his office door, all of which I have removed. The others are for his personal use at home, I presume, and I have placed them with his personal effects which you have asked to review."

St. James personal effects, including his clothing, had been placed in three sacks by the desk. Lestrade, Macintosh and Holmes began to go through them, one at a time. Lestrade took the lead, taking out the contents of each sack, then passing the item to Holmes, who passed it to Macintosh, who returned it to the sack of origin. There were no irregularities noted. At the conclusion of this examination, Kingsley rang for a page and instructed him to have these delivered to the home of St. James. The office had been cleaned in our absence and a new odor of cleanliness had replaced the stench of death which is so familiar to a medical man.

The page had no sooner left the room, when another appeared accompanied by two very impressive figures. Impressive because of their height, manner, and dress. The page announced, "King George Tupou II of Tonga, and his Prime Minister, Robert An'aga."

The Prime Minister who had followed the King, stepped forward to greet us. He was a tall man, probably six foot two or three inches in height. He was probably a man in his early fifties.

His features were not like those of the King. His skin was white, his hair brown mixed with a little gray, and his features were somewhat sharp, a little like that of Holmes. He was a healthy and robust appearing man, perhaps a little on the thin side. His brown eyes were large and penetrating. He walked with the grace of a jungle cat. There was something familiar about this man, but I could not put my finger on it.

"We are very sorry, gentlemen. We read about this tragedy in The Times. We had become very fond of Mr. St. James."

At this point, Kingsley stepped forward with outstretched hand and introduced himself. The Prime Minister clasped the hand and introduced himself and then introduced the King. Kingsley continued by introducing us all, beginning with Lestrade.

The King addressed Holmes, "Mr. Holmes, I am honored to meet you. I have followed your exploits with much pleasure. Dr. Watson has made your name a household word among the nobles of Tonga."

"Thank you, King George. You have to remember that it is Watson's flair for the tale that the readers really like."

King George Tupou II was a large man. Not just tall as his Prime Minister, but fleshy. His hair was black and thick. His round face was high-lighted by two large black eyes. His lips were a little large, but easily exposed large, starkly-white teeth. The whiteness was accentuated by his suntan-colored skin. I should say quite simply that he looked Polynesian. He was formally attired in a black suit with tails and vest and a red band of silk with an embroidered golden crown, crossing his breast under the coat diagonally. The Prime Minister was in a carefully tailored, dark-gray business suit with vest. They made quite an impressive pair.

It was at that point that Miss Talcan entered and announced that two gentlemen from Sotheby's were here for their appointment and then introduced Malcolm Hathaway, the Manager of Sotheby's, and his associate Tobias Wecht. Kingsley made the introductions of our party beginning with the King.

"I cannot tell you how shocked I was to learn about the tragedy of Mr. St. James, gentlemen. Dreadful matter. Can I assume that our plans are still in place? That you want us to look over these artifacts and advise you of how we might fare at an auction?", inquired Mr. Hathaway.

"Yes, certainly," responded Kingsley.

"I understand that the only inventory that you have is in Tonganese?"

"Mr. Kingsley," said the King, "Dr. An'aga has made a translation of the inventory into English which we have had copied. One for you, Mr. Kingsley and one for you, Mr. Hathaway."

Dr. An'aga passed the two large stacks of sheets to them. Kingsley then advised that the Governor and Deputy would meet the party at the vaults so that Sotheby's men could examine them. The King stated that he had brought four guards who could remain with the examiners and that we would not have to remain with them while they made their preliminary inspection. Because of the lateness of the day, it was agreed that they would only examine the contents of one vault. They would reconvene the meeting shortly before 5:00 P.M.

After Hathaway and Wecht had been safely tucked away in the vault with four Tonga guards and locked into the vault by the three locks, we returned to St. James' former office. Lestrade then entered the conversation.

"Mr. Kingsley, it is necessary that I inquire of King George and his Prime Minister concerning the death of Mr. St. James. I would prefer if we could meet alone with Mr. Holmes, Dr. Watson and, of course, Inspector Macintosh. Will that be possible?"

"Yes, of course," and with that he excused himself from the company, saying, "I will see you at 5:00 P.M."

We then gathered around the oval table and Miss Talcan entered with tea and small cakes. I asked Dr. An'aga if he was a medical man and he replied, "Yes, I am."

He told me that he had attended medical school in Sydney, Australia, and had what we know as a general practice of medicine in Nuku'alofa, which is the capital city of Tonga. The population of Tonga was probably less than 30,000 inhabitants although there was no accurate account of the exact number of people. His job as Prime Minister took little time, except on formal occasions, which seldom occurred.

Lestrade had moved into the conversation as soon as the fact was established that Dr. An'aga was a medical doctor.

"Did you know Mr. St. James before this meeting at the bank?"

"No, not personally."

"Tell me then, how did you know him?"

"I knew of him, you see, because we were cousins once removed. We have the same grandfather, Robert Murdock."

"Did St. James know of your relationship?", joined in Holmes.

"No, I did not think it a proper subject until we had put His Highness' business to rest."

"Can you tell us more about your grandfather," continued Holmes.

"Robert Murdock came to the island as a cabin boy of fourteen. He went ashore with two longboats full of men from Captain Cook's ship. They were brutally attacked and everyone was killed except grandfather who was raised in the household of a local chieftain. He was brought up in the ways of the nobles but the only restriction was that he was not able to leave the island. This continued for almost twenty years. The local chieftain was defeated and the conqueror, a Christian chieftain, allowed grandfather to return to England. While he was entering his manhood years, he met my grandmother, Annette Dubois, a French nurse working in the Methodist mission. When grandfather left the island, she was pregnant with my father. Grandmother married a local noble, whose name my father took."

"Why didn't your grandmother go with Murdock?"

"Grandfather did not want to take anything from this island. He wanted to return home and start a new life. Grandmother did not tell him of the pregnancy, but he had refused to marry her."

"There was a great dishonor caused to the French nurse," said the King in a slow speaking, deep, mellow voice, with his eyes looking down. "In our country, the worse crime that you can commit is to cause someone dishonor. It is worse than murder."

"'That was almost 100 years ago," said the Prime Minister. "It should have no bearing on the death of my kinsman. I am very sorry indeed that such a terrible thing happened."

It was at this point that Lestrade said to the doctor, "Dr. An'aga, I would ask that you remain in London until we can get at the bottom of this matter. We will want to talk again after the facts begin to unfold."

"Surely," replied the doctor, "I, too, would like to have this matter explained."

Lestrade continued, "Mr. Fawnsworth told us that you had an appointment last evening with Mr. Tu'ma. Did you make that appointment at 7:00 P.M.?"

"Yes."

"And what time did you leave the Bank?"

"Probably around 8:00 P.M."

"Were you with him all of that time?"

"Except for a short time that I went to the men's room."

"At what time was that?"

"I really don't know, but probably in the middle of our meeting. We had left about 5:00 P.M. from our meeting with Mr. Kingsley, we went to dinner and then I returned here."

Holmes addressed a dialogue to the King. "King George, can you shed any light on how this treasure ended up in your possession?"

"How exciting! I am going to participate in an inquiry from the world's greatest detective. It will be fun for me to help. The monarchy of Tonga has only been in existence since my great grandfather was able to consolidate the islands in 1845 and took the name King George Tupou I. What you have to remember is that from the beginning of our records, some AD 900, the Tu'i Tonga were sacred representatives of the Tongan gods and ruled our people completely until the end of the 15th century. Their power was very great, and my father left the Tu'i Tonga alone when he came to power. It was only after the death of the last Tu'i Tonga in 1865 that we discovered the gold objects which we have brought to England. They were in hidden chambers beneath his temple. My father could not believe his eyes. If the Europeans who visited our poor islands had ever suspected this treasure, they would quickly have conquered us and taken the treasure. Dr. An'aga has gone back through the records of the temple and it is his opinion that this treasure was acquired over some five centuries. Although we do not have many people living in my kingdom, Tongans have scattered in settlements all over the South Pacific Ocean, clear to the Easter Islands off the coast of South America. We probably have 5,000 Tongans in the Hawaiian Islands alone. These Tongans believed the Tu'i Tonga was their god's representative and anything that was beautiful would have been given to him. Before the Europeans came, Tongans had little use for gold, except for its beauty. It is our estimate that we probably have over 100,000 Tongans on these islands. Tongans have always been good sailors and in the past they were ferocious warriors. Cannibalism was practiced until the missionaries came and even now the practice still exists on some of the outer islands. Tongan War parties raided the coasts of Mexico and South America, plundering what they could during all of those centuries, and the gold objects found their way back to the Tu'i Tonga. That is the only explanation that we can give based on the records that we have found. We know of no gold ever produced on our islands. The Polynesians from Samoa who first settled here brought no gold. I believe that you would say, Mr. Holmes, 'when all other contingencies fail, whatever remains, however improbable, must be the truth'. The gold is here and we believe that it came from the Incas and the Aztecs. What a blessing it is for our impoverished people."

"Thank you, Your Highness, you certainly humble me by your obviously thorough study of my work. I have to agree. The specimens that I have examined show the Inca and Aztec origin. How are your plans for a protectorate status with England proceeding?"

Here the King proceeded to tell us of his trip to England and his meeting with Queen Victoria, the Prime Minister, various members of Parliament and foreign office representatives. He had been so impressed by all of the formal functions that he had attended, the food served and the guests that he had met. It was very obvious that he was duly stirred and appreciated very much the gracious hospitality which he and his Prime Minister had received while here in England. Through all of this, the response to Holmes' question was that it was pending and quite likely that Tonga would be offered a protectorate status by Great Britain, which will allow it to self-govern but receive the protection of Great Britain in its relationship with the world. What a long day this had been for all of us! Only Holmes had seemed to be more and more exhilarated. As I was about to doze off, Kingsley returned with Hathaway and Wecht. Sotheby's representatives were excited.

"Mr. Kingsley," said Hathaway, "there is no doubt that the treasure will bring 4-5 times its gold value after a commission of ten percent. The Gems are another matter, but the ones that we examined were exquisitely cut, large and deep in the European tradition. We believe that museums from all over the world will want to participate in an auction, so that we would need to allow probably sixty days' notice of any sale. The sale should be conducted at our gallery. Mr. Wecht would need to study each piece during that time so that we will have a correct description for the auction. We would like to do this at the gallery. He suggests that we should pick up a small box each day, receipt it, and then exchange it for another the next morning. We would not mind if His Highness wants a guard to accompany the artifacts. What do you say, Your Highness?"

"I am indeed pleased with the prospects of the sale. You should proceed as you suggest. It will be necessary to send several guards to accompany the artifacts so that they might rotate their duty."

Holmes asked Mr. Wecht about the treasure and its source.

"Mr. Holmes, the items I inspected were definitely Inca and Aztec creations. It is interesting that they come from different time periods. The Inca were originally a small warlike tribe, inhabiting the south highland region of the Cordillera Central in Peru. About AD 1100, they began to move into the valley of Cuzco, where, for roughly the next 300 years, they raided and, whenever possible, imposed tribute on neighboring people. Until the middle of the 15th century, however, the Inca undertook no major imperialistic expansion or political consolidation. Their furthest advance prior to this time was southward about twenty miles. Some of these artifacts come from this period. They do not have the quality of the later pieces but certainly bear the progression of antiquity. The rest seems to be divided into two periods. They are identified by the rulers of the time. The first is that of Pachacuti Inca Yupanqui in AD 1391 to 1471. He is ranked by some historians with the greatest conquerors and rulers of all time. The second was the reign of Pachacuti's equally capable son, Topa Inca Yupanqui, AD 1420-1493. The empire had reached about 2500 miles from north to south and from east to west about 500 miles. The quality of workmanship from both of these periods is exquisite."

Mr. Wecht continued. "Now for the Aztec artifacts. They were relatively newcomers to the area. After the fall of the Toltec civilization which flourished from the 10th century to the 11th century, waves of immigrants flooded into Mexico's central plateau area around Lake Texcoc. As they were late arrivals, the Aztecs were forced to occupy the swampy area on the western side of the lake. They were surrounded by powerful neighbors who exacted tribute from them and their only piece of dry land was a tiny island surrounded by marshes. The Aztecs were able to convert this disadvantageous beginning into a powerful empire within two centuries. This was due in part to their belief in a certain legend. According to this legend, they would establish a great civilization in a marshy area where they would see a cactus growing out of a rock and, perched on the cactus, an eagle eating a snake. The priests supposedly saw this when they arrived at this dismal swamp. This symbol is repeated again and again in their art. By 1325, they founded the city of Tenochtiti, which is the present site of Mexico City. Much of their artifacts surround their numerous gods who ruled over their daily life. Among the most popular were the sun god, moon goddess, rain god, and Quetzaicoati, who was the inventor of writing, and the calendar, which they really stole from the more ancient Mayan civilization. The Aztec civilization ended with the invasion by Hernan Cortes in 1521. The artifacts had to come from the period before 1521, although many may have been received as tribute and may pre-date the Aztec civilization. The emeralds were probably mined in Columbia and I rather imagine that the rubies came from the same section of the Andes. They are beautiful stones and cut with precision."

I suddenly and instinctively dived to the floor. It reminded me of the Afghanistan War. The sound was ear-splitting, resounding through this stone building like a cannon fired in a cave. Billows of smoke came down the hallway by our door, which had been left open to accommodate Holmes' pipe. Inspector Lestrade jumped to his feet and out the door he was in an instant, followed by Macintosh. Holmes and I followed leaving our fellow companions in bewilderment. Kingsley had remained with the guests.

Not knowing the source of the fire, Lestrade led the way to the stairway. The smoke was swirling upward like it does in a chimney in a strong draft and there really was nothing we could do except wait for it to clear. We could hear the clanging of the fire trucks and the shouts of men working below us.

"What fools we have been, Watson! We should have anticipated that our murderer would arrange to have the log books destroyed. We should have known that it would have been done after the nine-to-five shift had left for the day."

"What do you mean, Mr. Holmes?", muttered a surprised Lestrade.

"Our killer has destroyed the log books that would have shown us who were in the building when St. James was murdered. He probably sent some type of incendiary bomb to Kingsley in a package with a time device, knowing that Kingsley was engaged. It remained at the Registrar's Office until the explosion."

A number of the Bank employees had come out of their offices and were heading for the elevator and stairs. Lestrade directed Macintosh to send them back to their rooms until the matter could be sorted out. It was probably an hour before the smoke had cleared enough for us to make our descent.

The fire had begun on the first floor at the Registrars' Office. The Registrar had been out of his office at the time of the explosion, but two guards on the other side of the door had been badly shaken up and had been removed to the hospital. The Registrar's Office was destroyed by fire and water from the firemen's hoses. It was a stinking, smoking, charred mess. The Deputy Governor had taken charge and was directing security. An alternate doorway had been opened and the Registrar had set up a replacement office to handle people entering and leaving the building. Cleaning crews had begun to remove the smoking debris from the office. Building maintenance workers stood by ready to close up this fire-damaged entrance.

You could see through to the street, where the Registrar's Office used to be. There were constables and bank security guards protecting the front of the building. Fire Wagons had been pulled up to the site in haste without order. Firemen in their metal caps and protective clothing were scurrying to and fro, picking up hoses and equipment. Behind this frantic scene was half of London.

Holmes had looked through the rubble in the Registrar's Office without any apparent discovery. He did state that the registry books had been completely destroyed. He was able to point out to Lestrade where he believed the blast had occurred. There really seemed little doubt of that because of the blackened indentation in the floor.

I was glad to be back in Baker Street. Lestrade had taken over the management of the scene of the explosion and had sent us home by cab. Mrs. Hudson had saved, or, I should say, preserved our dinner for which we were both grateful. Holmes had a telegram waiting for him when we returned, but the only comment that he made was, "Good".

It was after 9:00 P.M. when we finished eating and had retired. I have to admit that we had several sherries that night to slow down the rapid pace of our minds from the day's cascading events. We talked little as we sipped the sherry. Holmes was in his introversion syndrome. I cannot answer for him, but I have never been so tired in my life. I do not even remember my head hitting the pillow.

Chapter III

THE CATCHING TOOL

We had no sooner finished breakfast and returned to our rooms, when the doorbell rang and steps were heard coming up towards us. Mrs. Hudson had announced our visitors, but the step of Lestrade was unmistakable. Both Lestrade and Macintosh looked worse for their wear. I doubt they had much sleep last night.

I should tell you that Holmes had advised me of his employment, but of course he said that we had been employed to represent the bank's interest, cautioning me against disclosing this fact to anyone but especially not to Lestrade. He advised me of the retainer being the same as last time. He went on to ask me to chronicle the fact that he does share his fees with me in cases in which I participate and I have to say that, although my part of the fee is not large, it is most generous for my contribution.

"Good morning, Mr. Holmes. You are looking fit, considering what we went through yesterday. You, too, Dr. Watson. Wonder if I might share some thoughts about the Bank of England matter with you gentlemen. I do want you to keep abreast of the developments in this case. Can we find a seat and visit with you?"

"Of course, we are interested in what you have found. Take off your coats and hats and join us by this fire," responded Holmes in a somewhat alert voice and manner. The swirl of smoke was emitting itself from his curved large-bowl pipe and, from his intake, you knew that he was enjoying it after such a good breakfast. There is nothing quite like an after-breakfast pipe.

"After I sent you and Dr. Watson home, we were able to secure the area and disperse the crowd. I was able to interview the Registrar who told us that a bank messenger from another bank had delivered a box, as you suggested, for Mr. Kingsley, around 3:00 P.M. He was an older gentleman in the uniform of a messenger. He instructed the Registrar that there was no urgency and that the package could be delivered to Kingsley at the time that Kingsley left the Bank. This messenger was a rather tall man, but walked somewhat stooped. His hair was gray and rather bushy. His bearded face was framed with horned-rimmed glasses. He wore white gloves. The messenger did require the Recorder to acknowledge receipt for the package. Then he was gone.

I had Macintosh check the trash bins in the area surrounding the Bank and about 100 yards south of Threadneedle Street, in a deserted alleyway, we found a trash bag which contained the uniform, gloves, wig, beard and receipt pad. Macintosh had other officers scour the neighborhood for any witnesses, but the buildings were generally abandoned . We were not able to find any witnesses who saw this messenger, his change of clothing or its disposal. It is possible that he made the change in one of the vacant buildings and simply dropped the bag into the bin.

They are rebuilding the Registrar's office now. They have worked around the clock on it. I did have the bomb section of the Yard examine the scene. They felt that an explosive device was used, probably TNT, but could not figure out the detonating device, nor explain the burst of flame that had enveloped the office."

"Holmes," said I, "you have made a lifetime study of explosives. What do you make of this?"

"Watson, the explosive material was trinitrotoluene. When there is a symmetrical mixture of 2, 4 and 6, out of the 16 different numbered trinitrotoluenes, you have what is commonly called TNT. The bomb section was correct. Without a detonator, it is a rather stable material and is easy to manage. I believe that the TNT was in the box with red phosphorus packing. The detonator probably contained a blasting cap and a battery or batteries of the Leclanch cell type connected to a filament that, when turned on, would create enough heat to cause the blasting cap to explode and detonate the TNT. The explosion would ignite the red phosphorus spreading flame around the area. There was a timing device to set close the circuit which started the process. I saw the remains of what appeared to be a small clock actually blown into one of the interior walls.

Without the Registrar's records, we have no way of being sure who was in the Bank at the time of St. James' death. We do know that we are dealing with a very cunning, intelligent and, perhaps, desperate assassin. We need to be on our guard and to try to see the moves he plans before they are executed. This man is dangerous and ruthless. Remember that, Lestrade, 'dangerous and ruthless'!

We are not dealing with an ordinary criminal. This person reminds me of Moriarty. Had I not seen him fall into the falls, I would swear that it was him. Be on your guard at all times."

"Thank you, Mr. Holmes, I surely will. Today, I want to visit with Mr. St. James' widow. I want to know what she knows about the family roots to Tonga and if Mr. St. James was ever contacted by Dr. An'aga or anyone concerning his grandfather. I would like to follow up with an investigation with Pa'uba Tu'ma who met with Dr. An'aga. Really, I have a feeling that Dr. An'aga has more to do about this thing that he is letting on."

"Lestrade, I would like to meet with the personnel manager at the bank and begin going through personnel files of the employees. I am afraid that we may need to go through all 1700 of them, or at least those who were working at Threadneedle Street. Would you authorize that?"

"Certainly, Mr. Holmes, we will appreciate any help you can give us."

Holmes excused himself and after a telephone call returned to join us.

"Sir Rodney will meet with us at 10:00 A.M. He wants to make the introductions and set the perimeters of our examination. Can we meet at the Bank at that time?"

"We will meet you there at 10:00, Mr. Holmes."

With that, Lestrade and Macintosh left our rooms.

I had planned to return to my practice today. Hopefully, my associate was able to cover for me yesterday. For some reason, in the spring there is just not as much illness. It has to be mental attitude and anticipation of the good weather to come. Holmes asked me to attend the brief meeting with Sir Rodney after which I could go to my practice which began at 1:00 P.M. We gathered ourselves together and traveled by cabby to the scene of the bombing. What a mess! The outer stone wall where the Registrar's Office had been was about halfway rebuilt. The workers were like ants, crawling all over the scaffolding. Carts full of stone were on the street in front, waiting for their turn. We met Lestrade and Macintosh at the temporary Registrar's Office and were promptly ushered to the Office of the Solicitor General which was located on the 2nd floor. The lifts were back in operation, but the smell of smoke lingered. Workers and cleaners were everywhere.

Sir Rodney greeted us all by name. He looked tired and concerned. He asked Holmes what he had learned, but Lestrade, somewhat offended that it should not have been directed to him, volunteered a brief up-date. He then advised that Holmes would like to review all personnel files.

At that, Sir Rodney adamantly replied, "The security of the Bank of England is at stake here, gentlemen. We cannot, for security sake, turn over the personnel files to anyone without a court order. We cannot have employee information in the hands of the public or anyone. I will make this one concession: I will allow Mr. Holmes the privilege of going through them, but he alone. What do say you to that, Inspector Lestrade?"

"Agreed, Sir Rodney."

"The files are neither to be copied, nor removed from the Bank. Mr. Holmes, you may make notes, but they, too, must be left at the Bank. Will you accept these conditions?"

"Of course, Sir Rodney, I fully understand. I do however have one request. I would ask that the personnel manager orders each employee to prepare and submit on one sheet of paper and, if necessary, they may use the back of the sheet, a statement in the employee's own handwriting, not printing, furnishing us with the information requested on this questionnaire." With that Holmes gave us each a copy of the following questionnaire:

1. Name

2. Sex

3. Height

4. Nationality

5. Department

6. Job description

7. How long employed by the Bank

8. Where were you between 7:00 P.M. and 8 P.M. on the night of March 15, 1896?

9. If you were in the Bank between those times, list the names of anyone that you saw during that that time period. Please describe where this occurred and whether anything unusual happened.

10. Were you on the 4th floor between those times or on a lift which stopped on the 4th floor? If so, list everyone you saw and, if

unknown, include a description of that person.

11. If you were in the Bank working during those times, list the names of all employees that were with you and whether or not anyone left the office. If so, who and how long were they gone and for what purpose if you know.

12. From the day of the murder of Mr. St. James to this date, have you observed anything unusual occurring on the Bank premises? If so, please give details.

13. Have you had any medical training? If so, please detail.

14. Do you have any knowledge of any facts concerning the death of Mr. St. James or the bombing? If so, please give details.

15. Were any guests assigned to you between 7:00 P.M. and 8:00 P.M. on the date of Mr. St. James' murder? If so, please state the guest's name and address, the purpose of the visit, the time of the visit and what occurred during the visit. If so, did this guest ever leave your presence during the visit?

16. Print your name, office location and phone extension or number.

17. Sign this information sheet with your own signature.

18. Date the document and turn it in the Personnel Office on the date completed. We ask that this be done within 24 hours of this request.

"These sheets do not contain home addresses or other incriminating identification. Without the answers to these questions, we do not have anything that tells us who was in the Bank at the time of the murder. I would like to be able to remove these sheets from the Bank for examination. They will all be returned to the Bank after the examination has been completed. I want everyone who works in the Bank, from the Governor down to the cleaning lady, to furnish us with this information. It is absolutely essential. I ask that you trust me in this regard as I really do not wish to say more about this at this time. It will all be explained later."

"Mr. Holmes, if the request was made by anyone but you, I would refuse it without hesitation. I will agree to it subject to the terms which you have set out. The information is to be confidential and guarded. The sheets are to be returned after your examination to me personally."

"Thank you, Sir Rodney. Once we have learned from the employees who were guests, we will need a letter to go out to the guests who were on the premises between 7:00 P.M. and 8:00 P.M. with a short questionnaire. This should request a handwritten reply. I would like this letter to go out over your signature as Solicitor General in the form set out on this sheet."

With that, Holmes passed two handwritten sheets to Sir Rodney and Lestrade, which set out the following form:

Bank of England letterhead

Name and address of visitor

(printed letter)

Dear Visitor to the Bank of England:

Our staff has indicated that you were present on our premises on the 15th of March, 1986, between the hours of 7:00 and 8:00 P.M. It was during this time that Mr. St. James, the Manager of our Note Department, was murdered on the premises.

Scotland Yard has requested that we send you the attached form and they request that it is replied to immediately. They have asked that your response be on a single sheet of white paper and in your own handwriting. Failure to make a prompt response to this request will necessitate a visit from Inspector Lestrade or one of his staff.

We are sorry for the inconvenience and appreciate your cooperation.

Your humble servant,
Rodney Grope
Solicitor General

"Are you requesting that I send this letter, Inspector?"

"Yes, Sir Rodney, I am. Mr. Holmes and I are working together on this case. This will save the Yard hundreds of hours of foot work."

Sir Rodney and Lestrade then read the questionnaire:

Please furnish us with the following information in your own handwriting on a single sheet of white paper.

1. Name, address and phone number.

2. Your employer, address and phone number. If self-employed, so indicate.

3. Were you a visitor at the Bank of England on the 15th of March, 1896, between the hours of 7:00 and 8:00 P.M.? If so, please state:

A. The purpose of your visit.

B. The person or persons you visited.

C. The office number of your visit.

D. Did your hosts, or any of them, leave your presence between those hours? If so, please give details.

4. Were you personally acquainted with your host or hosts? If so, please describe your relationship.

5. Were you on the 4th floor between those times or on a lift which stopped on the 4th floor. If so, list everyone you saw and, if unknown, include a description of that person.

6. Did you observe anything during your visit at the Bank on the 15th day of March, 1896, which you consider unusual? If so, what?

7. Have you had any medical training? If so, please give details.

8. Were you personally acquainted with Mr. Godfrey St. James? If so, please give details setting out your relationship and the last time that you saw him.

9. Please sign this information sheet with your own signature and date it.

Thank you for your cooperation.

"Yes, Mr. Holmes, that will be fine. Exemplary job," Lestrade said rather formally as if it were his idea all along.

You could see that Lestrade was puzzled. His face was contorted and his brow wrinkled as if in a frown. He acted as if he were playing a card game without a full deck. I think that it was the requirement that the response be handwritten that was causing this contortion. Obviously, his brain could not figure it out. I was not surprised.

"That will be satisfactory, Mr. Holmes. Let me take you to the personnel manager who will implement this program. His name is Mr. Paul Bodmin and I have alerted him to your visit. I don't want you to think that I am beginning to anticipate you, Mr. Holmes, but it seemed a rather natural course."

Down the hall a few doors to the right, we met Mr. Paul Bodmin. He was a rather studiously appearing man, small in stature, probably 50 years of age, thin and concentrative. He was the type of person that you would not see in a crowd. Non-descriptive, I guess, would describe him.

Sir Rodney made the introductions. He then instructed Bodmin to allow Holmes to examine all personnel files. There were to be no exceptions. Holmes was to be provided with a good sized office with a conference table and comfortable chairs. Adequate lighting would need to be provided. Bodmin had said that he had such a room, near the files which Holmes could certainly use.

Sir Rodney then went into the requirements of the questionnaire, the personnel manager's letter to the employees, Sir Rodney's letter and the visitors' questionnaire. All of these were to be printed. It was agreed that the personnel manager would not sign the employee letters, but just show his name and title at the bottom of the page. Sir Rodney wanted to review the letters sent out over his name and he would sign them personally. I rather expected that from a solicitor.

Bodmin would provide Lestrade, Holmes and Sir Rodney with a list of these two categories and furnish a report on who had responded with the date of the response.

Sir Rodney stressed to Bodmin that this meant all persons who worked in the bank from the Governor down. It should include any Directors who had any active function in the bank, other than attending the Director's meetings.

"All questionnaires are to be turned over to Mr. Holmes who has authority to remove them from the premises. They will be returned to the bank after he has done his research. Mr. Holmes, and Mr. Holmes alone, shall have access to all personnel files. This includes yours, mine and the Governor's. Mr. Holmes shall not remove any part of those files from this office. He is not to take his notes out of here without my expressed written permission. Is that understood?"

All of us reflectively nodded assent.

"Does that about cover the matter, gentlemen?", questioned Sir Rodney and there was no question as to who was going to be in charge of this campaign. He was indeed impressive and commanding.

"Right, Sir Rodney," responded Lestrade.

"Excellent," replied Holmes. "I will need a four-to-five-foot conference table, not wider than three feet, along with three swivel chairs, preferably comfortable ones, three bright lights and a free standing chalk board, probably not longer than six feet long, delivered to Baker Street."

The Solicitor General, who had been acting more like a general than a solicitor, turned to Bodmin and directed, "See to this immediately."

"Yes, sir," retorted Bodmin, his small frame growing taller as if he were trying to come to attention. I rather expected a salute.

"Gentlemen, is there anything else?"

"I would like to begin reviewing the personnel files tomorrow morning, beginning at 8:00 A.M. if that is satisfactory with you, Mr. Bodmin? This will give you some time to set up the office."

"I will look forward to working with you, Mr. Holmes and should you need anything, please ask for it. I will also get you a pass. It will be at the Registrar's Office tomorrow morning when you arrive. The requested furniture will be delivered to your quarters this afternoon. Sir Godfrey will have to sign the requisition and he has your address."

I then left for my office. Holmes returned to Baker Street to prepare for this furniture. Lestrade and Macintosh were left to their investigation.

Chapter IV

THE CEREBRATION

I must admit that I was relieved to return to my practice of medicine and involve my mind in something else than the bank murder and explosion. Even with a thorough bath, I felt that I reeked of smoke. It was late in the day when I arrived at 221B Baker Street. Holmes had already eaten and was in the basement setting up his command center. He had taken the rooms formerly occupied by Mrs. Hudson's son before his marriage some ten years ago. There was the table, three well-padded swivel chairs with rollers on their legs, a large chalk board, and three bright lamps on metal tripod stands, probably six feet tall. It looked like daylight. The floor was tiled and the room almost gave a hospital appearance. Holmes was arranging paper and pencils on the desk. He was actually humming one of his favorite violin melodies, the name of which I can never recall.

"What do you think of it, Watson?"

"Impressive, Holmes, very impressive," said I. "What do you plan to do with it?"

"Catch us a diabolic killer, my dear Watson."

"And just how will we do that?", asked I.

"By cerebration!"

"Come, now, Holmes, how in the world will we catch this murderer by just thinking?"

"Watson, you and I are going to cerebrate the traits which this killer has and our old friend Dr. Knoepker will help us transform those traits to handwriting. This will lead us to a narrower group of suspects and I am sure, to the killer."

"Dr. Knoepker?"

"Yes, Watson, he should be here in about three days. Mrs. Hudson has agreed to let the spare bedroom that she has on the first floor. He is excited by the prospects of using graphology in crime detection. If you are game for it, after your supper, we can see what we have. I can honestly say that I have never needed your help more. I need the input from a different perspective for balance. What do you say, Watson?"

"I am here to be utilized, Holmes. Although I do not share your enthusiasms on this pursuit, I will give it my best stick. See you after supper."

With that I left Holmes to his paper and pencils and went upstairs to eat Mrs. Hudson's fare. After supper, when I returned, Holmes had begun putting traits on the chalk board. He had written on the chalk board:

- Very intelligent
- Analytical
- Ruthless
- Violent
- Deceitful

"I agree with everything but deceitful. How do you know that he is deceitful?"

"Elementary, my dear Watson. He disguised himself as the deliveryman or, at the very least, had someone else disguise himself."

"How in the world can you go through all 1700 personnel files and questionnaires and make any sense of this?"

"By elimination, Watson. We must eliminate those who are not likely to be the killer. For instance, I think that we can exclude women in our first examination. What do you say, Watson?"

"I certainly agree, Holmes."

Holmes then placed a heading on the chalk board:

FIRST ELIMINATION

- Women

"Holmes, what about short men? You had originally indicated that the killer would have to be at least six feet three inches."

"Good, Watson. Later I revised it because of the type of murder weapon but he would have to be at least six feet tall. Let's add that to our Elimination List:

- Men under six feet tall.

"Holmes, how about people who were not in the building at the time of the murder?"

"Watson, if the murderer is deceitful, could we trust him to admit that he was in the bank at the time of the murder?"

"It seems to me, Holmes, that with as many employees in the bank at that time, the murderer would have to be named as being here. If the questionnaire indicated that he was not here and the witnesses said he was, it would certainly pin the tail on the monkey. If he is very intelligent, it seems to me that he would not run that risk."

"Excellent, Watson! See what a help you have been already. Let's put that on the board as well."

– Those employees who were not in the building at the time of St. James' Murder.

"Watson, how about those employees who were working with other employees between 7:00 to 8:00 o'clock and did not leave the room?"

"Well, Holmes, so long as it was clear that they were with another employee or visitor during that time, it should eliminate them as a suspect."

"Question 11 covers other employees. I agree with you in your original hypothesis. The murderer was in the building and would have been seen by others and, if working with others, would have left their presence. Those employees who were working with others during this critical time and did not leave their presence could not have been our murderer. I do not want to include visitors as there could be collusion."

"Of course, Holmes, I agree. Put it up there with the others."

– Employees working with other employees between 7:00 and 8:00 P.M.

"Holmes, what do you think of eliminating employees without medical training?"

"Watson, I am not sure that this murderer would have ever divulged his medical training. It might also be that he learned this art in some kind of ceremonial training. If he had thorough medical training, why is he here as an employee? It could be that something occurred that would make him hide the training. I would rather not exclude that class in the beginning.

Now Watson, let's make a list of classes of suspects with the facts that we have at this point."

"Holmes, what about men who have known medical training?"

"Bravo, Watson, let's put in on the board."

CLASSES OF SUSPECTS

– Men who have known medical training.

"Let's put up Aztecs and Incas."

"Certainly, Holmes, and how about Tongans or, better still, South Pacific Islanders?

"Sterling, Watson!"

 – Aztecs and Mexicans

 – Incas and Peruvians

 – Tongans or South Pacific Islanders

"Watson, think with me on this point: St. James was having trouble in the Foreign Department. My logic deduces that a supervisor in the Foreign Department would be a likely suspect. I dismiss the Domestic Department, because St. James was having no difficulty there. The only person there that we know of that would benefit by St. James' death is Kingsley and he is eliminated as he was not on the premises."

"Quite right, Holmes, I concur."

"The only other suspect would be a visitor who was on the premises between 7:00 and 8:00 P.M. and who is not otherwise eliminated."

"Yes, I have to agree with that."

"Alright, Watson, let's see what we have cerebrated:

The murderer:

1. Is a man

2. Is six feet or more tall

3. Was either a visitor between 7:00 and 8:00 P.M. on March 15, 1896, or a bank employee who admits that he was in the building at that time

4. If an employee, was working alone or left other employees during this period

5. Could have medical training

6. Fits into one of these categories:

a. Aztec or Mexican

b. Inca or Persian

c. Tongan or South Pacific Islander

d. Is in supervision in the Foreign Department of the Bank of England

e. Was a visitor at the time of the murder.

7. He has the following traits:

a. Very Intelligent

b. Analytical

c. Ruthless

d. Violent

e. Deceitful"

"That is utterly amazing! Cerebrate you say. Deduction, I call it. It certainly gives us a lot fewer suspects to examine."

"Elementary, my dear Watson. Let's get some shut eye. Tomorrow is going to be a busy day. Thank you again for all of your help. You have done an admirable job, old friend."

With that we retired to our rooms and slumber.

Chapter V

ELIMINATING THE NEGATIVE

As Watson was not with me, I feel that I must chronicle what occurred at the bank. I arose early to meet my 8:00 A.M. appointment. I left Watson in his usual state of slumber. The serenity of the day was only disturbed by his gentle, rhythmic snoring.

At the Registrar's office, I was issued an identification card and allowed to go to the second floor offices of the personnel manager, Paul Bodmin. I was ushered into his office where he greeted me with every courtesy. I advised him that I felt that my presence could create a danger in his department. I then made the following requests: a guard be posted on my office door 24 hours a day; all of the personnel files be removed to my office and stored in fire-proof filing cabinets; all mail addressed to me should be opened in a vault in the gold cellar and any package addressed to me, to him or his department should be placed into a remote vault in the gold cellar and unopened for a period of 24 hours.

Inspector Lestrade was to be advised of their arrival so that his explosive unit could make their examination. In no event would any parcels or other communication be delivered to me at my office here. After Lestrade's examination and clearance, I would then make my inspection.

"This will have to be cleared with Sir Rodney, of course, Mr. Bodmin."

"Mr. Holmes, the room that I have selected for you has only one entrance which has a solid oak door. There are three large windows, but they are inaccessible from the outside. Our personnel files are in fire-proof filing cabinets. I will have them moved to your room, as it is large enough to accommodate them. There are six file cabinets and they are locked at all times. I alone have the keys, except for the Governor. I will take your other requirements to Sir Rodney for approval. I would have no problem in implementing them. What kind of trouble do you expect?"

"Once our murderer knows that I will be going through the personnel files, he will become apprehensive, or probably paranoid is a more fitting description. The worst fear that a person can have is the fear of the unknown. He simply does not know what I am looking for and does not remember what information that he gave you when he applied for a job with the bank. Our murderer has killed once and tried a second time with the bomb. We must expect that he will go to no end to protect his secret. We must be on our guard at all times. He will be most interested in knowing what my findings are. Sir Rodney has required that my notes be kept here and I must be certain that they are protected. This diabolical fiend can be expected to do the unexpected and we must carefully plan for it. I want two brackets placed on the door for padlocks. These should be of such a nature that they cannot be removed from outside of the door. I will furnish my own padlocks. I will need the keys to the personnel filing cabinets and I request them at this time. We will also use the lock on the outside of the door and I will need all keys to it as well. It is imperative that you do not have any keys to the cabinets or the door. It could mean your life. The patrol should check on the officer guarding the door at least every 15 minutes and preferably on a staggered basis. By this I mean sometimes eight minutes, sometime twelve minutes, sometimes fifteen minutes, but never longer than fifteen minutes."

"I understand the gravity of the situation, Mr. Holmes, and want you to know that I fully appreciate what you are saying. Let me go down to Sir Rodney's office and get clearance before I start these project. It will only take a few minutes."

With that he left and returned very promptly. I hardly had time to do more than to look around his office and look at the filing cabinets which surrounded his outer office when he returned.

"It is done, Mr. Holmes."

He gave instructions to his assistant and returned to me.

"What else might I do for you, Mr. Holmes?"

"Mr. Bodmin, it is very important that you mention to no one, except of course Sir Rodney, what we have talked about. I mentioned packages, but failed to include that any packages, from without or from within, are to be placed in the holding vault. Any inter-office communication should be opened in the gold cellar vault. My hours should not be discussed as I will be working at different times and sometimes late a night. I do not want anyone to know if I am here or not. I know that your patrols do not carry firearms. I would like you to get authority from Sir Rodney to allow the guards at my door to carry side-arms. We must make this murderer know that we mean business. The more we protect this office, the more he will want to enter it and determine where our investigation is taking us. I would ask you to secure heavy drapes for the three windows. I do not want inquisitive eyes to know whether or not a light is on in the room and certainly I do no want to give him an opportunity to assassinate me while I am at my task. Yes, there will be an attempt to enter that office."

"I will clear that with Sir Rodney, but you know, of course, that all of these changes are highly irregular, Mr. Holmes."

The workman had already arrived and had begun removing the file cabinets to my office. Mr. Bodmin surrendered his keys to the cabinets and my front door and actually seemed a little relieved to pass this responsibility on to me. I signed the tendered receipt.

"Mr. Holmes, have you concluded that our murderer is an employee?"

"No, Mr. Bodmin, I have not. It is quite possible that he has an accomplice who is. What my senses tell me is that the murderer fears that these records will somehow lead us to him, directly or indirectly. At this point, I do not feel that he is trying to eliminate me.

"Mr. Bodmin, I need to ask you some other questions. Do you have any Mexican employees?"

"Yes, we do. I believe about twenty."

"I would like a list of those employees."

"Do you have any Peruvian employees?"

"They work in our Mexican Department and there are some in our South America Department."

"Yes, about the same number and they also work in the South America Department."

"How about South Pacific Islanders?"

"I would say that we have about fifteen in the South Pacific Department."

"Are some of them Tonganese?"

"I can't be sure as the Tonganese are scattered all over the South Pacific clear to Easter Island, but I am sure that we do."

"Can you furnish me with a list of these employees?"

"Surely, Mr. Holmes, I should have it for you by this afternoon."

"I would like to have the names of all department heads in the Foreign Department below Mr. Farnsworth. You should not disclose this request to anyone except to your assistant who prepares it. The assistant should be admonished not to divulge this request to anyone. Is that understood? "

"Yes, Mr. Holmes, it is understood. I will have the list to you by this afternoon."

"How are you coming on the questionnaires?"

"They are at the printers. We should have them by tomorrow or, at the latest, the next following day."

"Excellent! When they have been completed by the employees, I would like them placed in a box file, in alphabetical order. The request is that they are to be returned in 24 hours so that they probably should come in the following day from their delivery. They should be delivered immediately to me and if I am not in then, the box should be left with the guard in front of my door."

Mr. Bodmin nodded assent. He was already tired of all of my requests at the start of his busy day. I excused myself to begin my work. The files had been placed in my office and I hung up my coat and hat and began to pursue the files. I found them to be in alphabetical order which was reassuring. It was in less that an hour when I noticed a uniformed, armed guard at my door and workmen were beginning to install my padlock and drapery brackets. I thought it best to venture out to purchase my locks and, also, it seemed a good idea to avoid this confusion.

On my way out, I met with the Captain of the guards and advised him that I wanted to meet all guards on my door and asked that they not be substituted without my being advised. I felt that this was very important for my security and I was becoming somewhat apprehensive. It was just a feeling, but one that I did not like. The smell of the smoke still lingered in the great building from the explosion in the Registrar's Office and the image of that complete destruction was firmly implanted in my mind.

I returned after a very good lunch with two American Yale locks. I approached the closed doorway and the guard introduced himself to me. "I am George Wallace, Mr. Holmes. I was here this morning when you were working in your office. The Captain asked me to make the introduction as you requested. If I can be of any service to you, just let me know."

I firmly grasped the outstretched hand, and said, "George, I am glad to have you here. I hope that it will be uneventful, but I must warn you. For your own safety, be ever vigilant!"

I inspected the latches for my locks and they were as requested. They could not be removed from the outside of the door. I found four sheets of paper on my desk as promised, listing the names that I had requested. I then locked the door from the inside and began with my first list of names.

I started with the Mexican list. There were 19 names, five of whom were women. Of the remaining 14, I was able to eliminate nine of them as being under six feet tall. All five of those remaining had come from Mexico City which is where most of the remaining Aztec live. In reviewing their personnel files, I found that three gave their religion as Catholics and two gave their religion as Aztec. Catholicism had been forced upon the Mexicans and it was common knowledge that, even though they considered themselves Catholic, they might still worship Aztec gods.

I went through the files of Rigoberto Gomez and Luis Gonzales who had given their religion as Aztec. Both of them worked in the Mexican Department and were accountants. Both spoke English fluently. Both were in their mid thirties and neither had indicated any medical training. Their records were good. Then it occurred to me that I had the cart before the horse. I needed the questionnaires to complete my elimination. I was moving too fast for my facts. It still would be good to get some of the preliminary work out of the way. The other three, who were not eliminated at this point, were Felix Sigueiros, Jose de Alarcon and Carlos Orozco.

When I looked at my timepiece, it displayed the hour to return to Baker Street. I didn't realize how quickly time had passed. I placed my notes and the furnished lists in the third file cabinet from the right and locked it.

As I exited the office, I said "Good night" to George. I locked the door from the outside and put my Yale padlocks in their latches. It then occurred to me that our murderer would know that I was not in the room if it were padlocked. I guess we all have days like that. Nonetheless, I wanted the protection of the three locks, including the door lock. I certainly did not want the keys to the padlocks to be copied, so I did not want them out of my possession.

Watson and I had gathered for dinner. We discussed our day. He was quite pleased with his practice and interested in my findings and application of our cerebration. After dinner, I went to my command center and Watson went to the fire with his after-dinner pipe to read his medical journals.

The next morning when I reached my office at the bank, I met Franklin Wren. He introduced himself as one of my assigned guards and I recognized the name from the Captain's list.

"Mr. Holmes, this morning a package arrived for you marked 'personal' and it has been taken to a separate room in the other end of the gold cellar."

"Thank you , Franklin. When the patrol next checks your station, please have them ring up Inspector Lestrade at Scotland Yard and have him send his explosive team to check it out."

"Right, Mr. Holmes. The patrol should be here anytime now."

"Franklin, should there be any commotion in the hall, do not leave your post here. Do not leave your post here for any reason. Is that understood?"

"Yes, sir, I understand. Do not leave my post for any reason."

"Good. That is right, Franklin, not for any reason. Please pass those instructions on to your relief and ask that they be relayed to the next guard."

"I will, Mr. Holmes."

I unlocked the door and took the locks in with me to begin my quest. There I remained all day and was able to limit the 21 Peruvians to three, mainly because of height. Those remaining were Jose Pizarro, Ramon Trujillo and Simon Chimbote. I did review their personnel files but did not find anything significant. I felt that I would do a more thorough job after we had the questionnaires back and after I had made my further elimination.

The South Pacific islanders totaled 22, with seven women, but left eight who were six feet in height or more. The Polynesians are big people. Their names were Alfonso Reyes, Martin Louis Aguela, Pa'uba Tu'ma, Rufino Nervo, Jonah Heiau, Jesus Nani, Ar'got Pe'ute, and Rit'na Je'ra. I remembered that Pa'uba Tu'ma had been with Dr. An'ago at the time of the St. James' murder. They ranged in different ages and talents but there was nothing significant at this point. Again, I felt that closer inspection was a waste of energy when probably two thirds of the suspects would be eliminated by our questionnaire.

At that point there was a knock at the door, and Franklin announced, "Inspector Lestrade to see you, Mr. Holmes."

I opened the door, replaced the padlocks, locked the door and greeted Lestrade.

"You were right, Mr. Holmes. There was a bomb in the box. Similar to that which took away the Registrars' office. We could not dare open it in the bank, so we removed the box to a field. We dug us a hole and tried to open it with a long tree trimmer. It was at that point that it exploded. It was more incendiary than explosive and fire shot out of that hole like it was the devil's pit. Good for us that our men were dressed for it."

"Good work, Lestrade. The game is afoot. We can expect the killer to intensify his efforts to destroy the personnel files and, perhaps, me as well. This might be the time for you to consider putting a constable outside in the hallway as an extra deterrent. What do you think?"

"Well, Mr. Holmes, this seems to be the center of criminal activity for the whole of London. I'll set up round-the-clock constable protection in the hallway just outside of the Personnel Office door."

"Good, Lestrade. I would like to take you to lunch and discuss it with you. It would be interesting to hear how your investigation is progressing."

I learned very little from Lestrade. His meeting with St. James' widow had revealed no knowledge of Dr. An'aga. Pa'uba Tu'ma had confirmed the meeting and the fact that An'age had been gone for some 20 minutes during the meeting to go to the men's room. Nothing unusual had taken place. Tu'ma was Tonganese and had been acquainted with the doctor before the meeting. It was not a close relationship according to Tu'ma. Lestrade still had his suspicions about Dr. An'aga's involvement in St. James' death. I did get Lestrade to agree that I could send a constable or a person dressed as a constable to also roam the building. He would give the name of Christopher Smoggin. I assured him that I would take personal responsibility for his actions. He agreed to advise the constables that this person was his man from the Yard and they were to assist him if requested. It was to my great surprise that he agreed to this. There had been a lot of pressure on him because of this murder and he was willing to take some risks to get it resolved.

I then made a stop on the way back to the bank and was able to meet with Sir Rodney. He had been very aware of the bomb sent to me. He agreed that Watson could enter my office there upon the condition that the personnel files were not unlocked. This would give me a chance to do some investigation, with the killer thinking that I was in the office.

It was by this time late in the afternoon, so I returned to Baker Street and my old friend Watson.

"Watson, I need your help tomorrow. What do you say?"

"Of course, Holmes, I can make the arrangements. I am here to aid you in any way I can. What do you want me to do?"

"I want you to pack a lunch, load up on your medical journals and go to my office in the bank. It could be dangerous for you. You should bring your service revolver. Sir Rodney has agreed to your entry into my office if I lock up the personnel files while I am gone. This leaves you all alone with your journals and gives me the opportunity for some interesting investigation."

"Is that all, Holmes? It doesn't seem very important to me."

"It is of the utmost importance, Watson. You are my most trusted friend. I need you there tomorrow."

"Right, Holmes," replied Watson, taking on a new air of self-importance.

Holmes then gave me the three keys to the door, with instructions that I was not to allow the keys out of my possession and that I should lock the door from the inside after I made my entry. The locks were to be brought into the room with me and replaced when I left. He further cautioned me that I was not to open the drapes. I seldom questioned Holmes' methods but this seemed rather odd to me.

When I arose in the early morning light, which was against all instincts, Holmes was already gone. I arrived at the bank and met Johnathon Wilson, the armed security guard in front of the door to Holmes' office. He was not impressed with my story and was not going to let me in. It was at that point that a constable, Christopher Smoggin, entered the doorway and advised the security guard that Dr. Watson was to be allowed to enter the office. The security guard reluctantly allowed me to release the locks and open the door. It

was a stuffy place, with the odor of stale tobacco permeating the room. The drapes were drawn and it was completely pitch-black. The lights brought life to the quarters. So I began my strenuous endeavor, after first placing my loaded service revolver on the desk in front of me.

I had to leave the office several times during the day to take care of those personal matters a gentleman must respond to. With each exit, I replaced the padlocks and, upon my return, removed them, as instructed. There was a constable in the hallway, but it was not the nice gentleman, Christopher Smoggin, who had assisted me that morning.

By mid afternoon, I had just begun to tire of my medical journals. My eyelids were heavy and I was yawning. It was at that point that all thoughts of sleep left me. There was a loud explosion below me and it seemed that it was just outside of my windows. I jumped to my feet, opened the door and asked the security guard what had happened. He knew nothing more than I did. The constable in the hallway had run past the door. Then appeared Christopher Smoggin.

"Ere ye be all right, Dr. Watson?"

"Yes, I think so. Tell me what has happened? What was that explosion?"

"It was a bomb meant for your office. It was lowered by rope from the roof. When I made my inspection of the roof, I saw the rope that held it outside of your office windows. I cut the rope just in the nick of time. The bomb exploded on its way down to the ground. I do not believe anyone was injured."

"Good grief!", said I. "Lucky for me." Holmes was right. This had been a dangerous assignment. I asked Constable Smoggin if he had seen anyone on the roof and he told me that there was no one there when he found the rope. The other constable returned to his post and confirmed that there had been no injuries, but some windows had been blown out on the first floor. I put in the rest of my day. As I left the office, there were two boxes stacked in front of the door. The security guard advised me that Mr. Bodmin had personally placed the boxes there and that no one was to be allowed to look at them except Mr. Holmes. With his help they were moved inside of the office. The door was locked as I had found it and I was off for the comfort of Baker Street. I don't mind saying that I was relieved to get there. I couldn't wait to tell Holmes of my adventure.

I almost ran up the stairs to our flat. I burst the door open and said, "Guess what happened to me today?"

"The someone tried to blow you up, Watson."

"How in the world did you know that, Holmes?"

"Ere ye be all right, Dr. Watson."

"Holmes, you make me feel ridiculous. Were you really Constable Smoggin?"

"Yes, Watson. I had to be to move around the building. Sorry for the deception, but I felt that it was for your own safety. It was a very interesting day thanks to you making it possible."

I really was put out at this constant deception. It was at that moment that I noticed a rising form from the chair in front of the fireplace. The form rose and rose and rose. It was Dr. Knoepker engaging his muscles to raise that six foot six inch frame to tower over me. This graying, clean-shaven man glared out at me through large, gray eyes and the same boyish grin, wide and showing all teeth.

"Good to see you again, Dr. Watson. How have you been?"

"Very well, thank you," said I. "If Holmes would just not try to fool me all of the time. I feel so foolish."

"Did it ever occur to you, Dr. Watson, that Mr. Holmes is paying you the extreme compliment. If he can fool you, he should be able to fool anyone. Who knows him better?"

"Quite right. Never thought of it that way. Quite right, indeed. I forgive you Holmes."

"Thank you, dear friend."

I made inquiry of Dr. Knoepker's long trip and found that it had been a good one. He had taken the same route that we traveled. He was excited at the opportunity of working with Sherlock Holmes on a case. I am sure that it will be one of his papers. We ate dinner and retired to the war room, where Holmes succinctly brought Dr. Knoepker to date on events. What Holmes did not know was that the questionnaires had been returned and placed by his door. He was pleased that they were back and ready for examination. Holmes was very particular in detail of the murder and St. James' body. He went through what traits that we thought the murderer had, which were still on the chalk board.

a. Very intelligent

b. Analytical

c. Ruthless

d, Violent

e. Deceitful

Holmes showed Dr. Knoepker the Questionnaires which we requested to be filled out by the employees and visitors in their own handwriting.

"Dr. Knoepker, what I would like for us to do is to create a handwriting that would contain all of these traits and any others that we might add so that we might compare it to the questionnaires. We have also set up by cerebration our requirements at this point and if the suspect does not fit in everyone of them, he is eliminated. The requirements for our murderer are:

The murderer:

1. Is a man

2. Is six feet tall or more

3. Was a visitor between 7:00 and 8:00 P.M. on March 15, 1896 or a bank employee who admits that he was in the building at that time

4. Could have had medical training

5. Fits into one of these categories:

a. Aztec or Mexican

b. Inca or Peruvian

c. Tongan or South Pacific Islander

d. In supervision in the Foreign Department of the Bank of England

e. Was a visitor.

Holmes explained that we felt that the murderer would have to admit that he was in the building at the time of the murder, because he would have been seen at some point by employees of the bank. Holmes explained how he had made a preliminary elimination of suspects and would check the names for their questionnaires and make further eliminations. He then suggested that we continue with his game of cerebration of the murders traits as we perceived them.

Dr. Knoepker volunteered, "It seems to me that this must be a very concentrative person to have put all this together. This means that his handwriting would be smaller than normal."

"Sterling!", exclaimed Holmes. "Let us put it with the traits."

f. Concentrative in nature

Dr. Knoepker proffered again: "It seems to me that any person who could commit that deed and live with it must be totally emotionally controlled. His handwriting would probably be vertical or even backhanded."

"Splendid," retorted Holmes, adding another trait to the chalk board.

g. Totally emotionally controlled

Holmes was being caught up by his own game. "If you consider the detail and planning that he has shown, I feel that you would have to say that he sets his goals very high for himself. Look at the bomb lowered to a point just outside my office window. If neither of you object, I am going to add:

h. Sets goals high for himself"

Holmes suddenly exclaimed, "Oh, what a fool I have been! If our murderer is so intelligent and deceitful, he will be suspicious of the requirement that the questionnaire be done in the preparer's handwriting and not in printing. He will have someone else make his answers to the questionnaire! But by our elimination process, there will not be many to check and we could use the new Registrar's book to see his real handwriting. If the signature differs from the questionnaire, we probably have our man. We could also check the handwriting from the personnel files against the questionnaire. We may be very right after all, but for the wrong reason. What irony!"

"Holmes, it is obvious that this man has very much determination and persistence. Look at his two attempts to blow up the personnel files."

"Good for you, Watson. Let's add them to our list:

i. Determination

j. Persistence

We would have to say that he is cautious. His disguise. His approach to the bombings. Let us add:

k. Cautious

Dr. Knoepker, I know that you have to be tired after your long trip. I want to put you to bed so that we can get up early and go to the bank. We will also talk about your fee and expenses. I will need to get clearance from Sir Rodney, the bank's attorney, but I want you to go through the questionnaires for this profile in my office. I would ask that you make up a handwriting composite which you feel shows all of these traits so that we can get some idea of what we are looking for. I will be continuing with my elimination and will need to have access to the questionnaire file. It should be a good day for us. I have asked Mrs. Hudson to wake us up at 6:00 A.M. and we should leave about 7:45 A.M. Will that be all right?"

"It will be fine, Mr. Holmes. I am excited about the prospects of this experiment. I will probably have trouble going to sleep. See you in the morning."

When I arose, Holmes and Dr. Knoepker had already left. What I did notice was the uniform of Christopher Smoggin draped over a chair. Disgusting was what it was! Trying to fool his friend. But then again, maybe Karl was right. Who else would be better to test a disguise on?

CHAPTER VI

THE MURDERER'S HANDWRITING

If this story is to be complete, it is necessary that I chronicle the events which have followed. I feel that I am invading Watson's territory. Watson gets such pleasure from his chronicles of our adventures and does it quite well.

Dr. Knoepker and I arrived by cab to the bank at 8:00 A.M. As he was a stranger to the bank, it was necessary to escort us to Sir Rodney's office. I explained who Dr. Knoepker was and what he would be doing and Sir Rodney was obviously impressed. I told him briefly of our trip to the continent and our meeting with Dr. Binet. He seemed very interested in the rate of accuracy of Dr. Knoepker's unusual ability. I explained that at this point we would both be working with the questionnaires and I needed to have access to the personnel files. I assured him that only in rare instances would Dr. Knoepker even see the information contained in them. This he reluctantly accepted.

"Now I understand why you wanted the questionnaires to be hand-written," Sir Rodney's grated voice announced. "You are a sly devil, Mr. Holmes. It is no wonder that you have such a notable reputation. Dr. Knoepker is your secret weapon. I am not going to stand in the way of that. I will advise Bodmin immediately. I will keep your little secret between us.

Mr. Holmes, that was nasty business yesterday. It was a good thing that Scotland Yard was here or we would have lost you. I have asked security to patrol the roof of this building and to place a permanent guard there at all times."

I felt a wry smile begin to capture my mouth, which I immediately squelched. I thanked Sir Rodney and complimented him on making a wise decision. Sir Rodney's secretary accompanied us to the Personnel Office and she instructed Mr. Bodmin that this gentleman would be working with me and that it was perfectly all right. Bodmin then advised the guard with instructions to pass this new order along to his reliefs. This gentleman's name was never spoken. Bodmin had been uniquely curious, but I let it feed.

There was a long table at one side of the room with two wooden chairs. We placed the boxes of questionnaires on one end and Dr. Knoepker seated himself next to them.

"Dr. Knoepker, I should prefer to call you either Karl or Knoepker, so that we do not arouse any more apprehension than we have. Really, I would prefer Karl. I should be pleased if you would just refer to me as Holmes. Can we agree on that?"

"Surely, Mr. Holmes, I mean Holmes."

Karl then proceeded to outline his plan. He would first work out the handwriting that would indicate the characteristics of our killer. He then would begin to go through the questionnaires, noting any unusual writing. I would proceed with my elimination of suspects, checking the handwriting of the suspects in the personnel files with the handwriting on the questionnaire.

It was almost noon when the big German rose slowly out of his chair. "Holmes, this big body of mine is screaming for sustenance. Do you suppose that this is a proper time for a break and some lunch?"

I immediately agreed and apologized for my concentration. I explained to him that, when I am on a case, I sometimes do not eat for days at a time. I could hear Mrs. Hudson's scolding. I reached for our coats and hats and we were off.

The guard introduced himself as William Slatterly, which I returned with my full name and that of Karl, but did not include his last name. I learned that Karl had completed his composite of traits which we would go through after lunch. Lunch with Karl was an event! I have never seen anyone eat so much. How he savored each bite. I am surprised that after lunch he could bring that big body up out of his chair. It did seem to take quite an effort.

As we went down the second floor hallway to our office, we met Inspector Lestrade.

"Mr. Holmes, it was a good thing that your officer Christopher Smoggin was here yesterday. That bomb outside your window would have cleared out the office and everyone who was in it. This is a dangerous place. Who is this gentleman with you Mr. Holmes?"

"This is Karl, Lestrade."

"Doesn't he have a last name, Mr. Holmes?"

"I have brought him in to assist me in my investigation. He is from Germany. His only knowledge of this affair is what I have told him. I do not want to give out his identity to anyone at this time, Lestrade."

"Oh, come now, Mr. Holmes. I am in charge of this investigation and Scotland Yard is entitled to know of anyone on these premises, particularly a foreigner."

"Lestrade, I will advise you of everything in a day or two. Please indulge me. It is important for my investigation to be completed without any more interference than I have had. You are the one who came to me and asked for my help. I have gone to considerable expense in both time and money to make this assist, so for God's sake, let me do my job."

"Oh, very well, Mr. Holmes. I don't see how a day or two will make any difference."

Lestrade's authority had been questioned and he was flustered by the secrecy which I maintained. His face was contorted so that his mustache went up on one side of his mouth and was straight on the other. It was a funny sight, but I assure you that I did not laugh or even smile.

After removing the padlocks, we entered the room and Karl had pulled up the second chair to the table where he had been engaged. He gave me two sheets of paper with handwriting on them and some explanation beside them.

"Let's take the traits as you have listed them and I will explain how the trait is shown. I ask that you remember that, although I am speaking with firm conviction as if stating absolute fact, the conclusions are mine alone and you must always consider the fallibility of my judgment."

I assured him that I did.

"The first trait which you have listed is:

1. Very intelligent

_M_   _M_ _M_   _M_ _M_   _M_

This is shown by the loops of the 'm' and 'n'. These loops are not in fact loops, but are pointed like a tent, or even a straight line. They are not rounded. Here is how they might look:

2. Analytical ability

You may remember that the valleys between the loops, if made like a 'v', this would indicate analytical ability. The more pronounced the 'v', the more that ability.

3. Ruthless

I have not been able to find a singular handwriting symbol to illustrate this. Tyrannical, which is the absence of kind qualities, is close. A domineering personality, almost caustic, would be shown by arrow-like T-bars written to the right and downward, coming to a point. They are very dark in relationship to the rest of the writing and where they are completely on the right of the stem. This is the worst form and one which I believe that the killer possesses.

4. Violent.

A violent personality is shown by an intense emotional reaction. The handwriting would be very dark and the writing, depending on the instrument, would almost appear to bleed. It might be combined with temper which is shown by inflexible strokes that are short and at the beginning of a word.

5. Deceitful.

There are two types of deceit: self-deceit and intended deceit. Self-deceit is shown by a beginning loop in small circle loops that you find in the 'a', 'o', the bottom loop of the 'd', and the top of the 'g'.

The intentional deceit is shown by double loops: one in the beginning stroke and one in the ending stroke of the letter.

In either event, the loop is closed.

We discussed this other form of the same letters in Leipzig. If a person has a very deep secret, they will bury a tick-mark or stroke inside the closed loop of these letters. It need not be in every one of these letters, just one is enough. I feel that we will find this stroke in our killer's handwriting.

6. Concentrative in nature.

This is shown by small handwriting. The writing would appear smaller than a normal handwriting.

It is also shown by an 'i' and 'j' dot, carefully placed above the letter, rounded rather than a dash or little 'v'. I do not mean a circle for the dot, which means something entirely different. It shows a non-conformist. A person who must be himself and does not go with the group. I would say that a circle writer is full of idiosyncrasies. Sorry that I got off the main trait, but I did not want you to misunderstand about the dot.

7. Totally emotionally controlled.

We have a writer who is a vertical writer, with his handwriting going straight up and down or even slanting to the left, back-handed. Considering the events, I would rather think that it would be a back-handed writing.

8. Sets high goals for himself.

This takes us back to the 'T' and its wondrous tales. The bar would have to be placed rather high on the stem.

9.Determined.

Determination is shown by a straight down-stroke below the base line that are heavy. Look to the 'y' and 'g'. The length of the stroke indicates the lasting quality and the width of the stroke indicates the intensity. If the stroke curves, the determination weakens. The stroke should end bluntly and should be relatively constant in its width. If it is greatly exaggerated and gets much wider as it proceeds downward, it may be all bluff as opposed to true determination.

10. Persistence.

This shows the spirit that does not admit defeat. It is shown by tied strokes in the handwriting.

11.Cautious.

Words at the end of a line ending in a long dash for a final stroke shows a cautious nature. Also look for dashes within the line that have no real purpose, other than to fill up space."

"Karl, I sure appreciate your support," I told him. "How would handwriting show a deliberate person?"

"Holmes, it is shown by separated stems as in 'd' and 't'."

"Karl, did you tell me that a strong-willed person crosses his 't' with a heavy line in relation to the rest of his writing?"

"Yes, Holmes, with a heavy 't' bar."

We both went back to our tasks. I was working on my elimination and Karl was reviewing all of the questionnaires. The visitors' questionnaires had been brought to us. There were 42 visitors who were on the premises at the time of St. James' death.

Three days passed quickly. I really did not know where they went. The last two nights when we went home to Baker Street, I noticed that we were being watched as we left the bank. We had been in the habit of leaving at 5:00 P.M. to get home for Mrs. Hudson's fine dinner. Last night it was a tall elderly man reading a newspaper and tonight it was a chimney-sweep.

It was at that moment that it occurred to me that there was to be an attempt on my life. The killer could not get to the files. The knowledge from the files had been passed on to my scrutiny. Why should he not eliminate me! By this time it was a well known fact in the bank that I was on the case. Thanks to Watson's stories, I loomed as the greatest threat to this man's life. Of course, he would murder me. I should also tell you that Lestrade had put an around-the-clock guard at Baker Street. By simple deduction, this murder attempt would occur either on my trip to the bank or upon my return to Baker Street.

I said nothing of this to my colleagues during Mrs. Hudson's wonderful dinner. Mrs. Hudson rather enjoyed Karl and particularly his love of food. What praise he lavished upon her! I don't know if we can ever make her happy again. I don't think that his boyish grin is ever broader than when he is being fed good food.

After dinner we adjourned to the war room to discuss the case. It was at that point that I asked Watson if he would take over the chronicle and he agreed.

Holmes told us that there was to be an attempt on his life. He explained to us that he had been watched the last two nights as he left the bank and that he felt that the attempt would be either on the way back to Baker Street or on the way to the bank. He planned that Karl would go by his own cab to the bank in the morning and would return alone to Baker Street. It was at this point that he furnished Karl with a set of keys to the outside door of his office at the bank.

There would be a new boarder in our rooms at Baker Street, another German by the name of Heinrich Wolfgang.

"Where in the world will he sleep? ", said I.

"Don't worry, Watson, it should only be for a few days. Wolfgang will get authority to act for me in the event that anything should happen to me. He will work with Karl on the investigation and will have the keys to the files. I will get this clearance tomorrow. The details need to be worked out with Lestrade who will pick me up in the morning."

"What in the world is going to happen to you, Holmes?"

"I am going to be murdered, Watson!"

"You have to be kidding, Holmes! I am not ready to lose you."

"With the help of Lestrade and both of you gentlemen, we will let our killer think that he has eliminated me. There will be a lot of details which you will have to work out, but you will have Wolfgang here to help you."

"Holmes, poppycock, I don't want this Wolfgang here, I want you here."

"Watson, who do you think Wolfgang is?"

"Now I see, Holmes, sorry that I didn't catch on sooner. I just could not bear the thought of your death."

"Me, neither, Watson," quipped Holmes.

Karl just roared with laughter. I don't know what he thought was so funny.

"You two are something else! What a dialogue! I am ready to play my part. What makes you so sure that you will survive this attempt?"

"Our killer does not want to be on the scene when the murder occurs. The exception to that was St. James' death. However, that could not be helped. The bombs, the disguises and more than anything, his use of explosives, would have me conclude that it will be a bomb with a timing device. I am hoping that I will have an opportunity to get out of the cab before the explosion. Time will tell."

They both reported on their progress and it was still inconclusive at this point. Karl had found some interesting handwriting indicating an untrustworthy person, but not with the traits of our killer. He was trying to develop it. Holmes had received the Tonga file and had handwritten letters of Dr. An'aga to the bank.

We then adjourned to make ready for bed.

Chapter VII

THE CHARADE

When I descended the staircase, I found Holmes fully dressed and standing by the front door. He had a large sack, which appeared to be filled with his old typical clothing and a small traveling case.

"Where are you off to, Holmes?", I asked.

"To the bank, Watson, via Lestrade. His carriage approaches now. Karl has already left. See you tonight, old friend."

With that he was off. I followed my nose to the dining room where my breakfast awaited me. I then made my hospital rounds and went to the office for my afternoon patients.

At the end of our work day, Holmes met me at our rooms. He was electric with excitement and suggested that we meet in the war room before dinner. We found Karl already there and going through papers at the table.

"Gentlemen, I have met with Lestrade and advised him about you, Karl. He seemed somewhat relieved but does not share our enthusiasm concerning graphology. I have established the identity of Heinrich Wolfgang, who now has a pass at the bank. Wolfgang has met two of the guards who understand that he will be working with us. He has also met Mr. Bodmin. Sir Rodney was puzzled with this new character, but seemed to understand the game that was afoot. Tonight, I will advise Mrs. Hudson that Henrich will be staying with us and not to concern herself about him. Either Heinrich or I will be here for meals, not both. No questions asked."

"How is your investigation coming, Karl?"

"Very good, Holmes, very good indeed. I have found two employees who are in supervision who really cannot be trusted. I have not found our killer. I think that you are correct. I do not think that our killer has used his own handwriting for the questionnaire or has attempted to alter it. We will have to go to the Registrar's books or to the personnel files to verify this. How is your elimination proceeding?"

"I have completed my initial elimination of the Mexican list. I had made my original elimination to five, two of whom indicated that their religion was Aztec. Only two of them were in the building at the time of St. James' death. Felix Sigueiros and Louis Gonzales. I have checked their handwriting in their personnel files and it is the same as on the questionnaires. They do not have the characteristics which we feel our murderer would show. It is interesting to note that Sigueriros is an Aztec high priest and well trained in the old rites. Neither has had any medical training, at least according to the files. I do not feel that our man is here.

I have also done my elimination with the Peruvians. Initially, I had eliminated all but three because of their height. Simon Chimbote was the only one on duty at the time. He has been with the bank for 10 years. He has a good record and there is nothing to indicate that he has any involvement. No medical training. He is an accounting clerk in the South America Department. He is a man in his mid fifties. He actually has a deformity in his left arm and hand. His handwriting shows none of the traits that we are looking for.

The South Pacific Islanders were initially limited to eight, but only three were on duty at the time. They were Pa'uba Tu'ma, Ar'got Pe'ute and Rit'na Je'ra. I have not made any further elimination at this time. Tu'ma was meeting with Dr. An'aga at the time of St. James' death.

I have been most interested in the Asian and African Departments. I have met with Miss Daisy Talcan and requested the files on all pending matters. It looks like Egypt is about to issue 5,000,000 pounds worth of notes and currency. She said Karnak is in charge of the matter. I understand that the gold bullion has been approved and is in the gold cellar at this moment. They are adapting a new value for this issue and it will be coordinated with the British system. One Egyptian pound will be equivalent to a British Pound Sterling with coinage to match. I have been studying all afternoon to try to understand Egypt and its relationship to England.

Today, the Khedive rules Egypt and he has since 1867. This was a title the sultan of Turkey gave to Ismail Pasha who was then head of the Egyptian state under Turkish rule. It comes from a Turkish word, khedive, which means prince or ruler. Before that time, the ruler of Egypt had been called wali, or viceroy, a title of less dignity. Since 1849 with the death of Muhammad Ali, Egypt came increasingly under European influence. Ismail Pasha increased the national debt by borrowing lavishly from European bankers to develop the country and pay for the Suez Canal which was opened in 1869. These spendthrift rulers drove the country into bankruptcy and ultimately into the control of their British and French Creditors. Egypt had agreed to let the Suez Canal Company, a French company, operate the canal for 99 years. When this financial catastrophe hit Egypt, it sold its share of the company to Great Britain. In 1876, the government appointed two British and two French officials to manage its financial affairs. In 1881, a revolt broke out to free the government of non-Egyptian control. The army became the real power behind the Khedive. After bloody rioting in Alexandria in 1882, British troops put down the revolt and have occupied Egypt ever since. Tawfik Pasha, the Khedive, had appealed to the British for help. Our interest stemmed from the Suez Canal as the short route to India. We promised to evacuate the country once order had been restored. That promise has been conveniently forgotten. Tawfik remained on the throne as a figurehead prince. The British counsul-general was the real ruler of the country. The first counsul-general was Sir Evelyn Baring who took over in 1883. He is still there but is known as Lord Cromer since 1892.

I should also point out that during this period Egyptian agriculture was so completely dominated by cotton grown to feed the textile mills of Lancaster, England, that grain had to be imported to feed the rural population. Under Lord Cromer's control the entire debt to Britain has been paid.

Can you imagine parents naming their son Evelyn Cromer? Think of the fights that he had to have had growing up. To top it all, when he was knighted, he became Sir Evelyn. I am sure that took a lot of explaining. Sir Evelyn had to be pleased when he could be called Lord Cromer.

There is a nationalist movement led by Mustafa Kamil, a European-educated lawyer who is backed by Tawfik's successor, Abbas II. He agitates for self-government for Egypt and an end to the British occupation, but is largely ignored by British authorities.

I will be most interested in reviewing these files. I should say that Karnak's handwriting does not contain the traits of our killer, but I have not compared it with his personnel file."

"I am impressed, Holmes. You certainly are doing your homework. You as well, Karl. Very impressive!"

After their gracious acknowledgement, we adjourned to Mrs. Hudson's dining table. It seemed to me that every meal was not only different but somewhat more elegant than the one before. There was no doubt in my mind that Mrs Hudson enjoyed Karl's flattery as well as his appetite. With each meal, I found myself looking forward to the next!

After our fine meal, Karl and Holmes adjourned to the war room to go over papers and I sought out the over-stuffed chair in our rooms by the fire with my journals.

At breakfast, Mrs. Hudson told me that Karl and Holmes had left separately about a half-hour before.

At the end of my day, I returned to Baker Street, and was waiting for the return of my friend. I must confess that this was a sherry day if you know what I mean. In fact, I was on my second one when the door to our rooms burst open and there stood a rather large man, slightly stooped, who was assisted by a cane.

I immediately stood up, somewhat startled.

"Look here, my good man, what is the meaning of this intrusion? I suppose that you are here to see Holmes, but he has not returned from his work. You should call for an appointment."

"It would do no good, Dr. Watson. Mr. Holmes has been murdered!"

"Murdered," said I. "How can that be?"

This man was speaking in a foreign accent. German, I believed. His aging face was framed with a mass of gray hair which bushed out in all directions and even enveloped his face. His eyes were sharp with a twinkle of mischief. His eyebrows were thick and heavy and, of course, as gray as his hair and beard. As he walked over to me, I noted that he was walking with a slight limp in his right lower extremity, probably an old war injury. He wore gloves on his hands. He was in a brown tweed suit which appeared to have been slept in. He looked like he came right out of rural town in the south of England.

"Murdered he was. Mr. Holmes was returning from the bank just an hour ago, when his cabby asked if he might detour to drop off a birthday present to his mother. He turned off of Marylebone Road onto Harley Street and stopped in front of an abandoned tenement. He said that he would just be a minute and bolted from the cab. I don't suppose that it was more than three minutes before a bomb obliterated the cab and poor Mr. Holmes. His body was removed to the morgue at Scotland Yard."

I was so grief-stricken at this sudden report that I could hardly form words in my mouth. It was then that this pitiful creature introduced himself to me.

"Dr. Watson, I am Heinrich Wolfgang."

"Holmes! Is that really you under that blanket of hair and whiskers? What a ghastly prank to pull on an old friend. I think that I am having a coronary attack."

"Sit down, my dear friend, and let me get you another glass of sherry and I will tell you all about it. It would probably be a good thing to get Karl and meet in the war room and I will explain what has occurred. There, there, Watson, you will be all right. Come with me. Oh, bring your glass of sherry."

I was still a little short of breath as a result of this shock, but the sherry did help. There we were again, sitting around the table. Holmes began to relate: "When I met with Lestrade yesterday, we established a procedure by which we would act if my life was threatened. He agreed to have his men follow my cab to and from the bank. This is where I was sure that an attempt on my life would be made. Yesterday, I took some of my old clothes. Those, Watson, that you have made me known for, down to the deerstalker hat. Lestrade agreed to secure a cadaver scheduled for burial in potter's field and dress it in my old clothes. My clothes were first partly burned to give the appearance of fire. The cadaver, dressed in my old clothes, was loaded from the morgue into Lestrade's carriage and was to be returned after my trip if not needed."

"What in the world is potter's field?", inquired Karl.

"Karl, potter's field is a free burial ground for strangers, criminals, and persons who are too poor to pay for the expense of a funeral. The Bible story of Judas Iscariot tells of the first plot of ground known as a potter's field. After Judas betrayed Jesus Christ to the high priests of Jerusalem for 30 pieces of silver, he returned the money to the priests. They would not use the money for their temple. Instead they bought 'the potter's field to bury strangers in'. This comes from Matthew 27:7, I believe. The field is located in the Valley of Hinnom. It is an ancient long-used cemetery and contains clay used for the making of pottery, which gave it its name, potter's field."

"Really, Holmes, where do you store all of this knowledge, much less have the time to acquire it? You are indeed unique."

I was so flabbergasted that I really could not respond. I didn't want them to know that I had no idea where the term came from. But the look that I got from Wolfgang's twinkling eyes acknowledged receipt of that message.

Holmes continued to narrate: "When I left the bank today, a cab was waiting for me. It was driven by a cabby who resembled the description of the messenger who delivered the bomb to the bank. He asked me if he might not stop at his mother's flat on our way to deliver her birthday present. I agreed to this and was instantly on my guard. We turned off of Marylebone Road onto Harley Street and stopped in front of what appeared to be an abandoned building. He excused himself, telling me, 'Governor, I will just be a couple of minutes.' He bounded from the cab with a package in his hand. When he passed through the doorway, I left the cab and signaled to Lestrade's men. I went across the street and went into a stairway that used to be an entrance to a basement flat and waited. In about three minutes there was a terrible explosion and fire covered the street. The cab had been completely destroyed. Lestrade's men came up to the scene and placed my substitute body in the middle of the fire. The coroner's office was called for a wagon and a fire brigade was dispatched to the scene. There were no bystanders. Lestrade's men traced the cab, which had of course been stolen that very afternoon.

Watson, do you remember Dr. Mortimer O'Reilly?"

"Yes, of course, " said I, "he is that nice Irishman from the Coroner's Office at Scotland Yard."

"Exactly," responded Holmes, "and he is the one who will take care of the body, right down to the casket. There will be a guard on the casket which is closed and will remain so until the burial."

"What about the funeral?"

"Watson, you know that I am not an active church attender and we have really not discussed my religious beliefs. I want you to know I do believe in a supreme order of things, whatever you want to call it. This intelligence exists in the universe and in us all. I am grateful for it. Suffice it to say, you will officiate at the funeral, which I request be short."

With that, Holmes read a short passage which comes from Latin, which he said might help me officiate. He then gave me the copy.

"Happy the man, and happy he alone,

He, who can call today his own:

He who secure within, can say,

Tomorrow do thy worst, for I have lived today.

Be fair or foul, or rain or shine,

The joys I have possessed, in spite of fate, are mine.

Not Heaven itself upon the past has power,

But what has been, has been, and I have had my hour."

"Watson, you will need to engage a hall to have the funeral. I do not want the funeral in a church if you please. It probably should be set for four days from now at 2:00 P.M.. With a little bit of good fortune, we may not have it at all. We all have a lot of work to do and time is short. I think that I have found our man. I will need to go back to the bank after dinner and continue my investigation. Karl, tomorrow we can go down to the bank together and check my results."

Mrs. Hudson was becoming quite impatient. We all went upstairs for another wonderful creation. I will hate to see Karl return to Leipzig. Holmes explained to Mr. Hudson what charade was afoot and assured her that he was very much alive. He did caution her to play the part of the bereaved housekeeper for a few days.

Chapter VIII

THE CIRCLE CLOSES

I awoke in the morning as tired as I was when I went to bed. This Holmes situation had really disturbed me. I had bad dreams all night and actually had to get up twice. I don't know why this shook me up so much. I guess that it was the fact that someone had tried to kill my best friend and, what's more, almost did. The thought of Heinrich made me chuckle. He was enough to frighten small children but in a comical way. After groping my way to the breakfast table, I learned that Holmes and Karl had already gone. The morning paper was folded and sitting on my plate. When my weary eyes caught sight of the headlines in the opened paper, I thought my heart would stop.

"SHERLOCK HOLMES MURDERED"

The article went on to give the details of the murder, which I already knew. The article did state that Holmes was working on the St. James' murder case and Lestrade was quoted as saying that he believed that the murders were connected. No suspects to either murder had been found, but Lestrade in his usual over-confident manner indicated that an arrest in the St. James' murder was imminent. I sometimes think that Lestrade could not find his own nose if it weren't attached. It is a good thing for him that Holmes is still alive!

Breakfast helped. I really felt a little sorry for my patients of that day. I got home a little early and napped in my favorite chair, only to be awakened by footsteps and loud voices at my door. There stood Holmes and Karl. They were exhilarated and smiling like boys on allowance day. That would be a little hard for Heinrich to do, but that was what he was doing.

"Sorry, old chap, we did not know you were sleeping," said Holmes.

"Quite all right, just resting my eyes. Pray tell me what you two have been up to!"

"We know who the murderer is, Watson. We will announce it tomorrow at the bank. I would like you to be there as well if you can arrange it. Please bring your service revolver. I do not want to tell you more about him at this time."

"Certainly, Holmes, I think my patients will enjoy my associate after today. Been a rough one for me. I will look forward to it. Hope that it is not too early in the morning, Holmes."

"9:00 A.M."

"Fine."

"Let us adjourn to the war room and we will tell you of Karl's other findings."

We were seated at the table, when the big German rose and went to the chalk board.

"Watson, if I may call you Watson, our murderer has a very bad temper. This is shown by a straight inflexible line which precedes letters that do not start on the base line. The 'M', 'N'. 'B', 'F', and 'P' are good examples of where you might find it.

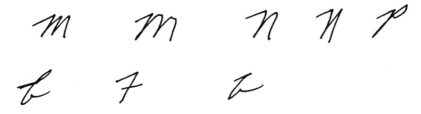

I have also found these signs in the handwriting of Bertram Woolrich who is an accountant in the Domestic Note Department. He is very sensitive and will offend very easily. If you recall, it is shown by large upper loops.

Woolrich has very controlled emotions. Actually he writes with a back hand. His loops are closed, but not deceitful. His writing is heavy which indicates deep, long-lasting feelings. He would not show this temper or deep feelings unless hurt very, very badly. If he ever did show it, I feel that he could be homicidal. Tomorrow, we will recommend psychological help. He is a bomb waiting to explode."

Holmes then reported that he had met with Bahadus Meerut.

"Meerut is head of the Asian Department. He has been with the bank for almost 20 years. His hair is coal-black with very black eyes and eyebrows framing a light-brown, clean-shaven face. He is a man in his early fifties, with a slight build, probably not over five foot nine inches tall. You would describe him as wiry, but not thin. His black hair was neatly trimmed and appeared to be stuck down with a hair-dressing of some type. He was on the premises at the time of St. James' death, but I eliminated him because of his height and his handwriting.

I should also report that Karl and I have reviewed the Tonga file and examined Dr. An'aga's handwriting. We do not feel that he has any of the traits that our murderer would possess. He gives us an alibi for Pa'uba Tu'ma, who was only alone for a very short time. There was not enough time for him to have been the murderer and he had no idea that Dr. An'aga would excuse himself.

We also reviewed the two remaining South Pacific Islanders and their handwriting proved negative as well."

Karl then continued with his findings. "I was in for a little surprise in the Indian Department. There is an accountant who works in that department named Jinnah Patel. He is Hindu. Hindus are divided in about 3000 castes and belong to the caste of their parents. They cannot leave it and most are loyal to it. Patel's handwriting shows a desire to acquire things which includes money. This is shown by little hooks at the beginning of strokes.

He also shows the double loops for intentional deceit: one at the beginning and one at the ending of the loops that form the letter. You find these in the 'a', 'o', the bottom loop of the 'd', and the top of the 'g'. The loop of the letter must be closed.

His writing is very small, showing a concentrative nature. He sets his goals high. He is one smart fellow. His 'M' and 'N' loops are pointed, almost a straight line.

It will be our recommendation that his books be very carefully audited. He is a young man in his late thirties. At least young compared to me. I should also say that the Hindus follow the occupation of their parents and that is just what Jinnah has done. His father is also an accountant. There has been quite an unrest among the Indians against the British; one might even say hatred. You know that there are over 300 million of them."

Holmes quipped, "We did it to ourselves. Between the East India Company and its greed, bringing poverty to many Indians, and the Sepoy Rebellion in 1857, it is a wonder that we are still there."

"What was the Sepoy Rebellion?"

"Karl, I enjoy your inquisitive mind. Indian soldiers, called Sepoys, started the rebellion when British officers ordered them to bite open cartridges greased with cow or hog fat. The religious beliefs of the soldiers forbade them to obey the order. The Hindu soldiers could not eat beef and the Muslim troops were forbidden to eat pork. So they fought us. There is still much bitterness there and this is the beginning of the independence movement in India."

With the end of the report, at Holmes' request, we adjourned to our quarters for a glass or two of wine before dinner. We were celebrating their day and I was celebrating feeling better after my nap. After another great feast brought about by the culinary prowess of Mrs. Hudson, we adjourned. Holmes began playing his violin. It had been so long since I had heard him play and I retook my favorite chair by the fire. Indeed, it seemed like home again.

Chapter IX

THE FINAL STROKE

We gathered in the Court Room at the bank exactly at 9:00 A.M.. Lord Kensington had already taken his exalted seat at the head of the great table. He was surrounded by Sir Charles and Sir Rodney. Kingsley was there as well as Fawnsworth. King George II and Dr. An'aga were taking their seats. Karl, Heinrich and I were walking to the table, when a man I had never met entered the room. Fawnsworth stood and introduced us to Said Karnak who is in charge of the African Department.

He was a large man in his early forties. His build was that of a trooper in the Coldstream guard. Tall, straight, muscular and with a military bearing. His frame was large, but not fat. His lips were thin and tight and he had a somber air about him. There was a large bushy mustache which turned up on its ends much like what the Americans call a Handlebar mustache. It was thick and black, matching his bushy hair and eyebrows. He appeared nervous and apprehensive. His black penetrating eyes combined with his other features to give a somewhat sinister appearance. He took a seat next to Fawnsworth.

Lord Kensington called the meeting to order and turned the meeting over to Heinrich Wolfgang. There was puzzlement in the eyes and manner of those at the great table. Heinrich arose slowly, saying nothing, but intently studying those assembled. With a dramatic gesture, Heinrich reached above his head and removed his wig. He then withdrew a towel from his pocket and removed his makeup, revealing Sherlock Holmes. There was such a gasp in the room and then silence. Karnak was white.

Holmes stood and, with somewhat a flair for the theatrical, addressed the group: "I have found the murderer of St. James and he is in this room. It is you, Said Karnak."

With that dramatic announcement, Karnak pushed his chair back and took a revolver from his pocket, pointing it at Holmes.

"Won't you ever die, Holmes? I am leaving this room and no one must follow me. To do so would mean your death. What I have done was for Egypt and freedom from British oppression. Long live Egypt!"

He backed his way to the door and as he opened it, still facing the gathering, Lestrade and Macintosh grabbed his gun and disarmed him. Karnak struggled and shouted out a fury in Egyptian tongue which I could not understand. Never have I seen a man

with such temper. His contorted face brought a tinge of fear to my senses. The four constables who had followed Lestrade into the Court Room subdued Karnak and placed him in handcuffs. He was still screaming in Egyptian and kicking wildly at his captors as he was dragged out of the door.

"Good job, Lestrade!", exclaimed Holmes. "Very good, indeed!"

Lestrade and Macintosh joined us at our table.

"Mr. Holmes," said Lestrade, "just how did you figure that this Karnak was the one?"

Holmes had sat back down at the table and poured himself a glass of water. He then began his narration:

"Said Karnak is an Egyptian and fanatical member of the Mustafa Kamil movement. I do not doubt that this Kamil, an attorney by the way, is behind what has occurred here. Kamil is so close to Abbas II, the current Khedive of Egypt, that quite possibly some of this 5,000,000 pound currency and coinage would go to the benefit of the independence movement. But to make sure, they developed a plan to issue an extra 1,000,000 pounds of gold tola bars that weigh 3.75 ounces. These are not numbered. They are certified by the melter, who, in this case, would be the Thompson Motherhead Group as they are the only refinery in London. Some might be in kilo bars which are pocket size bars which can be carried in the pocket and are now so popular on the continent.

What occurred is that the shipment of gold to back the issuance was delivered and placed in a vault. The gold value was certified by the bank's metallurgist, William McBeth, and arraignments were made with the Sothis Engraving Company, Ltd, for the printing of the notes and for their coordination of the coinage. This is an Egyptian company that is well respected in the bank note printing circles. If you recall, Watson, the name Sothis is the ancient Egyptian name for the star Sirlus, the Dog Star. It became more important than we thought.

When the bank received another shipment of gold from Egypt, it was placed into the same vault and stacked next to the certified gold that was there. There was no need for inspection, as the value that was required to issue the guaranteed currency and coin had already been certified. Lord Kensington, Sir Charles and Mr. St. James were all present when this was done.

This is what bothered St. James. He thought it strange that additional gold would be sent. The three of you returned to the vault so that St. James could inspect the new bars and he found that they had been mingled. He took the numbers and melters' name off of each. What he had found the night of his murder was that these bars were already in the inventory of the bank and when checked closely, he found the duplication. He checked the vaults where they were located and found that they were still there. The transfer had not been made.

By simple deduction, he realized that he had counterfeit bars probably of lead or some other metal which had been caste with the identification numbers of the real bars and shipped to the Egyptian vault for substitution. They would transfer the real gold bars for smelting into tola bars, replacing them with the counterfeit bars, with the correct numbers, to back up the issuance of coin and currency. As Karnak was in charge of this, it would be an easy matter to make this substitution for a shipment to Sirlus. That gold had already been certified and would remain in the bank to back up the currency and coin to be issued. The substitution would not be discovered. As near as I can figure, there was enough to be equivalent to 1,000,000 pounds sterling of tola or kilo bars, all virtually unquestioned.

There has to be a member of the Mustafa Kamil movement at Sothis to make this work out. The surplus gold tola or kilo bars would be transferred to the Kamil group to fund its fight for Egyptian independence from England. Simply put, Egypt only had an interest in the 5,000,000 pounds of notes and coinage. The bank had certified the equivalent of that sum in gold in its vaults and they would have that sum of notes and coins. This surplus could be diverted to Kamil without any suspicion.

This transfer of gold for coinage has just been made. The certified bullion that is left will support the currency that will be issued. Lord Kensington, Sir Charles and Mr. Kingsley were all present. What occurred is that the counterfeit bars have replaced the certified ones in the vault and the real gold bars have been transferred to Sothis along with the gold bars for coinage to be made into tola or kilo bars to be delivered to Kamil or his followers.

Sir Charles, is your brother-in-law still managing the Thompson Motherhead Group?"

"Yes, Mr. Holmes, he is."

"We must contact him immediately to stop the melting of the gold bars and request their transfer back to the Bank."

"I will do that immediately after this meeting adjourns. What about the way Mr. St. James was murdered?"

Karnak knew that St. James was getting close to discovering this plot. He knew of the Tonga matter and had observed the artifacts that St. James had taken to his office. It was an easy matter for him to get another member of the Kamil movement to furnish him with the leather straps. It was a macabre affair, designed to confuse us."

"Lestrade, you will need to ferret out our accomplices at Sothis Engraving."

"Right, Mr. Holmes."

"I would like to give special thanks to Dr. Karl Knoepker, who is perhaps the leading graphologist in the world. He has helped me compose the handwriting of our killer by the traits that we felt that the killer possessed. Karnak had the symbol of a deep secret. His secret was that he was a fanatic, active in the Egyptian independence movement. The questionnaires were a big help to secure handwriting samples. We figured that the killer would substitute his writing. Karnak did and this gave us our first positive suspicion of this guilt. We found in his personnel file the murderer's handwriting and we knew we had found our man. Agnes Heathrow, an employee in the Foreign Department, was on the elevator at approximately 7:30 on the evening of St. James' death and saw Karnak get off on the 4th floor. Karnak, in his questionnaire, made no mention of seeing Miss Heathrow.

Karnak had been an assistant in the coroner's office in Cairo while attending the university there. There was no doubt that he had the knowledge and skill to dissect a cadaver. I verified this by telegram and was assured that he had been quite competent in that endeavor.

When I reviewed the files in the Egyptian matter, I found that a splotch of blood had attached itself to the back of one of the pages. When Karnak removed the file from St. James' office, he was wearing gloves. Once outside, he inspected the file and unbeknown to him, when handling the pages, left a perfect fingerprint to the back of the sheet in the drying blood. I verified this by the personnel files, which require fingerprints.

I should say that we have not been able to use them effectively as yet, but one day they will be of great importance in finding the identity of the perpetrator of a crime. Here there was no doubt. The fingerprints matched perfectly.

Lestrade, if you will have his shoes analyzed and look into the stitching between the soles and the shoe, you will find St. James' blood. When we looked at the rags used to wipe up blood, I noted that there was a trace of shoe polish. The blood had been wiped off of the murderer's shoes. As this was not visible to the naked eye, Karnak continued to wear the same shoes and is wearing them today. New shoes would be out of character and would focus attention on him.

Well, Lestrade, that about takes care of your murder. I would appreciate it, when you give your story to the press that I really was not murdered, but that charade was part of your plan to capture the murderer. Please bury my substitute and he may have the casket for his trouble."

"Very well, Mr. Holmes. I do appreciate your help in this case. I had better get off to Sothis. Come along, Macintosh."

With that, Scotland Yard left us.

"Holmes, you absolutely amaze me. This is the second time that you have come to our aid. I really hope that it is the last time we need you," retorted Lord Kensington.

Holmes then asked Karl if he would tell them of his other findings. Patel in the Indian Department and Woolrich in the Domestic Department were discussed. They agreed to carefully go through the work of Patel and to have their psychological adviser counsel with Woolrich.

Dr. Knoepker continued, "What I have found is that, on a whole, your staff is not self-motivated very well. The 'T' bars are just not high enough on the stem."

He then gave a short course on the subject with chalk board diagrams.

Sir Rodney then inquired, "If a person learns to cross the 'T' higher on the stem, will that mean that person is setting his goals higher for himself?"

"Yes, it is my belief that it is so. It will be one of the most difficult things a person can do. By conscientiously trying to change your handwriting, you are in fact intentionally changing your personality. Motivation also would help. I would suggest incentives, praise and recognition."

Holmes was obviously pleased. Everyone graciously thanked us and we left for Baker Street. Karl had become a member of our family. It was with much sadness that I said "Goodbye" to him. He was homesick for Leipzig and his students. We were all glad that he had come. Holmes really appreciated working with him in this case. The quality of our meals certainly declined with his leaving. I certainly would look forward to a return visit, soon!

I should tell you that one morning some thirty days from Karl's departure a messenger from the bank was at our door with a letter addressed to Holmes. It was the same blue stationery.

22 May, 1896

My dear Mr. Holmes,

What a pleasure it is to report that Mr. Karnak has confessed to his deed and is scheduled for trial in the fall.

We have recovered the bullion and the Egyptian business is resolved.

I should like to report on the Patel matter. You would favor me if you would pass on our thanks to Dr. Knoepker. We found that Mr. Patel had been transferring funds to his own account, using a fictitious name. He had transferred some 50,000 pounds which have been recovered. He is in jail waiting for trial.

As to the Woolrich matter, I'm pleased to report that he is presently under psychiatric treatment and is making great progress. He is now showing his emotions and expressing his feelings. He is even trying to reduce the loop in his 'd's. His wife and family have asked me to express their gratitude. We are assured that he will make a complete recovery.

Enclosed please find bank notes which we hope will compensate you for all of your efforts on our behalf. Thank you all for helping us again. Good job, Mr. Holmes! Lord Kensington has asked me to express his personal gratitude on behalf of all employees at the bank.

The same psychiatrist is helping all of us at the bank with our self-motivation. Even I have begun crossing my 'T' stems higher.

> Your humble servant,
> Rodney Grope
> Solicitor General
> Bank of England

The Bab Deception

A Sherlock Holmes Adventure

by Paxton Franklin Watson

You cannot imagine the extent of Uncle John's note-taking in this exceptional adventure of the great detective. Sherlock Holmes' research file filled two folders. These records give us an insight into the religious beliefs of Mr. Holmes, and, for that matter, those of Dr. Watson.

It was early August of 1896 and we had suffered an unusually hot summer, which, obviously, had no intention of leaving. Holmes was restless and had been playing somewhat energetically on his violin since dinner. I had just finished the Daily Mail which was a recently introduced London newspaper.

An article had been taken from "The Humanitarian", which was a journal published in London by Victoria Chaflin Woodhull, titled "The Scientific Propagation of the Human Race." Rather dry, I might say.

The "Evening News" told of the death of Alfred Bernard Nobel, a Swedish chemist and inventor. His Will was quoted whereby he gave the major portion of his estate, involving millions of pounds, to a trust. I thought this might be of interest to Holmes and would give us a subject of discussion, and might break his boredom.

"Holmes," said I, "did you see in the News that Alfred Nobel died and set up a trust to provide awards granted annually to persons or institutions for outstanding contributions during the year previous in the fields of physics, chemistry, physiology or medicine, literature, and international peace?"

"Yes, Watson, I have read it," Holmes retorted, without dropping a note or sharping a flat. "It seems the least that he could do."

"What do you mean, the least that he could do?"

"Watson, Nobel found a safe way to handle nitroglycerin after blowing up his younger brother and four other people. This new product called dynamite will blow up tens of thousands more. Why shouldn't he encourage humanitarianism?"

"Holmes, dynamite has many peaceful and valuable uses, such as in mining and in clearing land. He didn't invent nitroglycerin, he merely made it safe to handle. If you look to the Will, it is clear that he intended that the interest on this money be divided into five equal parts and that the earnings be distributed annually."

"That was noble, indeed. Noble! I made a pun without intending one, my dear friend, please forgive me!", Watson chuckled to himself.

Holmes, intrigued by a Nobel defense, put his violin on the table and took his faithful pipe from his purple dressing gown, settling comfortably into his large chair in front of the fireplace.

"I know, Watson, that you are trying to help me overcome my boredom and that is indeed noble and for which I am grateful. Rather than continue in this vein or Baden-Powell's victory in Rhodesia of the Matabele revolt or even Kitchener's campaign against the Mahdi in Sudan, why not talk about the occult, which I have been studying these past two months. I would very much like your thoughts on the matter. It has fascinated me."

"The occult? What do you mean? Spirits? It's all nonsense, you know. As a medical doctor, I can tell you that when you are dead, you're dead. There is nothing more to it."

"Watson, as a detective, it would be a great help if the murdered victim could come back to us and tell us who did him in. This is what the spiritualist believes."

"It's all poppycock, Holmes!"

Ignoring my protest, as if I had never rebuffed him, Holmes continued, "My study takes me back to the first grave of man that contained some of his personal possessions. It is at that time that man and woman began to believe that there was a spirit in this body which went on to another place.

About 530 BC, the philosopher Pythagoras founded a school of philosophy that was more religious and mystical than the Ionian school. It fused the ancient mythological view of the world with the developing interest in scientific explanation. The system of philosophy that became known as Pythagoreanism combined ethical, supernatural and mathematical beliefs into a spiritualistic view of life. They taught and practiced a way of life based on the belief that the soul is a prisoner of the body which is released from it at death. It is reincarnated in a higher or lower form of life, depending on the degree of virtue achieved.

They taught that the highest purpose of humans should be to purify their souls by cultivating intellectual virtues, refraining from sensual pleasures, and practicing various religious rituals. My violin is grateful to them for their discovering the mathematical laws of musical pitch.

It is this belief in the soul, or something in us that lives on after the body dies, that is the basis of all religions. We humans want to think that we will go on living in some form. We then set conditions for ourselves, which, if met, hopefully would qualify us for this extended life. We cannot agree on these conditions, and that is the reason that we have so many different religions."

"My God, I had never thought of that. Simply put, Holmes, I must think more of what you have said. It is indeed a heavy subject."

"Watson, psychic research began in earnest in 1882 with the formation of the Society for Psychical Research in London by Henry Sedgwick, a prominent philosopher. His co-founders included the noted physicists Sir William Barrett, Sir William Crookes and Sir Oliver Lodge, and philosophers Frederick W.H. Myers and Edmund Gurney. They are all respected members of the academic community. Their goal is to study psychic phenomena and to rationalize them in both religious and scientific terms.

The following year, Sedgwick met with William James, the eminent Harvard psychologist and philosopher, who in turn founded the American Society for Psychical Research in 1885. James, along with several other psychologists, focused on studying the spiritualist movement and its mediums who claimed to be able to communicate with the spirit world.

Rather than trying to prove the truth of spiritualists and mediums, both groups sought to understand the paranormal in logical and rational terms. They were fraught with difficulties almost immediately, as numerous mediums were revealed to be frauds, forcing scientific inquiry to turn away from the seance room."

"Holmes, I know that I am a bit of an agnostic, but how do you rationalize all of this with Christianity?"

"Watson, first you have to realize that there are less than 1/3 of the world's population that are Christians. The chief characteristics of all religions are a belief in a deity, a doctrine of salvation, a code of conduct, the use of sacred stories, and religious rituals."

"What occult are you studying about?"

"Occultism comes from the Latin word 'occulere', 'to hide'. It is a belief in hidden or mysterious powers not explained by known scientific principles of nature. In medieval times, it was the alchemists, astrologers, seers and others who practiced this science of experimentation and they were in conflict with orthodox religion. These were really the early scientists and were frequently called magicians and sorcerers because of the mystery attributed to their investigations by most of their contemporaries.

It was Franz Mesmer in the late 18th century that developed a concept of animal magnetism. He believed that certain individuals possess occult powers, comparable to the powers of the magnet, that can be used to invoke the supernatural. This has taken the form of spiritualism today, a belief that the spirits of the dead may manifest themselves through the agency of living persons called mediums."

"Holmes, you can't be serious about this balderdash. It's not like you and your scientific methods."

"Old man, I merely said that I had been studying the subject. It includes other things than talking with the dead. The human mind is a wondrous mechanism, only a small part of which we use. It is logical that some people have a greater capacity than others. It is also logical that some of us use our minds more, hopefully developing our abilities. It is not impossible that some of these minds can read other minds. In fact, I think it very likely.

I also think that our minds do communicate with each other on the subconscious level. Have you ever met someone for the first time and found that you like them very much, or have you met a very charming person, who immediately you do not trust. It seems possible to me that some of these minds may be able to sense into another dimension. Much like the blind developing acute hearing or a heightened sense of feel or smell.

Watson, one of the most amazing parts of the occult is Astrology, the science that describes the influence of the stars upon nature and mankind, which was practiced by the earliest civilized peoples of the earth. Men of great learning and power have followed 'the handwriting on the wall of heaven.' Hippocrates, the father of medicine, Vitruvius, the master of architecture, Placidus, the mathematician, were also astrologer-scientists. Pliny, Galen, Ptolemy, Galileo and Copernicus believed in the influence of the planets upon human life.

The Holy See can boast of several astrologer-popes, including John XX, John XXI, Sistus IV, Julius II and Calixtus III. According to a legend, Maresilio Ficino, the astrologer to the household of Lorenzo the Magnificent, casting the horoscopes of the children of that illustrious de Medici, predicted that little Giovanni was destined to become a pope. He became Pope Leo X.

The four greatest conquerors of historic times, Alexander the Great, Julius Caesar, Genghis Khan and Napoleon I had constant consultation with their astrologers.

Michael de Nostredame, better known as Nostradamus, is history's most famous seer. He was astrologer and physician to King Henry II and Charles IX of France. The prophecies of Nostradamus were read all over the world. He prophesied the great fire of London in 1666, the French Revolution, and the advent of Napoleon centuries before these events occurred. The man died in 1566."

"Amazing, utterly amazing, Holmes! What do you make of it?"

"I can only approach it with logic, Watson. A horoscope is a map or diagram of the heavens' cast for a particular moment of time and read in accordance with well-established rules. A horoscope is calculated by a mathematical process. Those who practice it say that it is free from the elements of chance or divination, and predictions are deduced in a strict mathematical way. The key is 'deduced' and someone has had to determine what the inter-action of these planets will be. Astrologers differ on these effects.

One cannot deny that great and learned men who have studied the stars have believed in their influence. One only has to look to the tides. Certainly, the sun has an effect on every life form on the planet.

As to the legends which have been passed down, one can wonder if the seer's prediction did not drive the subject to accomplish his predicted mission. Like so many things that are predicted or forecasted, you only hear of the ones that worked. How many have failed? You also have the power of the mind working to find the prediction true. A wise man, with knowledge of the person and subject, can predict to some degree what that person's future will be. He can say he saw it in the stars to give it some mystic, where in fact it is logical, common sense."

"How about Nostradamus' predictions?"

"I have no explanation, Watson. It just wasn't a lucky guess. Let me read his prediction of the London fire in 1666, a hundred years after his death:

'The blood o' th' just requires,

Which out of London reeks,

That it be raz'd with fires,

In year threescore and six.'

Watson, it defies reason. There is no explanation except that he did foresee the event from the stars. His prophecies continue until the year 3797. Mankind will have to be the judge of his accuracy.

I ponder the thought that there exists a collective unconscious, a reservoir of data that the unconscious mind is able to tap. Learning may be training one's conscious mind to reach this reservoir."

"Holmes, wasn't it Homer that blinded himself, so that he could look within for the source of knowledge?"

"Quite right, Watson, but the writings are not clear that he ever found it. We have other fortune telling tools among the occult including palmistry, which is really the study of the human hand, phrenology, the study of bumps on the head, Tarot cards, I Ching, and numerology.

Napoleon and his wife Josephine were fervent believers in the science of palmistry, which I do not believe is a science. My brief study of palmistry indicates that much can be learned from the shape and texture of the hand, fingers, and nails. I must admit that they have developed quite an impressive identification: Jupiter; Saturn; Mercury: upper Mars; Luna and the plain of Mars. I regard all of these as mere flattery for the hearer. It seems that people are not satisfied where they are and want to be told of something better yet to come, or be complimented by some good trait that is found. Pure entertainment, Watson, if you like that sort of thing."

"Women seem to be fascinated by fortune telling, Holmes. Where do witches fit into this occult thing?"

"Witchcraft is not based on dogma or a strict set of beliefs, but rather finds its inspiration in nature, revering the movements of the sun, moon, and stars, the flight of birds, the slow growth of trees, and cycles of the seasons. Many people believe that the term occult is synonymous with witchcraft. Witchcraft is usually thought of in its traditional sense; as heresy prosecuted first by the Catholic Church and later by Protestant sects.

There are two strains of witchcraft commonly referred to as 'white' and 'black.' White witchcraft is usually based on Celtic, Dianic and other pagan fertility beliefs. Black witchcraft or Satanism involves devil worship, satanic practices and sometimes perverted sexuality, human sacrifice, and murder. Satanism is the worship of Satan as a superior, or preferred, god. Its structure reflects an inversion of the Christian belief system.

Covens of witches are traditionally made up of 13 members, usually of both sexes, and preserve and pass on the knowledge and rituals gained by centuries of practice. They were called Wicca or Wicce, from the Anglo-Saxon root word meaning 'to bend or shape.' Those who could shape the subtle forces of nature to their will were often the teachers, healers and midwives of every community. Covens are autonomous units and there is no central authority. It is a small community of friends. The Book of Shadows is perhaps the only text that exists which covens would have in common and it is more poetry than doctrine.

Witches are known to practice certain arcane spells and to be skilled in magic, which is viewed as a combination of abilities, intuition and scientific principles based on mystical knowledge. They believe that magic is accomplished by creating a force field of energy that is channeled by complementary opposites, namely woman and man. They call this process the polarity theory. The woman represents the life force and the male represents the death force, each dependent on the other when life and death are seen as moments in a never-ending cycle."

"Holmes, can witches really cast a spell on someone?"

"They can cast anything they wish, but it isn't going to affect you unless you believe it will. I firmly believe that it is your own mind that causes the accomplished mission, if it occurs. I cannot measure the effect of a coven of witches thinking of bodily harm about a person. We know the old Christian saying, 'Seek and ye shall find.' What if the thing sought is to harm another?

All religions and occult practices are firmly founded upon a fear of the unknown. We know that fear and anxiety can cause ill health. Religion, through faith, puts our fears and our anxieties to rest. The occult tries to explain the unknown through the study of nature."

"Where does that leave me, Holmes?"

"You are fine, Watson, you have faith in yourself and in our friendship and, on most days, your fellow man. You believe in knightly honor and you are on your quest all the time to find and help people in trouble."

"That was very gracious of you Holmes," said I, feeling somewhat comforted by his words.

"Watson, how would you like to attend a seance with me?"

"Certainly," I retorted. "It should be entertaining, to say the least, but what is the occasion? You are not planning another adventure with Professor Moriarty?"

"Now, indeed, that would be interesting, but I hadn't given it a thought. I am rather content to have that arch-criminal out of my life. No, you see, I have been following the career of the flamboyant medium, Daniel Webster Rainbe. This Scotsman's seances were accompanied by such unusual effects as disembodied hands and an accordion that played under its own power. During his seance, his body seemed to elongate itself before the eyes of the participants. He conducts these in full light. They have never been able to produce evidence that Rainbe had relied on trickery.

His most astonishing seance took place back in 1868. While in a trance, the medium's body was mysteriously transported out one window and back in another. Lord Dramsley reported to the Committee of the Dialectical Society in London, 'The distance between the windows was about seven feet, six inches and there was not the slightest foothold between them.'

I think that this man would be worth a session. I will try to arrange a meeting tomorrow.

Did you know that Abraham Lincoln regularly attended seances? He was attacked as a spiritualist by the Cleveland Plain Dealer, an American newspaper. His comment was that, 'The only falsehood in the statement is that half of it has not been told. This article does not begin to tell the wonderful things I have witnessed."

With that, we called it a night and retired to bed. My mind was whirling with these thoughts of the occult. I finally had to get up for another glass of sherry before falling to sleep.

Chapter 2

I had just returned from a most exhausting day of practice in Kensington and found Holmes playing a rather sad song on his violin. It seemed to me that his boredom had reached his psyche. He was intently serious as if in deep thought. His opened research books were stacked on his laboratory table. I thought to myself that it was probably more of the occult. Hogwash. I had really had enough of patients this day but greeted him cheerfully, "Hello, old chap, I see you are enjoying your friend. How has your day been?"

"The moat of boredom surrounds my castle, Watson."

"Lower the drawbridge and let's see what excitement we can concoct."

"Right you are, Watson. Tell me about your day."

It was at that moment that a bell was heard at the door below and voices came up the stairs. Mrs. Hudson announced, "Inspector Lestrade and another gentleman to see you, Mr. Holmes."

I hurriedly responded instructing her to send the gentlemen right up. I was relieved in the hope that this might indeed be the cure that the doctor in me was looking for and, as it developed, it was.

"How have you been, Mr. Holmes, and you too, Dr. Watson? You remember inspector Bradley Macintosh?" Lestrade never changes.

"Yes, of course," responded Holmes. Macintosh had been one of the brighter stars in a very dull police experience for Holmes. "We are fine. How can we be of help?"

"Mr. Holmes, we have just come from South Norwood where we found the bodies of two men, Sir Randolph Gretzinger and his man servant, Rafid Alhawaj. The bodies were found by Lady Merryanne Gretzinger, Sir Randolph's widow, when she returned from Sussex not more than two hours ago. She had been visiting her daughter for the past three days. There seems to be no motive and we are puzzled as to what caused their deaths. We are here to ask you to assist us in our investigation if you would be so kind."

"Lestrade, has the scene been disturbed?"

"Not at all, Mr. Holmes."

"Get your coat, Watson, and let's be off. The castle drawbridge has been lowered."

"What's that you say, Mr. Holmes, the castle drawbridge has been lowered?"

"Lestrade, it's just a private joke between us. Pay no attention, please."

We then left our rooms on Baker Street by police carriage to Tennison Road near the Crystal Palace. We stopped in front of a three-story brick townhouse, surrounded by uniformed constables. We were immediately ushered into the house and to the study of Sir Randolph, where his body slumped in the chair behind a large over-sized walnut desk.

"This is where we found him, Mr. Holmes. Nothing has been moved."

"Watson, would you assist me in examining the body?"

I responded affirmatively and approached Sir Randolph with Holmes. As we approached, I was immediately aware of an ether-like odor.

"Chloroform, eh Watson."

"Most assuredly," said I.

At my request, the body of Sir Randolph, fully clothed, was removed to a nearby couch. When his body was righted, there was a book on his lap. It was beautifully bound in dark red leather and trimmed in gold. On the front of the book was an Arabic inscription which I could not translate. The book was given to Holmes and then to Lestrade. The clothing was loosened. I then began a thorough examination of the body and could find no evidence of trauma. It appeared to me that he had suffered a hemorrhage of some sort, but only an autopsy could tell us for sure.

"Hey, Watson, what is this?", said Holmes, raising up the right hand of Sir Randolph, and pointing to the right thumbnail. "See the little bit of blood under the fingernail. This is where the poison was injected, probably by a hypodermic needle."

"Quite right, Holmes. Amazing, just amazing! I don't know how you do it!"

"Lestrade, we now would like to examine the other body."

We were then taken into the kitchen where crumpled on the floor was the body of Rafid Alhawej. The same odor of ether was present and a quick look at the right thumb showed the same trace of blood under the fingernail. Both of the victims did not show evidence of violence or other trauma. I felt by the condition of the bodies that they had been dead since the morning of that day, but I knew it would take the coroner to make that determination. A search was made by Holmes to find a needle capable of injecting whatever substance had been inserted into their bodies, but none was found. We returned to the library where Holmes examined the desk and the floor around the chair where Sir Randolph was found.

"Lestrade, can you tell me about Sir Randolph?"

"Yes, Mr. Holmes, Sir Randolph retired last year after 30 years of service with Her Majesty's Foreign Service and had been the Ambassador to Persia for the past 10 years. Since his retirement, he had been working for a newly formed company called the Anglo-Persian Oil Company. I really know very little about it. Apparently they have been negotiating with the Shah of Persia for the right to drill for oil. He was a man 57 years of age, married to Lady Merryanne and had two daughters who have married and live outside of London. Lady Merryanne indicated to me that he had no enemies and got along well with everyone. She has been in shock and has withdrawn to her quarters with a nurse sent by her doctor."

"Lestrade, I should very much like to talk to her when she is able. There is so much here which I do not understand."

"Right, Mr. Holmes. We have advised her daughters and Macintosh advised me they are on their way to London. We should be able to visit with her in the morning."

Lestrade had picked up the intriguing dark red book and began fanning the pages of its text. "What do you make of this book?"

"That book is called the Bayan which means revelation. It was written by Mirza Ali Muhammad of Shiraz and proclaimed as God's word in May of 1844. He became known as the Bab, which means the gate, because he is considered to be the gate or door to spiritual truth. This was written to supersede the Koran. It is in opposition to basic Muslim theology.

The Bab declared that the prophets were divine manifestations of God himself and that he, the Bab, was one of the prophets, equal to Muhammad in importance and the precursor of an even greater

'Manifestation' which was to appear 19 years after the founding of Babism.

Babism forbade polygamy and concubinage and sought to alter many other Muslim customs. It proclaimed the coming of an era in which all religions would be united under one spiritual head. The Bab founded a group of 18 disciples, 17 men and one woman, and the faith spread rapidly in Persia until the accession of Shah Nasr-ed-Din. The Shaw, persuaded that the tenets of Babism were destructive of Islam and a danger to the state, initiated violent persecution of the Babists. An estimated 20,000 Babists were massacred. After two years of civil war, their rebellion was put down and the Bab, although he had not taken part in the revolt, was imprisoned and executed at Tabritz in 1850.

In 1863, Mirza Hoseyn Ali Nuri, a follower of the Bab, called Bahaullah, which means the splendor of God, proclaimed himself the promised 'Manifestation' and, on the basis of Babism, founded a new faith called Baha'i. He, too, was sent to prison where he died in 1892 and his son Abbas became the new leader of this faith. He is called Abo ol-Baha, servant of the glory. He is a political prisoner as we speak."

"Holmes, how in the world do you get all of these facts and remember them. It is disgusting. I have never heard of the Baha'i religion."

"Watson, there are probably 2,000,000 members of this religion and it is rapidly expanding throughout the world."

"Mr. Holmes, do you think that this Baha'i thing has played any part in these murders?", queried Lestrade, obviously perplexed as reflected by his contorted brow.

"Not likely, Lestrade. It is a non-violent sect, an offshoot of the Shiite sect of Islam, and they have passively tolerated persecution for almost 50 years. The Bab and Bahaullah place themselves with Zoroaster, the Buddha, Jesus Christ, and Muhammad who, they believe, all brought a series of divine manifestations into the world. No, I feel that someone wants us to believe that this was revenge of some kind, but I do not know how it would involve Sir Randolph. Our murderers want us to believe that this murder was somehow caused by members of Baha'i."

"Murderers? Holmes, how do you know that there was more than one?"

"Elementary, my dear Watson. As we know that Sir Randolph and Rafid Alhawaj were chloroformed and there is very little sign of struggle, we know that our victims would have to have been held while the chloroform was administered. Hence, murderers; two or more murderers. It is also obvious that Sir Randolph was expecting them. He was seated at his desk and the man servant had allowed them to enter and had returned to his chores in the kitchen. It is probable that the murderers, or at least one of them were known to Sir Randolph. Because of his background in foreign service, the murderers likely include a member of the staff of one of the embassies, probably persian. I could not find his appointment book, which would have identified our culprits. It has been conveniently removed."

" Mr Holmes, is it all right to have the bodies removed to the Yard for an autopsy?"

"Yes, Lestrade, of course. We can do little more with them than speculate. We will need a thorough autopsy."

Lestrade then delegated the removal to Macintosh, who had been rather quiet during the investigation.

"Mr. Holmes, what do you think killed them?"

"I feel that a poison was used that comes from the animal kingdom, namely a snake. The venoms are broadly categorized as hemotoxic, which destroys blood vessels and causes hemorrhage, hemolytic, which destroys blood cells, or Neurotoxic which causes paralysis in nerve centers that control respiration.

As the cadavers were natural in color, rather than blue, it rules out the latter, which eliminates the cobras and coral snakes. Probably hemotoxic, as hemolytic would take too long.

The murderers wanted to blame these deaths on the Baha'i, so it logically follows that this poison comes from Asia. Of the snakes in Asia, the odds are that the poison came from a viper, probably a pit viper. Many of these vipers have a deep hollow in the side of the head which is connected with the brain by a well-developed nerve which acts as a sense organ. It is highly sensitive to heat and helps it to locate and secure its warm-blooded prey.

As the pit viper has a pair of long, hollow fangs in the upper jaw, there is no way that a snake could inflict the wounds which we have found.

When the Babists were persecuted, many went to the north to Azerbaijan. In the arid and semiarid lowlands of Azerbaijan, there is an Asian snake called Russell's viper, Vipera Russelli, which would be a likely candidate.

If these murders are staged to blame the Baha'i, then what better way than to use nature's poison from an area that they populate in large numbers. This land was part of Persia until 1828.

The venom could be easily removed. Its effects depend on the amount of venom delivered and the size and condition of the victim. Although these victims were both large men in apparent, good health, the amount of venom could be increased to compensate. Using the thumb would speed up the poison's lethal effect, because there is an artery there. Yes, gentlemen, I feel our killer is a pit viper from Asia."

"Lestrade, I should like to examine the scene carefully and, if you have no objection, would like to open the drawers of the desk to see if we can glean some direction in our puzzlement."

"Fine, Mr. Holmes, I will assist you."

"No, I would rather conduct my own examinations if you will indulge me. You know my methods are somewhat particular to my personality, but I will report back to you when my work is done. It would be most helpful if you or your men check the neighbors to see what they might know of this."

"Of course, Mr. Holmes, I quite understand," retorted Lestrade, somewhat offended by his rejection. "Dr. Watson and I will have a look around outside. Macintosh, will you take a couple of constables and check with the neighbors to see if they observed anything around this house today?"

"Certainly, Sir," retorted Macintosh as he left the room.

Almost an hour passed before Holmes appeared and invited us into the study. "It is most baffling to me. Our killers have left no trace of themselves. No ashes, hairs or smudges. The desk is orderly and the mail neatly opened and stacked. I find nothing in the desk that would refer to any work that Sir Randolph may have been engaged in concerning the Anglo-Persian Oil Company. This is odd, indeed, and makes me reach the conclusion that any documents concerning that company have been removed. As soon as we can meet with Lady Merryanne, we may find out what his involvement was in this oil company and who else he was working with. This could shed some light on the motive of these murders, and give us direction in our investigation. It is premature to attempt to draw a conclusion without all of the facts. Like playing whist without a full deck. I should be extremely interested in the results of the autopsy. So, urge the coroner to look closely for evidence of poison and, if possible, to identify its source. Lestrade, did your investigation with the neighbors turn up anything?"

"Not a thing, Mr. Holmes. The nearest neighbor, a writer named Doyle, has just returned from Egypt, where he has been following the Kitchener campaign for the press. We could not find anyone who saw or heard anything."

"Bad luck, Lestrade. We are ready to return to Baker Street and will await your call to meet with Lady Merryanne."

Holmes was in deep and serious thought on our carriage ride home. It was not unusual for him to be so introverted when confronted with such a mystery. It was as if his mind had left his body and what was left did not want communication. Swirls of smoke circling his head confirmed that there was life under his deerstalker's hat and, by the volume of smoke, I knew that he was churning the matters at hand.

Mrs. Hudson had held dinner for us. How splendid a woman she is! Although Holmes ate very little, we enjoyed the meal in silence. After dinner, Holmes went immediately to bed.

Chapter 3

When I awoke, Holmes, still in his dressing gown, was reading The Times. He greeted me rather sarcastically because of my late slumber. It was my day off and, as was my custom, I never passed up a chance to take the rest that my body deserved. Besides, yesterday had been somewhat fatiguing to say the very least.

"Already eaten, I suppose?"

"Yes, Watson, over an hour ago, but Mrs. Hudson is expecting you. You are right on schedule, old man. The Times has covered the murders we attended yesterday. Lestrade found it necessary to mention our consultation. If I am not mistaken, it will bring us some new clients."

"New clients? What do you mean, Holmes?"

"Baha'is, Watson, Baha'is."

"What in the world for, Holmes?"

"To clear their name. The strange thing is that we rather need their help more than they need ours."

"Holmes, it is too early in the day to play games with me. Suffice it to say that I don't really understand and further, at this hour, I don't want to."

With that, I left him to find my morning tea and breakfast. When I returned to our rooms, he was fully dressed.

"Get cracking, Watson. Mycroft has summoned us for a parley and Lady Merryanne will take tea with us. This will be quite a social day."

"What in the world does Mycroft want with us?"

"I rather imagine, Watson, that it involves the Gretzinger matter. The Times has alerted him to our involvement. Older brother does not show much interest in me unless I am involved with something that he is entangled with."

"Get cracking, you say. All right, I'm cracking."

In a short time we had engaged a cab and were on our way to the Diogenes Club, Pall Mall, to meet with Mycroft Homes. Mycroft was seven years senior to Sherlock and would be almost 50 years of age. I can only recall two meetings with him. I remember the suggestion of uncouth physical prowess encased in a huge frame. His intense, gray eyes, firm expression, and clarity of thought hypnotized one captured in his presence. Holmes had always said that Mycroft was perhaps the most brilliant mind in the world, but lacked the patience for details, which is Holmes' stock and trade.

After dismissing our cabby, we were ushered into the lobby of this prestigious club founded by Mycroft and where he maintained his life. We were then escorted by lift to the third floor where his suite was located. We were expected and the page escorted us to the massive door, which he abruptly opened, allowing us to enter the large office and conference room of Mycroft Holmes.

"Sherlock, good of you to come. How are you? It is been several years since we were together. Dr. Watson, the shadow and chronicler of the great detective. Good to see you again. Please have a seat here by my desk."

"I have summoned you, Sherlock, because you are getting in over your head! I felt that I need to inform you of the game which, you might say, is afoot. I want you to know that I am speaking to you from the highest circles of the British Government. Yes, gentlemen, Queen Victoria herself. With all of the British interest in manufacturing and trade, colonization and development, there has been too little emphasis on petroleum. We must develop petroleum resources and quickly. Since a Canadian Geologist, Abraham Gesner, discovered kerosene in 1852, a great interest has been taken in this black gold. Today, the refined oil is used for lighting lamps. It is petroleum's chief product.

The Queen's Council felt that with the advent of electric lighting, petroleum would be replaced over perhaps a fifteen-year period. Thomas Alva Edison's carbon-filament lamp of 1879 gave us the direction. There seemed to be no urgency.

Then we had the advent and development of the internal-combustion engine. This did not become relevant until Gottlieb Daimler developed his four-cycle, single-cylinder motor which was patented in 1887. The V-type engine gave more power and was adopted by a French manufacturer Levassor who launched experiments in 1891 and has been producing automobiles since 1894. Just last year, the first car, propelled by the Daimler engine came in six hours ahead of the second car at the Paris-Bordeau Race. The Duryea brothers of the United States brought out their horseless carriage in 1892. Haynes and Winton have produced cars there. Henry Ford produced his first car in 1893. Today, there are probably only 8-10,000 motor cars in the world.

These combustion engines will operate everything in the few years ahead. We can project at least 300,000 automobiles within the next ten years and, beyond that, who can guess the astronomical numbers they may reach.

These engines run on what is called 'gasoline', which is a by-product of oil refining. It used to be discharged into the streams when refining kerosene because of its explosive nature.

Suddenly the British Government is negotiating contracts around the world for the exploration and development of petroleum. If it is not successful, the government itself could possibly fail.

That is where Sir Randolph Gretzinger comes in. He served Her Majesty faithfully as her Ambassador to Persia. Our geologists have determined vast amounts of petroleum in southwestern Persia. Sir Randolph was the closest friend of Shah Nasr-ed-Din who was assassinated early this year. He was also a close friend of the Shah's family and his successor Shah Muzaffar al-Din. After his retirement last year from the Foreign Service, the Queen asked him and others to form the Anglo-Persian Oil Company and to seek an exploration agreement with Persia. We were advised that Shah Nasr-ed-Din had agreed to give this company a 60-year-development agreement for all of Persia. While the financing was being secured and the documents drawn, the Shah was assassinated. The turmoil that followed and the succession of Shah Nasr-ed-Din and his new ministers have caused delay after delay. Sir Randolph was well known to the new Shah and, only last month, the new Shah had verbally agreed to honor his father's agreement. Now we have these new murders. I should also give you another vector for consideration.

During this century, Persia came under the influence and at times the actual control of England and Russia. England wanted influence over Persia so they could protect India from the French under Napoleon, and later from the Russians. Russians wanted control of Persia so they could have an outlet to the Persian Gulf. Russia defeated Persia in 1827 and by the treaty of Turkmanchai, it gained the land north of the Aras River, giving it the outlet to the

Persian Gulf. English and Russian influence especially on Persia's trade has been increasing since the early 1800s.

The Queen's Council believes that Russia has been cursed by the same short-sightedness that we have and, suddenly, is making a desperate move to get the vast petroleum resources of Persia under its control.

We don't think that the Russians are doing the actual assassination or killing, but believe that they have hired assassins of the Muslim faith, giving them a religious motive to discredit the Baha'is. There is certainly no love lost between them.

Our one hope is to get Lady Merryanne to take her husband's place in this negotiation. She, too, was a close friend of the members of the old Shah's family. Perhaps, she will be able to call in Sir Randolph's marker so to speak.

The president of the Anglo-Persian Oil Company is Lord Trimble Norbridge and its treasurer is Sir Girard Wendelbone. Fine chaps. You should also know that your friends at the Bank of England have agreed to finance this exploration, but it is guaranteed by Queen Victoria herself. The Empire itself may be at stake."

"Brother, what is it that you wish me to do?"

"Sherlock, do what you do best, catch the murderer or murderers, and do it quickly. I must ask you both, in the name of the Queen, not to mention what I have just related to you. I would ask that you encourage Lady Merryanne to take her husband's place and emphasize the importance to the Empire, but not in detail. It would be bad for any high government officials, other than those working with her husband, to contact her. Trust me, the Russian intelligence service functions very efficiently in England."

"Mycroft, I will need the services of our Persian Embassy. I want to know the precise details of the death of Shah Nasr-ed-Din including the cause of death.

I would like to know if a copy of a religious text of the Baha'i called the Bayan was found with the body."

"I will order a dispatch today. The foreign office here may already possess that information. I will inquire and advise you by messenger."

"Mycroft, it would be a great help to me if you could secure from our foreign office a list of all personnel in the Russian and Persian

Embassies here in London. I would like as much information about the staff as possible: job, title, age, idiosyncrasies, personalities, description, date of assignment to London. I would be particularly interested in education and, specifically, if anyone has letters in geology."

"Of course, Sherlock. I will gather what we have and get it to you right away. You do need to know all the players."

With that, the meeting adjourned with formal salutations, including a firm handshake from that huge man. I was always relieved when a meeting with Mycroft was over.

Chapter 4

"What do you make of all this, Holmes?"

We had come to the Crown and Goose known for its excellent food. I had just ordered the ploughman's lunch and Holmes a shepherd's pie. My pint of bitters was at hand and Holmes had a lager with lemonade.

"Interesting, indeed, Watson. Knowing why it occurred does not find who did it, but it is certainly a long step towards our destination. Good to see Mycroft, again. He doesn't seem to ever change."

"No, he doesn't, Holmes. Same big fellow. Why are you interested in the details of the Shah's death?"

"I feel that we will find a pattern there. If so, it will help us better understand our murderers."

After a leisurely lunch, we hailed a cab and were off to Scotland Yard. Holmes and I went to Lestrade's office, and then the two of us followed him to the Office of the Coroner. It was good to see my colleague again. Dr. Mortimer O'Reilly greeted us in his pleasant Irish manner.

"What have you found, Doctor, in the Gretzinger matter?"

"Inspector, we have found that Sir Randolph and his man-servant died from a rather large dose of venom, injected by a needle into their right thumbs. Death was rather immediate. Both victims suffered a severe hemorrhage and died in a matter of minutes. The time of death was established as having occurred between 10:00 A.M. and 10:30 A.M. They had both been chloroformed, and there was a residue in the tissues of the nose as well as the mouth. There was no evidence of trauma, except as noted, and some redness to the forearms, near the wrists, of both men. The venom type is classified as hemolytic and matches perfectly to that of an Asian pit viper."

"Vipera Russelli," interrupted Holmes.

"Why, yes, Mr. Holmes, exactly. How in the world did you know?"

"By deduction, Doctor, but I must admit that it was only a theory. I am indeed grateful for your confirmation. Did you find the victims in otherwise good health?"

"Yes, Mr. Holmes, the body and organs did not show evidence of disease or deterioration, except what was caused by the venom of Vipera Russelli."

"Thank you, Doctor," said Lestrade. "Mr. Holmes, we must be off to Lady Merryanne's house for tea, lest we be late."

The three-story building looked almost naked without the constables. We rang and were greeted by a young lady in her early thirties, who introduced herself as Heather Stone, the eldest daughter of the Gretzingers'. Lestrade made our introduction in somewhat an awkward manner and we were ushered into the presence of a very lovely and charming woman, Lady Merryanne. It was obvious that she had been under sedation and was captured by grief. The large pupils of her enormous, enchanting, gray eyes told the story. She was seated as we entered, very straight, and quickly rose to greet us.

Inspector Lestrade clasped her outstretched hand and introduced himself and then stated to her, "This is Mr. Sherlock Holmes and Dr. John Watson who are assisting the Yard in our investigation. I want to extend Scotland Yard's sympathies to you, Lady Merryanne, and want you to know how much we appreciate your seeing us today. There are a number of facts which we must have if we are to solve this case. We will be as brief as possible, but I hope that you understand the importance of this meeting."

Lady Merryanne was a well-figured, petite woman, dressed in black. Her form reminded me of my departed Mary. Her features were distinct and kind, except they showed the powdered-covered trail of many tears. She had attempted a partial smile as she shook our hands. Her nose wrinkled with the smile. Her flowing, shiny, gray hair had been tied behind her head and fell onto her back, like a pony's tail. This woman was very much a diplomatic soldier, and gave a distinct impression that she would do what she must do to complete this difficult task.

"Please be seated," she invited, pointing to the sofa and surrounding chairs. She seated herself in one of the middle chairs facing the couch, where we all sat.

"How may I help you?"

"Lady Merryanne, how long had you been gone from your home?"

"Three days, Inspector."

"And the purpose of the visit was to visit your daughter's family?"

"Yes."

"And you returned from Sussex late afternoon, yesterday?"

"Yes, the 2:45. I arrived here close to 4:00 P.M. You know what I found. I called Scotland Yard and then called my children."

"Lady Merryanne, were you aware of your husband's business activities?", asked Holmes.

"Yes, Mr. Holmes, Randolph and I were always very close. We would always discuss what he was doing. He retired from the foreign service, or I should say 'we' retired last year. The government asked him to help form a company that would begin oil exploration in Persia. He had been working on this project since the fall of last year. He went back to visit with the Shah to work out the details of a 60-year-exploration agreement with Persia. Our geologists had determined that there was a vast amount of petroleum there.

Randolph indicated that he and the Shah had entered into this agreement, but financing and documentation needed to be completed. Before this could be consummated, the Shah was assassinated.

It seemed that we would have to start over. We journeyed back to Persia for the funeral and visited with his son, Shah Muzaffar al-Din. The new Shah indicated that, as soon as the period of mourning was over and his government was established, he would complete his father's agreement. Randolph was only now ready to go back to Persia and complete this agreement."

"Do you have any idea who would have profited from your husband's death?"

"No, Mr. Holmes. Randolph was a gentle man, well liked by all who knew him. I would have known of any threats or even fears."

"Did Sir Randolph keep an appointment book?"

"Yes, Mr. Holmes, a red, leather-bound one. There was a page for each day. Each year he would purchase a new book, and he would make notes on the page, noting occurrences. The next day, he would go to the next page, and then when the two pages were finished, he would turn it, placing it under a large rubber band. It was in this way he recorded the events of his life, or at least the last ten years."

"Where did he keep it?"

"In the center of his desk."

"We did not find one. Would you check and see if you can find it?"

She excused herself and returned to the parlor promptly.

"It is gone Mr. Holmes. Someone has taken it."

"Lady Merryanne, I would appreciate it if you could get us 1895's appointment book. Would you see if you have it?"

Again, this graceful lady excused herself. In a few minutes she returned with a red, leather-bound book.

"Here it is Mr. Holmes."

"Lady Merryanne, is this the same color, size, and style as the missing book?"

"Yes, Mr. Holmes, he would buy the same style each year. It made for neater storage."

"Would you mind if I took it with me for review?"

"Will that be all right, Inspector?"

"Yes, Lady Merryanne. I will see to it that it is returned to you."

"How long have you known Rafid Alhawaj?"

"He has been in our employ for over six years and returned with us to England. He was a devoted and competent servant and a good friend."

"Did he leave a family?"

"No, Mr. Holmes, he did not. He was orphaned early in his life and raised by the Christian missionaries in Persia. Ours was his first job."

"Are you acquainted with the Royal Family of Persia?"

"Yes, Mr. Holmes, our families were together on all holidays...ours and theirs. The first wife of Nasr, the mother of Muzaffar, who is now regarded as the Queen Mother, and I spent much time together. I could never pronounce her name, so I asked her if I could call her Victoria, which pleased her very much. It got so that I called her 'Vicki', which she liked just as well, if not better. Vicki and I would horseback ride, shop, sew, walk in the garden, and of course, when our husbands were engaged, enjoy tea time."

"Do you know who Sir Randolph met with yesterday?"

"No, Mr. Holmes, I do not. I know that his business with the Anglo-Persian Oil Company brought him into contact with Sir Girard Wendelbone and Lord Trimble Norbridge and he has met with the staff at the Bank of England. He has also had emissaries from the Shah. He would lunch with members of the foreign office and there was, of course, his club."

"Lady Merryanne, I believe that you will be asked to replace your husband in negotiating with the Shah. I would urge you to accept it. Should you accept the post, I would also ask Lestrade to post at least two constables around the clock to see after your protection. I would also like to provide you with suitable servants. This should not be for a very long period. I believe you would be in danger. What your husband was doing is of extreme importance to the future of England. The task has now fallen to you."

"Mr. Holmes, I am not emotionally able to make any judgment at this time, but I can assure you that if it is important to the Empire, I will somehow manage."

"I am sure, Lady Merryanne, I am sure. Please let me know if you accept this post."

"Yes, Mr. Holmes, and I will advise Inspector Lestrade as well."

"Lestrade, do you have any further questions of Lady Merryanne?"

"No, Mr. Holmes, not at this time. I feel we have imposed enough."

We rose abruptly, shaking the hand of our gracious hostess, thanking her for her hospitality, and we each bid her good-bye.

Lestrade dropped us off at Baker Street, just in time for supper.

Mrs. Hudson reported that two rather large foreign looking gentlemen had called while we were out. They insisted on seeing Mr. Holmes today on a matter of great urgency. Because of their perplexed and somewhat frantic manner, she had made an appointment for them to meet with Holmes at 7:00 that evening. The card read 'SUHAIR TAWFIK'.

"Does this mean anything to you, Holmes?", said I.

"Watson, I think we have had a visit from the Baha'is."

Chapter 5

We had no sooner eaten and retired to our rooms and donned our lounging jackets, when the bell rang below us, and I could hear the steps of Mrs. Hudson on the old wooden floors, coming from the kitchen. I arose and went to the door and invited her to show the gentlemen up. Holmes met them at the door, pipe in hand.

Both men were dressed in business suits and well groomed. Their complexion was light brown, hair and eyes dark black, and their faces clean shaven. I would judge them both to be in their early forties, about six feet in height, and they seemed trim in form and somewhat athletic.

One of the gentlemen spoke up. " I am Suhair Tawfik and this is my associate Al-Jodaly Alheloo. Which of you is Mr. Holmes?"

"I am, Mr. Tawfik, and this is Dr. John Watson, my colleague of long standing. Please sit down and tell us of your mission. I should tell you that I have been expecting you since the article appeared in the paper concerning the Gretzinger matter. You are from the Baha'is, are you not?"

"Why, yes," replied Mr. Tawfik, "how in the world would you ever know that? "

"Elementary, Mr. Tawfik. As soon as I found the Bayan in Sir Randolph's lap, it was obvious that someone was trying to discredit the Baha'is. I know of the gentle nature of the faith emphasizing the spiritual unity of mankind. Even after the massacre of 20,000 of your followers, or, more particularly, followers of the Bab who authored the Bayan, there has been no reprisal taken in those 46 years."

Mr. Tawfik's eyes were large and strained as if he were looking into your soul. This fixed, penetrating stare, which made me a bit uneasy, looked fanatical, except for his gentle, kind, and pleasant features of his face.

"Mr. Holmes, I am honored that you have become acquainted with our faith. So few people even know of it. Yes, we have suffered persecution from Persia and from Islam. Even now, our leader Abo ol-Baha, the servant of glory, is a political prisoner of Persia. It is for him that we speak. We wish to employ your services to find the murderer of Sir Randolph and Rafid Alhawaj, who was a member of our faith. We feel that the real motive will be revealed or at least the fact established that the Baha'is had no responsibility for these deaths.

I should also point out that earlier in this year, Shah Nasr-ed-Din was assassinated. He was the Shah who ordered the Bab to death some 46 years ago. In his room were found three pit vipers of the Asian type. On the table by the bed was our sacred book, the Bayan. The newspapers pointed out the facts which implied our involvement, causing our leader deep spiritual pain."

"What else do you know of the death of the Shah?"

"Mr. Holmes, our followers in the palace reported that loud screams came from the Shah's bedroom. By the time that they could break down the door, they found his body on the floor, between the bed and door, very dead indeed. Two of the vipers had gone to the floor and the third was found in the bed. It appeared that he had been bitten at least six times, perhaps more."

"How do you explain the quickness of his death?"

"Mr. Holmes, it was common knowledge that the Shah was suffering from a bad heart condition. We felt that the shock of the snake attack and their poison combined to impose a quick death.

We feel, Mr. Holmes, that these three deaths are from a common source. We have no idea who would want all three of them killed, nor do we know how they are connected. Who will be next? Our faith is expanding rapidly around the world. We cannot allow this sacrilege!"

"Mr. Tawfik, what is your position with the Baha'is?"

"I am one of the 18 disciples. The Bab founded the basis of this faith with 18 disciples and, after his death, Mirza Hoseyn Ali Nuri, a follower of the Bab, whom we call Bahaullah, continued with this plan. My duties include Western Europe and Al-Jodaly is my assistant. Our job is to preach our faith, organize churches, and serve our congregations. My title in English would be Bishop. The church uses lay ministers as teachers of the faith."

"How many members do you have in Western Europe?"

"Over 100,000."

"In England?"

"10,000."

"In London?"

"3,000."

"Amazing, absolutely amazing! I can't believe we have 3,000 Baha'is running around in London," said I.

"They are not running, Dr. Watson. They are doing what every other Londoner does: work, eat, live, play, and, of course, pray. They are from all races and feel that we will reach a time when we will all be under a single spiritual head...one religion. If we were created by a supreme being, it seems logical that there is only one. It is all right if he is called by different names. Mortals have a tendency to make this God their personal God. In simple truth, he is our God. Shouldn't we be able to find a simple way to thank Him without killing one another because of our different ways to say 'thank you'?"

"Sorry, old chap. I really didn't mean to insult you. I just had no idea. Holmes speaks very highly of your faith. Please, forgive me."

"Of course, Doctor. I always welcome an opportunity to practice my trade.

Mr. Holmes, will you let us employ you to find the murderer of Sir Randolph and Rafid Alhawaj?"

"Mr. Tawfik, I would be delighted to assist you in the investigation of these murders, but I will require more of you than my fee. Watson and I have relied on an unofficial force we call the 'Baker Street Irregulars'. This is a gang of street urchins, young boys, that roam the streets and alleyways of London. There is not much that they can't find if we know what we are looking for. In this case, I know what I am looking for, but it will not be found on the streets of London. I will need your Baha'is of London. We can call them the 'Baker Street Baha'is'."

"Mr. Holmes, the Baha'is will commit no crime, I should make that perfectly clear."

"Let me put it another way. There was a certain item of personal property belonging to Sir Randolph, which was removed at the time of his murder. It was stolen from his house. That was the crime. Returning it to its rightful owner would certainly not be a crime. Do you agree?"

"Yes, I agree. We will form the 'Baker Street Baha'is'."

"This will be a dangerous business, Mr. Tawfik. You must understand that. 'The Baker Street Baha'is' will be at risk."

"I will see to it that they understand the risks before becoming part of your plan. Pray, tell me more."

"I want to locate the appointment book of Sir Randolph, taken by the murderers."

"Holmes," said I, "it is preposterous that you think that the appointment book would still be around. I would have thrown it into the furnace immediately. It will give the names of the murderers. No, Holmes, that book is gone."

"Well, Watson, let's just suppose that Mycroft's theory is correct. That the Russians are involved. Assume that the assassins are hired. The book would have value to the Russians who are interested in the negotiations that have been conducted by Sir Randolph and this appointment book has daily notes of what has occurred. It would be invaluable. The person in London who would evaluate and draw conclusions from it would have to save it for any superior who might want to see parts of it for confirmation. Russians have a way of not trusting each other.

And more important than that, Watson, what better way to insure the silence of their involvement in the whole affair. The murderers would know that, if ever they ever told anyone, all the Russians would have to do is deliver the appointment book to the police and they would be convicted. It is rather ingenious. Yes, Watson, that book is locked up at the Russian Embassy."

"How, Mr. Holmes, will the 'Baker Street Baha'is' be able to help?"

"I am being furnished with a list of the personnel of both the Russian and Persian Embassies. I would like you to go over the list and tell me if anyone is a Baha'i. I think that it is likely as your faith has grown so tremendously in both of those countries. Let's take it a step at a time. If not, we will plan another method.

I will also get a job classification of the personnel and should be able to pick out those who would have an interest in this kind of business. I will also have some profile of each of their personalities, which should be of help. So, the game is afoot."

"Can you tell me why the Russians would want to do this?"

"In time, Mr. Tawfik, in time. I must get clearance to tell you more. Suffice it to say, it is but a theory, but one that sounds exceptionally logical to me."

"How much is your fee, Mr. Holmes?"

"1000 pounds. Five hundred now, and the balance on completion of the case."

"Agreed. I will have it delivered by messenger tomorrow."

"Please write out your addresses and phone numbers so I can advise you when the lists come to me. We will need to have another meeting. Time is of the essence. So is born the 'Baker Street Baha'is'. Thank you, gentlemen, for this interesting evening."

"We both have appreciated your courtesy and intellect, and will look forward to working with you. We shall advise Abo-ol-Baha of your acceptance. Good night to you both."

I saw our visitors to the door. Very interesting indeed.

"Holmes, you were right, again! Should be a little tiresome, but I must admit, I rather enjoyed it. The look on their faces. What astonishment!"

"Well, Watson, this detective has just engaged a force larger than the London contingent of Scotland Yard. What do you say to that?"

"It has been a good day for you."

"Us, Watson, us."

"Yes, of course, but this part of 'us' must get ready for bed. Early day, you know. Good night, Holmes."

Chapter 6

I returned from my day of hospital visits and office patients to find Holmes reading a letter.

"Watson, we have been formally invited to a seance at the home of Daniel Webster Rainbe. He is having such interesting other guests. It should be an exciting experience, to say the least."

"When is this event to take place?"

"Two days hence. It is in the afternoon at 3:00, and afterwards they will serve tea."

"Who are these interesting other guests?"

"Rainbe sent us the invitation, which lists all who are invited. We cannot of course be sure who will come, but Rainbe is in such demand that I doubt if any will fail to attend. They are probably like us, who have requested to be present. The first on the list is Victoria Chaflin Woodhull. Do you know who she is?"

"Yes, Holmes, she publishes The Humanitarian. A writer, too. Read her rather dry article just a few days ago. Something about propagation of the Human Race. She does not sound interesting to me."

"She is married to John Budduph Martin, a banker whose family owns Martin's Bank, which, by the way, dates back to King Edward IV and is older than the Bank of England."

"That does nothing for me, Holmes."

"Did you know that she was the first woman to run for President of the United States?"

"No, when?"

"In 1872. She ran on the Equal Rights Party against U.S. Grant and Horace Greeley. Black reformer Frederick Douglas was endorsed to run as Vice President, but I do not think that he ever acknowledged that fact. In those days, women could not even vote. She made a poor showing, but speculation had it that many of her ballots were cast aside and not counted.

She even argued before congress that the word 'person' as used in the U.S. Constitution included women when it said, 'All persons born or naturalized are citizens of the United States', and, of course, 'citizens' had the right to vote. Needless to say, she was unsuccessful.

She wrote a letter to the New York Herald announcing under the headline 'First Pronunicamento' that she was the most prominent representative of the only unrepresented class in the Republic: 'I announce myself candidate for the Presidency.'

She was an avid woman's right advocate, but extreme. Her attitude toward 'free love' was that love and sex are tied together and should only take place between people, men and women, who have a genuine affection for each other. Even a married couple should not have sex with each other if they feel no love for one another. She believed that sex should be as free and natural as eating or sleeping.

Her newspaper, The Woodhull and Chaflin's Weekly in New York City created the greatest scandal in the United States in this century. She printed the story of Henry Beecher and Lib Tilton, and their love affair. Beecher was perhaps the leading preacher in the United States, a great author and a spell-binding orator. His close friend, Theodore Tilton, sued Beecher in 1874 in Brooklyn City Court for alienation of his wife's affection and criminal libel. He asked for $100,000.00. The trial continued for six months. It was more like a carnival. Crowds stuffed themselves into ferryboats, like sardines. They fought to get a seat in the courtroom. Each day as many as 3000 were turned away. This provided nearby saloons with a booming business. It resembled a fairground with refreshment stands and souvenir booths. Tilton's wife, who had admitted the adultery to him, got on the stand and denied it. Beecher won.

Victoria and her sister, Tennie, were clairvoyant, which was exploited by their father during their young life. Victoria had seen a vision when she was very young. A beautiful young man in a dazzling white Grecian tunic had appeared to her. He looked like an angel. 'You will know wealth and fame one day,' he promised gently. 'You will live in a mansion, in a city surrounded by ships, and you will become ruler of your people.'

From the age of three, she showed signs of being clairvoyant. She had the rare ability of being aware of distant objects or future events, which could not have been known to her through ordinary senses. Sometimes, she would scare children by reading their minds. She could describe events before they happened.

Watson, you can see why I have shown this much interest in her background. She tells this story on herself. There appeared a vision in Pittsburgh. It was her beautiful young man in the Grecian Tunic, who had appeared to her in her childhood. 'Go to New York City,' he said, 'To seventeen Great Jones Street. There you will find a house ready and waiting for you and yours.' As he spoke, Victoria could see a picture of the house, its outside and then its interior. To the right of the entrance hall was a parlor and a staircase led to the upper floors.

'Who are you?' she demanded.

The robed figure reached out and began to write with one finger on the table top. The word written began to glow a name, DEMOSTHENES.

Next morning, she boarded the first train for New York and went to that address. It was a four-story brownstone house in a respectful section of the city. 'Is this house for rent?' she asked a matronly woman who answered her knock.

'Of course, dear,' replied the woman, 'We're moving to Buffalo in two weeks.'

The inside was exactly as she had seen in her vision. On a table in the parlor, she noticed a book. Stamped in gold on its cover was the title: 'The Orations of Demosthenes.' Her blood ran cold. She and her family lived in that house many years. While on a lecture tour, she was invited to attend the annual convention of the National Association of Spiritualists. They unanimously elected her their president.

Watson, she is a woman of about 60 years of age. I have seen her photograph at the time she ran for president. She was indeed a pretty lady. Her lips were determined and her stare penetrating. Her black hair was cut short on the sides and tossed back up on her head. Somewhat boy-like. Her ears were small and her face thin with a small pug nose. She always wore a single flower in her hair or on her blouse. It will be interesting to see how time has treated her.

When she came to England in 1877, she changed and turned conservative. She lectured on 'The Human Body, the Temple of God.' The stories in her newspaper reflect this same approach. What has happened to our revolutionary? Happily married, I dare say."

It was at this point that Mrs. Hudson's melodious voice reminded us of the pleasant experience, "Gentlemen, your supper is ready." We adjourned to take sustenance and reconvened back in our rooms with our comfortable jackets and our lighted pipes.

"It was a most enticing story, Holmes. I concede, she will be an interesting companion. Who is the next guest?"

"Alexander Franklin James."

"Never heard of him, Holmes. I suppose that he is a king or something like that," I said a little sarcastically.

"Not quite, Watson. But you have certainly heard of him. He is mainly known for his association with his brother Jesse."

"Jesse James, the outlaw and murderer! This is that Frank James who robbed all those trains and banks?"

"Most certainly, Watson, the very same. I saw an advertisement in The Times that he was coming here on a tour. He has been very popular since his acquittal of the charges of murder and payroll robbery. He was actually tried twice, you know. The books written about Jesse and Frank James have made them somewhat of Robin Hood figures. They hated the railroads because of all the ruthlessness they had experienced from them."

"How old of a man is he?"

"I believe that the paper said he is 53."

"I, for one, would not pay a shilling to see the bloke. He is an outlaw, Holmes."

"One thing I like about our criminal system is that an accused person is not tried in the press. In our former colony, they can report in the press an arrest or an indictment, which has the effect of making the public feel that a person is guilty before tried. That is very unfair and has ruined many a good name. You must remember that Frank James was tried by his peers and acquitted.

The next guest, Watson, is Arthur Conan Doyle. He is an eye surgeon, but does not practice. He enjoys his writing and has written two successful books, The White Company and Micah Clarke. He is a good writer and has just recently returned from Egypt where he was covering Kitchener's campaign against the Mahdi for one of the papers. He is even credited with introducing skiing to Switzerland. He has been active in the field of spiritualism and conducted experiments back in 1887 using an experienced medium named Horstead. He has written several papers about those seances, which he felt were successful. He is indeed a remarkable man. Although I have never met him, I feel very close to him. Strange indeed.

He is bringing a guest whom we have met, Lady Merryanne Gretzinger, Sir Randolph's widow. If you recall, when Lestrade reported on the neighborhood investigation, the closest neighbor was a family named Doyle. I believe that it is the Arthur Conan Doyle family. It is logical to me that Doyle has offered to bring Lady Merryanne to this seance so that she might reach her husband and receive some comfort. He is an avid believer of spiritualism.

We will also be in the company of Nickolay Romanovich, who is the Russian Ambassador to England. I know little about him, but believe that he has some degree of Romanov blood in him. Emperor Nicholas II married just two years ago to Alix of Hesse-Darmstadt, a German princess who took the name Alexandra when she converted to Russian Orthodoxy. They say that Nicholas has a tendency to rely for advice on his wife and is influenced by her mystical beliefs. It could be that the Ambassador's interest lies in pleasing the Emperess. And then of course, we must include ourselves."

"Yes, Holmes, and, of course, we are certainly the most interesting of the lot," I sarcastically replied. "I will look forward to it. Good night, old friend."

Chapter 7

The next two days passed rather quickly. My practice had been heavy and Mycroft had delivered to Holmes the information he had requested. Suffice it to say that the information concerning the death of the Shah was confirmed. The venom had been from Vipera Russelli as Holmes had thought and, of course, the Bayan had been left on a table. The murderer had not been found.

The Persian Embassy had a total of 50 souls in its contingent and the Russian some 85. Holmes had copied the names of all of them and furnished it to Tawfik, who was checking with the local congregations to see if any were members of Baha'i.

Holmes had been very interested in several at the Russian Embassy. His particular favorites were: Vladimir Isayevich who was the Trade Attaché, Gregory Yevgenyenich, Security Chief, and Alexander Zworykin, who was an Attaché Without Portfolio. Vladimir was an affable, charming man who was a salesman in all respects. Gregory had been reported as a hard, quiet, intent man, who looked like a policeman. Alexander had only been in London for about a month and had not been seen in the diplomatic circles. It was not known what his tasks might be. Holmes had felt that the Ambassador was not involved in the death of Sir Randolph as they had been friends for many years. If Mycroft was right, this would have been directed from the highest level and very, very secret.

As to the Persian Delegation, Holmes had no favorites, and, if his premise was correct, it could have been any one of them. Then again, it might be someone else altogether.

We prepared ourselves to go to the home of Daniel Webster Rainbe. Dress was to be informal. I must admit that I was not too keen on going to a seance. It was a spooky thought that made my blood run cold. I certainly did not believe that you could talk with the dead, and if any of the dead wanted to talk to me, I did not want to hear what they had to say. I had heard that many mediums do their seances in the dark and at least this would be in daylight. However, that consolation offered little comfort.

We arrived by carriage about ten minutes before three. Holmes had cheered me up by saying that you should never be late for a seance. The spirits get angry if you are late! All I needed was the thought of an angry spirit.

We were promptly ushered into a study with a long, large walnut conference table, surrounded by leather-covered arm chairs. Bookcases, running over with books, lined the walls on all sides

except for the ceiling-to-floor windows on the outside wall of the house and a large frame, on which was mounted a collection of daggers, unsheathed, with their scabbards beside them. There must have been ten of them, many with stones in the handles and scabbard.

Our host was seated at the head of the conference table. He stood up as we entered and welcomed us. "Please be seated, over here," he said, pointing to two chairs next to the inside wall.

He sat back down and began introductions. "To my right is the Russian Ambassador, Nickolay Romanovich. Next is Dr. Arthur Conan Doyle. Next to him is Lady Merryanne Gretzinger. On my left is Victoria Woodhull, Alexander Franklin James, Dr. John Watson and Sherlock Holmes. Thank you all for coming. I should explain that my contact in the spirit world is Kerstin, who was a Swedish school teacher of English in her past life. Her English is very British and distinct. When she takes over my body, you have to understand that she will be talking through my vocal cords not a woman's. It will be at a higher pitch, and she has a sing-song, Swedish lilt to her words. It should be charming to you, but realize that she is under quite a handicap, having to talk through me.

I will go into a trance, like falling asleep, and she will take over. I have no control over events. Sometimes the accordion, which I have placed on the table in front of me, will play. Sometimes a hand or leg will appear. You must realize that there are many evil spirits out there as well, who might try to take advantage of me. Kerstin protects me, so there should be no difficulty. It is possible to ask questions through Kerstin directed to anyone of that world and she will relate the answer from the spirit world to you if there be one. Sometimes, the spirit will talk through me. Are there any questions? If not, it is time to begin."

His body slumped down in the chair, and his head rested on his chest. He appeared to be in a deep, peaceful sleep. I could see the muscles of his face relax. He was a pleasant man in his early sixties with heavy, graying hair, long on the sides. His features were sculptured and distinct with thin lips now turned down somewhat, in slumber. He was a handsome man.

I should tell you that I was not comfortable sitting next to that train robber, Frank James. He was a big man both in height and weight. He had the look of evil. His brown hair had thinned on top and the front was bald. He had a mustache which hid his upper lip and turned down on each side. His thin lips were without smile. His large nose dominated his face, coming to a point. His cold, dark eyes were framed by narrow eyebrows and were without emotion, blank and staring. He generated the personality of a rock.

Victoria Woodhull was all that Holmes had suggested. Beautifully charming in her graciously aging way. What fire she had in her eyes. Like an imp or sprite from the woods. She had a smile that told you of how happy a life she had had. Dressed fashionably in a petite woman's way. She was wearing a single red rose in her hair.

The Russian Ambassador looked military in bearing, full beard, and sat very straight. A man in his forties, I would say, and pleasant. His round face went together with his body. He had eaten well. I would judge that he was suffering from gout.

Doyle was also a large man with a large frame, heavy brown hair, and receding hair line. He had a handlebar mustache, waxed to a point. His hair seemed oiled down. His lips were thin and firm. I thought it odd that he wore a gold ring on his left little finger. I wondered what the story was that went with that. His vest sported a watch fob with a key hanging down in the center. This man also had determined and penetrating eyes, was extremely confident and appeared domineering.

Lady Merryanne, wearing mourning black, seemed more in control than when I first met her.

"I am Kerstin and I am your spirit guide." At that moment, the accordion on the table began to play. It was an old drinking song, which I immediately recognized, "Comin Thru the Rye".

Victoria began to sob. "That was my nomination song at Pollo Hall. My sister Tennie wrote the words. What a memory that was."

No hands appeared to play the accordion and it had risen several inches off of the table. Then when one chorus was played, it returned to the table, silent, compressed as it had been. I can tell you that I have never seen anything like it. It made the hair on my arms stand up.

"Victoria, there is a spirit named Buck who wants to talk with you."

"Yes," said Victoria, " it is my father."

"Vicki, I want to ask your forgiveness for all that I put you through."

The melodious voice of Kerstin penetrated the room.

"Of course, Buck, you are forgiven."

"Victoria, there is also a beautiful young man in a dazzling white Grecian tunic who wants to speak with you."

"Demosthenes," cried Victoria, "it is Demosthenes!"

"You have known wealth and fame, live in a mansion and have lived in a city surrounded by ships. You will also become ruler of your people, in a city from which your husband comes. Farewell, Victoria, live well."

"Thank you, Demosthenes! Oh thank you for all you have done for me!"

Kerstin's voice sung out again, "I have a Robert Sallee James, who wants to speak with his son Alexander Franklin James."

"Frank, I am sorry that I left you all to go to the gold field. It was not a proper thing to do. Forgive me!"

"Yes, father," replied Frank. "Let me talk to Jesse."

"Frank, you know that Jesse is not of the spirit world."

It was at that moment that Frank bolted from his chair and stomped out of the room muttering profanity. Everyone overcame this abrupt action, not fully understanding it. Tranquillity again reigned.

Kerstin continued as if nothing had occurred. "I have a charming woman by the name of Mary...Mary Watson, who wishes to speak with John."

"John, you were a good husband and we had a fine life together. I want you to get out of your bachelor quarters and find yourself the right woman. You need a woman to complete your life."

"Of course, my dear, of course," I whispered, somewhat embarrassed.

"I have a man named Charles who wishes to speak with his son Arthur."

"Arthur, I miss you very much. Take good care of your mother, but I know you will. I liked the Stark Munro Letters and I am glad that you have found spiritualism."

"I will take care of the Ma'am, father. Thank you."

Kerstin's rhythmical vociferation continued, "I have a man named Randolph asking to speak with Merryanne."

"Merryanne, I am sorry that I had to leave you so suddenly. Know that I am all right and will miss you very much. Take good care of yourself."

"Yes Randolph, I will," Lady Merryanne said sobbingly.

"Lady Merryanne, ask Sir Randolph who his murderers are," directed Holmes.

Kerstin's voice directed itself to Holmes, "I cannot tell you the names of my murderers, but I can tell you that you will find out who they are."

Kerstin's symphonic utterance again came out, "I have a rather stern person who says that he is Alexander III of Russia and wants to talk with Nickolay."

"Nickolay, these are troubled times for Russia and for my son Nicholas II. Serve him well and give him good counsel, my kinsman."

"Yes, Your Highness, it will be done."

At that moment, a hand appeared in the air and went for the dagger mountings. Kerstin screamed, "It is a man who calls himself Moriarty, who wants to kill Sherlock Holmes. Daniel, Daniel, wake up, there is danger!"

The hand tore a dagger from the display and, in an instant, it was on its way directly for Holmes. He instinctively dropped to the floor and, with a resounding thud, the dagger struck in the bookcase behind his chair.

"Not a very good throw, Watson," exclaimed Holmes, coming quickly to his feet.

Holmes reached up and withdrew the dagger from its mark. He examined it carefully and placed it back in its display. He looked behind the frame and examined the wall around it.

Our host began to wake up. Kerstin was no longer there.

"What has happened?", spoke Rainbe in his own voice. "What on earth has happened?"

Doyle relayed the occurrences of the afternoon to Rainbe. Rainbe could not understand how this had occurred. Rainbe apologized to us all, and especially to Holmes. He seemed weakened by this seance and his assistant took over while he excused himself. And off we were back to Baker Street.

I do not think in all of our years that I have seen such an expression on the face of my old friend. It was a look of bewilderment, disbelief, frustration, and, yes, fear. He did not want to talk about it, and his mind seemed to be swirling in trying to solve an unsolvable problem. How could a dead Morarity hurl a dagger at him?

Chapter 8

After supper we returned to our rooms for our pipes. Holmes had been very quiet during dinner. We made ourselves comfortable and he poured us each a glass of sherry and we sat down.

"Holmes," said I, "that was quite a most unforgettable afternoon. What do you make of it?"

"Watson, it is plain to me that all of the information that Rainbe, or perhaps I should say Kerstin, passed on to us could have been known to Rainbe. The one exception is the disclosure that Jesse James was not dead, though shot in the back of the head on April 3, 1882, by a member of his gang. Photographs of his body lying in the wooden casket, with his hands folded, were in all of the papers. And yet, like folk heroes, rumors persist of sightings of Jesse James. Women claim to have been living with him and even having his children after his supposed death.

Let us look at what we heard, concerning Jesse James, with cold logic. It is either true or not. If not, then Rainbe can simply say that was what Kerstin was heard to say. He was in trance and, by his theory, not present. Jesse can't very well come forward from the spirit world if he is not dead. If true that Jesse lives, if found, he would be tried for murder, and, besides, it would prove that what Kerstin said was true. Frank James leaving the room the way that he did gave credence to Kerstin's words and to the rumor of the legend. I imagine that we shall read about this in The Times tomorrow."

Holmes had been looking into the stilled fireplace during this discourse. He now rose and went for another glass of sherry for both of us to my pleasure.

"Then Watson, there is the accordion. Even I knew of Victoria Woodhull's nomination song, 'Comin Thru the Rye'. How did that confounded thing play? I don't know, Watson, I just don't know. It has occurred in many of Rainbe's seances. Of course, not the same song."

"Well, Holmes, we saw it rise up and play. We heard it. How can we deny it?"

"Yes, Watson, we cannot deny that it raised up and played, but we can deny that it was done by a spiritual means. How many times have we heard someone say, 'I saw it with my own eyes?' Think of the magician who saws the lady in half or this Houdini. Things are not always what they seem. Remember that we did not see anyone playing it and therefore cannot just assume that it was a spirit. I rather think that is magic, Watson, and very good magic indeed."

"But what about the dagger that almost killed you? That floating hand that appeared from nowhere, hurling that dagger directly at you. You were lucky that you were not killed. What about that, Holmes?"

"Watson, old friend, look at the facts. That dagger was not meant to kill me. Your chronicle of our adventures has painted a picture of Moriarty as the devil himself. If that hand had belonged to my deceased arch-enemy, Moriarty, you can most assuredly have assumed that it would now be stuck in my body. The dagger went into the bookcase far above my head. What we saw was the hand remove the dagger, the hand throw the dagger. We heard what we thought was the dagger hitting the bookcase and saw the dagger, stuck in the bookcase.

Raine has had hands and feet appear at his seances for years. No one has ever proven any fraud in his seances. I must admit to you Watson that I do not know how it was done, but it was a magic trick as sure as we are sitting here. Rainbe is good, very good. This whole thing will be written up in the paper probably by Doyle who is quite caught up in this sort of thing.

There is something so familiar about this Doyle, but I just can't put my finger on it. He is a nice enough chap, Watson."

"What about Mary telling me to find another wife?"

"That is good advice for you anytime, Watson. You need a woman's care. It is not a revelation from your sweet, departed Mary."

"What about Sir Randolph telling you that you will find his killers?"

"Good friend, Watson, from all the glorification that you have given me from our humble adventures, most of London would take the bet that we would find the killers. It is time for us to retire. Pleasant dreams, Watson."

Chapter 9

I awoke rather late, as was my custom on Sunday, to find Holmes fully dressed.

"Sorry to do it to you, Watson, but we will have visitors within the hour. Baker Street Baha'is. The game is now surely afoot. Join us when you can."

"I'll make it, Holmes. Let me get my tea and breakfast."

I had no sooner finished dressing, when I heard the bell and footsteps on the hallway steps.

"Good morning, Mr. Holmes and Dr. Watson," greeted Tawfik.

He was accompanied by his assistant, Al-Jodaly Alheloo. His last name rather sounded to me like a bad yodel. Holmes and I returned the greetings of the day and Holmes invited them to be seated and immediately began his inquiry.

"What have you found, gentlemen?"

"We have five recruits for the Baker Street Baha'is, Mr. Holmes. We have three Baha'is at the Russian Embassy and two at the Persian."

"Please tell me who they are and what they do for their employers."

"At the Russian Embassy ,we have Rafid Ali, who is a domestic servant, and who cleans the building and grounds; Shalin Al-Hamdi, who is an interpreter; and Muayad Mohaned, who is a clerk in the trade office."

"Can they be trusted?"

"Yes, Mr. Holmes, they can be trusted. They would do anything to clear up the good name of Baha'i that is lawful ."

"I should very much like to meet with Rafid Ali. I do not want to involve anyone unnecessarily. Does he speak English?"

"No, Mr. Holmes, he does not. I will have to act as your interpreter. When do you wish to meet with him?"

"As soon as possible, Mr. Tawfik, as soon as possible. Please tell me about our Regulars who are at the Persian Embassy."

"Jamilah Mahmood is a Correspondence Secretary and Silham Al-Hazeem is a cook."

"Mr. Tawfik, did you read the Times this morning?"

"Yes, a very interesting article. Looks like somebody tried to kill you."

"It was made to look that way. The article went on to say that the deceased Sir Randolph Gretzinger's spirit told me that I would be the one to find his murderer."

"I think that the headline was, 'SPIRIT TELLS SHERLOCK HOLMES THAT HE WILL FIND HIS MURDERER'."

"Exactly, Mr. Tawfik. That creates some problems for us as the murderer or murderers know where to find me and are again dramatically reminded that I am on the case. I cannot make contact with the Persian Embassy for fear of jeopardizing our Baha'is. If my theory is correct, there is a likelihood that the murderers are part of that 50-person staff. I would like you to visit with our Baha'is, individually, and inquire whether or not there are any rumors about members of their staff fraternizing with the Russians. I should be most interested in knowing who these persons might be. Pledge them to secrecy and do not tell one about the other. Please do not tell them of our purpose."

"Of course, Mr. Holmes. We will take our leave and should be able to return within the hour. My recollection is that Ali has Sundays off. If I can't return by then, I shall call you within a few minutes."

Our Baker Street Baha'is then departed and I inquired of Holmes concerning the article in The Times. I fetched some more tea and took my position in front of the fireplace in my favorite chair, paper in hand.

Before I had finished the paper, Tawfik returned with his assistant and a stranger, who looked much like they did.

"Mr. Holmes, this is Rafid Ali of the Russian Embassy. Rafid, this is Sherlock Holmes and his friend Dr. Watson."

Holmes invited us all to be seated and began his chat with Ali through Tawfik, acting as interpreter. Holmes had his pad in hand and was looking at this rather thin, tall man with dark hair and eyes and with a light-brown complexion. Holmes' manner was friendly for Holmes, but intent. He attempted a slight smile as he began his questioning, but his penetrating eyes were affixed on the eyes of Ali.

Ali was nervous at this attention, but began to feel more at home as the interrogation unfolded.

"Mr. Ali, has Mr. Tawfik told you of why you are here?"

"Sir, only that I was needed by my faith to save our name. He said that I would not have to do anything illegal and that you would tell me what I must do."

"Did he also tell you that you must say nothing of what we discuss here or your mission to anyone other than us?"

"Yes, sir!"

"This is a dangerous assignment. You would be risking your life."

"Yes, sir, I understand," Ali answered through Mr. Tawfik.

"What is it that you want me to do, Mr. Holmes?"

"Locate a book, exactly like this one. It is a red, leather-bound appointment book. It will have the year marked on the front, '1896'. I do not want you to look inside of it, or remove it, just locate it. Is that understood?"

"Yes, sir, Mr. Holmes. It is understood."

"Exactly what are your duties in the Embassy?"

"I am a cleaner and work with a crew of 15 people, who keep the building and grounds clean. The assignments vary, but I work throughout the Embassy."

"Where do you sleep?"

"We sleep on the fifth floor. It is like a barracks. One large room for the women and one for the men."

"How long have you been here?"

"One year and a half. I have agreed to work for two years. At the end of that time, I will be returned to Azerbaijan and to my wife and son. Work has been hard to find back home, so I agreed to this work. The Russians feed and house us, so I am able to send most of my pay back home to support my family."

"How is the domestic contingent fed?"

"We are fed in a back dining room. We are usually the first to rise and, after a hard day, are ready to eat around 5:00 P.M. The others eat by class of jobs with the Ambassador and his close personnel eat around 8:00 P.M. I should also say that we are not fed very well, but we have plenty of potatoes and bread. Usually, there is a fish or poultry dish."

"Is there any schedule as to when you get fish or poultry?"

"We know that there is always fish served on Friday. I believe that it is the Catholic influence. It certainly does not offend the Muslim or Baha'i faiths and would please a Catholic. Poultry, usually chicken, is served on Sunday. I think that they want to start the week out with good food."

"Mr. Ali, does the Embassy have a safe?"

"Yes, sir, a very large walk-in one. There are many file cabinets lining the room, some of which are locked. It is fire proof and has a combination lock on the front. It is opened in the morning so that the staff can have access and is closed at 5:00 P.M. There are two security guards stationed there at all times that it is open."

"Where is this safe located?"

"It is located on the second floor."

"Are there any other safes on the premises?"

"No, sir, there are not. Some of the offices have locked desk drawers and some file cabinets have padlocks on them."

"Will you furnish me with a diagram of the entire building, showing me where everyone is located, and their jobs?"

"Yes, sir, but I have little education and am without drawing skills, so I will need the help of Mr. Tawfik."

"Mr. Holmes, we will get this done for you," said Mr. Tawfik.

"Do you Know Alexander Zworykin?"

"I clean his quarters on the second floor. I have seen him on many occasions working at his desk in the study off of his bedroom. He does not mingle often with the other staff members. He has only been with us about a month."

"What are his duties?"

"Mr. Holmes, it puzzles the cleaners. We do not know. We pretty much know who does what, and, of course, their ranking. His ranking is that of a top diplomat, but what he does, we do not know. He is gone from the Embassy daily, but we do not know where he goes."

"Does he have a locked file cabinet or desk drawer in his study?"

"He has a locked desk drawer, the bottom one on the right."

"Do you have keys to this drawer?"

"No, sir, only he has the keys to that desk. It was purchased shortly after he arrived and no one else, not even security, has keys to that drawer."

"Do you suppose that you could get me the manufacturer's name and any identification numbers off of that desk?"

"Yes, sir, I will try."

"Does the Embassy ever bring in repairmen who are not Russian?"

"Yes, of course, if we need a repair that we cannot do ourselves."

"Whom does the Embassy use?"

"Londondary Flat Maintenance Alliance. It is only a short distance from us and they have a variety of skilled repair people. They even do our chimney sweeping every year."

"When do they do this chimney sweeping?"

"About this time of the year, Mr. Holmes."

"How many sweeps do they send?"

"Four or five."

"Who requests the service?"

"The boss of our section. He is really one of us, but has the responsibility to see that we do a good job and that the Embassy is clean and functioning."

"Where does the Embassy buy its food?"

"Our meats we buy at Nikita's Butcher shop. Our other grocery needs are filled by the Pancras Wholesale Grocery."

"Do they deliver to you?"

"Yes, they do, Mr. Holmes."

"Does the embassy have anyone who is an engineer or geologist?"

"Not that I know of."

"Mr. Ali, you have been of a tremendous help to us. I want you to fix this appointment book in your mind. This is what we are trying to find. You should contact Mr. Tawfik should you see it. Please get me the manufacturer's name which will be on Mr. Zworykin's desk as soon as you can. I should also ask you to let me know if the Embassy decides to have their chimneys swept. I will be looking forward to the diagram of the building. Thank you for your help. Again, please do not mention this conversation to anyone. Your life could depend on it!"

With that and closing salutations, the Baker Street Baha'is left us. Holmes' questions puzzled me, but I knew that he had a purpose or he would not ask. The next day Tawfik delivered detailed drawings of the Russian Embassy and the name of the desk manufacturer to Holmes.

Chapter 10

Watson is already off for a busy practice day, so the task, poor reader, has fallen to me, Sherlock Holmes to chronicle this part of the epoch.

I had received word from Tawfik that there were no rumors concerning the Persian staff fraternizing with the Russians. I am not surprised as they have fought two wars this century and Persia lost them both. Yet, they have grown to depend upon each other for trade.

Tawfik also delivered a layout of the Persian Embassy, showing where everyone lived and did their business. The company that made Zworykin's desk was the Trafalgar Desk Manufacturing Company and their plant is located in the north at New Castle upon Tyne. The serial number was A76390 and it was called an 'Imperial Desk'. I was able to locate a sales office in London and I was off to see Mycroft, seeking his help.

I explained that I needed the master key for the lock in that desk. All manufacturers keep a master key that will unlock any desk that they have manufactured in that style. One master key for each style, which in this case would be for the 'Imperial Desk'.

I told him that I had reasonable suspicion that Zworykin was our man. I believed that he had Gretzinger's appointment book and that it had not been disturbed. It was a great insurance policy for the Russians and a road map of Gretzinger's meetings concerning the Anglo-Persian Oil Company.

Mycroft agreed with me that Zworykin would not share any of his workings with any member of the Embassy. After all, if our theory were correct, he had just caused the murder of a former British diplomat. We agreed, also, that Zworykin would have the appointment book in his personal possession and not in the Embassy safe. If his involvement were known, it could even cause a war with England.

Mycroft laboriously explained to me that normally, where there was probable cause, a court would issue a search warrant. The Embassy is a foreign country and, in this case, Russia and our courts have no jurisdiction over anything that goes on there. He also suggested that, if I got caught inside, I might never be heard from again, which was an uncomforting thought. It was a risk that I had to take.

Mycroft told me that I should not contact Trafalgar. If any word got out concerning my interest in a key that would fit Zworykin's desk, the appointment book would be destroyed or, at least, transferred out of this country.

He then offered to have The British Secret Service contact Trafalgar Desk Manufacturing Company and secure this master key for me. It would be the highest level of the international unit, so that no word of our request would get back to Lestrade. They would only be told that it was a matter of national security, and that the key would be returned. They would not be advised of its purpose or intended use.

"Sherlock, just how do you plan to use this master key? You can't very well just walk into Zworykin's office, unlock the desk and take out the appointment book!"

"The Baker Street Baha'is will check the drawer for me. We have three friendly Baha'is on the Russian staff. If it is there, as you and I seem to think it is, then I will have to devise a plan to get it out. It would be too dangerous for anyone in the Embassy to be involved in its removal."

"I see," said Mycroft with a wry smile beginning to dominate his features. You are working with the Baha'is. I am not surprised. Let's just say that you get this appointment book. Just what do you intend to do with it?"

"Give it to Lestrade."

"He will want to know where you got it. What will you tell him?"

"I haven't decided."

"You cannot tell him the truth. It could throw us into a war with Russia. It might even throw Persia back into war with Russia if Zworykin could be tied into the assassination of their Shah. These three murders have much similarity. It should be enough for Lestrade that it will name the murderers. The book could be identified by Lady Merryanne as authentic and she could also identify Sir Randolph's handwriting. That should do it for Lestrade. We cannot tell him of the involvement with the petroleum."

"The Baha'is have hired me to clear their name. I believe that Lestrade can do that once he knows that the murderers were not Baha'is and that the blame had been falsely placed. There is so much bitterness within the Shiite sect of Islam directed towards the Baha'is that the authorities may well believe it was just an attempt to discredit the Baha'is. But how will Lestrade figure that Gretzinger became a target?"

"Your Baha'is, Sherlock, your Baha'is! Once they are off the hook, they can claim a real friendship with Sir Randolph, which will satisfy Lestrade's motive. It is probably true as well as there are so many of them in Persia. Sir Randolph would have dealt with them for the ten years that he was there. He was such a gentle, pleasant man. I'll bet you can sell it."

"Mycroft, there is just one problem. I am dealing with Suhair Tawfik, who is the Baha'i spiritual leader in Western Europe. His faith has been blamed for three deaths. Two of them here and then we have the assassination of the Shah. Earlier this year when the Shah was assassinated, they found the Bayan on the table of his room. To get Tawfik's cooperation, I will have to explain your theory of what has really happened and why. I do trust him, Mycroft. Will you allow me to discuss this with him? We know that there was no love lost between the assassinated Shah and the Baha'is. My hope is that the Shah's assassination can be explained as a violent act, attempting to discredit Baha'i. The Shah's death would appear as revenge, but could be explained as an attempt to blame the Baha'is as it would be logical for them to want to get even with the Shah. Their leader even now is in a Persian prison."

"Sherlock, it is against my better judgment, but I will agree. I do not know how he can hurt our cause, but admonish him to keep this between himself and his leader.

Sherlock, just for fun, let's suppose that you get this appointment book. What do you think that this Zworykin will do?"

"He will surely leave the country."

"Will he try to get it back from you?"

"Perhaps. It depends upon how much time I have it in my possession before it is discovered. I believe that he will be able to figure out when it was removed with either of my plans."

"What about the assassins?"

"He will have to have them immediately killed so that they cannot identify him. He has the same problem we have in not wanting to start a war. I suppose that he could get them out of the country, but, once they are known, one of them surely would be caught. No, he would have to have them killed."

"I would be very careful, little brother. This is a dangerous game. I will get your master key for you, Sherlock, and should have it to you within two days. Good luck on your venture!"

Sherlock's chronicle comes to an end.

Chapter 11

I really saw little of Holmes the next several days. He would get up before me and arrive home before I finished my practice day. Our bathroom was a bloody mess. I could not figure out how so much dirt could be carried into the house.

A messenger from Mycroft had arrived this day, with a package for Holmes, which had delighted him. He had called Tawfik, who had come for instructions. The two of them talked very seriously for some time. Then Tawfik left and I really did not know what it was all about.

The following day, Tawfik had returned. He seemed especially pleased with himself. This meeting with Holmes was brief, but very pleasant. Both of them were grinning like Cheshire cats when he left.

It was on the following day that the most unusual thing occurred. It was my day off and in mid afternoon the door suddenly opened and there stood a red- haired man, mustache to match, with a top hat on and a scarf thrown rather carelessly about his neck.

"Look here my good man, you cannot just burst into our rooms without an appointment. Sherlock Holmes is not at home. You must make an appointment."

Here stood a chimney sweep, dressed in his full uniform with black all over his face and clothes.

"Aw, Govnor, I'm here to clean your chimney. I have also been asked to deliver a book to you. Here it is."

He then handed me a red, leather-bound book, with gold lettering which identified it as an appointment book for the year 1896. Was this the appointment book of Gretzinger? But how did he come by it? What was the meaning of this?

"Where did you get this book?", said I.

"I stole it, Watson."

He threw off his red wig, pulled off his mustache, and there stood Holmes, as dirty as ever, but identifiable. He gave me quite a start with his theatrics. He seems to delight in fooling me with his disguises.

"Let me have my bath, and I will tell you the whole story of what I have been up to, Watson."

After his bath, he came out in his dressing gown and poured us each a glass of sherry, which was my favorite pastime at the end of my working day.

"This book tells us who the murderers were. See here, it shows that Gretzinger had an appointment at 10:00 A.M. with Alhandi Jamilah, courier from the Persian Embassy. This is our man and the second man is probably a courier also as they were traveling together."

"Tell me how you were able to get this book."

"Watson, I learned the name of the manufacturer of the desk, which had been recently acquired by Zworykin, who was my chief suspect. With the help of Mycroft and the British Secret Service I was able to get a master key that would open the locked drawer of this desk. Ali checked the contents of that drawer which he told us about and confirmed that our appointment book was there. I am in the employ of the Londondary Flat Maintenance Alliance and have been these past few days. I am a chimney sweep. This is a busy time of year for them, so I have been earning my keep. After the book was found, I asked Ali to see if he could suggest to his boss of the domestics in the Russian Embassy that it was a good time for the chimney sweeps. Londondary was called and I entered as a chimney sweep. I went to the fireplace in Zworykin's study, unlocked the drawer of the desk and took out this book. We finished our work and I left with the book and here I am."

"Will they be able to trace you, Holmes?"

"Watson, I have used an alias. Nonetheless, Zworykin may suspect that I was the one who took it, or that I had it taken. In any event, he will consider taking it back from me. He will also consider killing Jamilah and his confederate to prevent tracing the murder back to him. Zworykin needs time to discover that the book is gone and then he will make up his mind. I rather think that the murders will take place immediately to protect the identity of Zworykin. I then look for him to leave the country. For reasons of my own, Watson, I do not want to deliver this to Lestrade until tomorrow morning. Yet, a visit to Scotland Yard would certainly take off any need for Zworykin to try to get the book back from us or commit any further mischief. Let me dress, and we will pay Lestrade a visit."

In twenty minutes, we were on our way to Scotland Yard.

"Good afternoon, Mr. Holmes and Dr. Watson. Do you have anything to report. I must admit that I was amused by the seance reported in the Times. It is nice to have the murdered victim have so much confidence in your ability."

"Lestrade, I just wanted to report that I believe that I will have the appointment book of Gretzinger tomorrow morning. This book should name our murderer. I want no credit for its solution, but I have two favors which I hope that you can grant. The first is that you will not ask me to tell you how I came in possession of this book. It can be authenticated by Lady Merryanne and she can identify Sir Randolph's handwriting."

"It is agreed, Mr. Holmes. No questions on how you came in possession of this book."

"The second favor is that I want you to keep an open mind during this investigation. I think that this crime has been done to discredit the Baha'is, and you will find in your investigation that they have had nothing to do with it. I would ask that you advise the press that this crime was committed to discredit the Baha'is who were friendly to Sir Randolph. This is conditional upon your investigation reaching the same conclusion as mine. If done to discredit them and if you find them innocent of any involvement, then we should take away the discredit. Suhair Tawfik is the spiritual leader of the Baha'is in Western Europe. I know how to reach him should you wish to talk with him during your investigation."

"Mr. Holmes, when the investigation is completed, if I do reach the same conclusion, I will certainly advise the press. I would like to meet with Mr. Tawfik if you will be good enough to set it up."

"Thank you, Inspector, until tomorrow morning. Say 9:00 A.M. at our place."

"Yes, Mr. Holmes, that will be fine. Good day gentlemen."

As we left the Yard, Holmes noticed a man watching us from the shadows. He was a foreign looking man by his manner of dress.

"Zworykin?", said I.

"Probably, Watson," retorted Holmes. "Hope so."

"Holmes, why won't you tell Lestrade where you got the book?"

"Watson, we took the book illegally. All Zworykin would have to do is deny any knowledge of it. You can bet that the murderers who could identify him will not be around to do so. If they are, then Lestrade can develop it. There is not enough proof to convict Zworykin. The disclosure would also create quite an international incident. Remember that Mycroft said that his intervention comes from the highest office in the realm. Queen Victoria does not want an international incident or a war. Watson, let it be."

Chapter 12

I had made arrangements for my associate to make my hospital rounds in the morning and, if necessary, my office patients in the afternoon. I wanted to be present at the conclusion of this case.

When I awoke, Holmes was already taking breakfast, but had laid open The Times. The large headlines dominated the front page: "TWO PERSIAN COURIERS MURDERED." Just as Holmes had anticipated, Alhamdi Jamilah and Abinuk Alhawaj were murdered in separate attacks last night. They were both knifed to death after a struggle. No motive was known as robbery did not appear a motive. They were not on any diplomatic mission at the time of their deaths. Scotland Yard was baffled.

I joined Holmes at breakfast.

"Looks like Zworykin has covered his tracks, Holmes."

"Yes, Watson, thoroughly. I would not be surprised to learn that he was already aboard ship on his way back to Russia. Look at it this way, he did complete his mission. The rest of this drama will have to be played out by the interested parties. Mycroft did advise me that Lady Merryanne had agreed to take her husband's place with the Anglo-Persian Oil Company. They are providing her with security.

I have also asked Tawfik to join us at 9:00. We might as well get the whole matter resolved. I have informed him of all that has occurred. He has consented to keeping the Russians out of it as long as the Baha'is are cleared and the deception rectified."

Promptly at 9:00 o'clock, Lestrade, accompanied by Macintosh, arrived. Tawfik followed them in as well, followed by Alheloo. They all joined us in our rooms. After proper introductions had been made, Holmes handed the appointment book to Lestrade. Lestrade went quickly to the day of the murder.

"What's this? This begins to explain those two knifings last night. Weird business. This Alhawaj must have been Jamilah's accomplice. Now, who would want to murder the murderers?"

"The person or persons who put them up to it, Lestrade," quipped Holmes. "Someone was afraid that they would be given away if you zeroed in on Jamilah."

"Can you shed any light on this, Mr. Tawfik," asked Lestrade.

"Perhaps, Inspector. These murdered men who were killed last night are not members of our faith. They are Shiite Muslims. The Baha'is are an offshoot of the Shiite faith. The book that was left in the lap of Sir Randolph at the time of his murder was the Bayan, written by the Bab. In our faith it replaces the Koran and is, so to speak, our Bible. The Koran is their Bible and they will not accept the Bayan. They see us as a threat to their religion. Our faith is a fast-growing, non-violent religion. The Muslims are not pleased with our growth and seek to discredit us anyway that they can. Sir Randolph was a friend of our faith. We can only assume that he was chosen as another way of trying to bring some shame upon our name. The people hired to do the job were killed to protect their superiors. It is a type of holy war."

"A holy war. Holmes, what do you think?"

"Lestrade, we know that Gretzinger was murdered. It was made to appear that the Baha'is did it. We now know who did it and they were not Baha'is.

You can check with the Embassy for any other motive, but this seems to be the only explanation, based on the facts that we have. Do we know of anyone else who would want to kill Gretzinger?"

"No, we don't, Mr. Holmes. Macintosh went to the Embassy last night and no one there has any idea of why these two couriers were murdered. Well, we have found our murderers of Sir Randolph. There has certainly been a speedy trial and execution. The only question now is who killed them? We have no leads, and the only explanation we have is that it must have been a battle in the holy war between the Muslims and the Baha'is. So be it. Let's return to the Yard, Macintosh. Holmes, mind if I take this appointment book with me?"

"No, of course not, and when you return it to Lady Merryanne, please give her this one for 1895."

Thank you, very much, Mr. Holmes. And of course, you too, Dr. Watson. Good day, gentlemen."

Holmes clasped Tawfik's outstretched hand with both of his.

"Thank you so much for your help in this delicate matter, Mr. Tawfik. Excellent job!"

"It has been a pleasure working with you Mr. Holmes. It has been a different experience serving as a member of the Baker Street Baha'is. Perhaps again, sometime. The balance of your fee will be sent by messenger tomorrow. Abo ol-Baha sends his special thanks for your assistance in getting this matter resolved. May the press treat us kindly."

At this point, I returned to my hospital rounds and relieved my associate. It had been a good day indeed. Sir Randolph's spirit was right, my friend Sherlock Holmes had found his murderer!

The next morning in The Times was another large headline: "MURDERS ARE PART OF HOLY WAR." It went on to say that Inspector Lestrade found that the two murdered men had killed Sir Randolph in an attempt to defame the Baha'is and were killed by their superiors after their role became known. The article explained in detail why there was so much animosity directed by the Muslims towards the Baha'is.

I should also report that in the International Section there was a notice that Alexander Zworykin had left by ship for Copenhagen, returning to Russia for reassignment.

That evening, at dinner, I asked Holmes about his interrogation of Ali. I just couldn't understand why he was so concerned about the eating habits of the cleaning people at the Russian Embassy. "Please tell me, Holmes, why you were so interested in the eating habits of Ali and his fellow workers."

"Botulism, Watson, Botulism."

"You were planning to poison them?"

"If I couldn't get in as a chimney sweep, I would need to go in as a replacement cleaner. To accomplish this, they would all need to be very sick.

It would have been the Sunday chicken, you know, Watson."

"Good grief, Holmes, what you won't do to get your man!" I must say that my dinner does not set well just thinking about it. It was good to get this case closed.

Three days later Holmes received a note from Mycroft thanking the little brother for his fine performance and conveying the gratitude of Her Majesty.

The Queen offered to knight Holmes, which he politely declined through a response to Mycroft. He mumbled something about having all the notoriety that he could handle because of my chronicles and that he certainly needed nothing more.

The Eight-Pointed Cross

A Sherlock Holmes Adventure

by Paxton Franklin Watson

It was late fall in the year 1897, quickly approaching the turn of the century. Holmes had been very much in demand and his talents had been sharpened by the challenges of his clients. I should point out that he had narrowly escaped a Girkus sword in the matter of the Hindu prince whose identity I am not at liberty to divulge because of national security considerations, but this only seemed to exhilarate him.

Holmes was taking his mid-morning tea before a crackling fire when I returned from my rounds at the hospital.

"Watson, we will have a morning visitor. Lord Calhoon of Scotland will be calling on us within the hour. Will you attend?"

"Delighted, Holmes," said I. "What is it all about?"

"Not exactly sure, Watson. Something about a drawing etched on the inside of some old shoulder armor. We will just have to wait and see."

I had no sooner cleaned up and made myself more comfortable, when I heard footsteps on the stairway to our rooms.

Holmes, in an instant, was at the door, ushering in a tall, dark-haired, handsome man. His features were pleasant and sharply defined.

"Please come in, Lord Calhoon, let me take your coat and hat. This is my colleague, Dr. Watson, and I am Sherlock Holmes. Pray tell us more about this armor."

We were all seated around the brightly burning fire when Lord Calhoon began to open a bulky package which he had set before him.

"Mr. Holmes, this is the suit of armor of one of my ancestors, Macalister Calhoon. He was the youngest son of Lord Colston Calhoon of Scotland, whose title has descended through generations directly to me. Macalister is a great uncle, much removed. The younger sons of our kinsmen went to the Crusades, and so did Macalister. He was killed in battle and, as was the custom of his order, his armor was returned to us and, in his honor, it was mounted in the great hall of our castle, where it has remained until the present day. An inscription was placed in the front of the armor, 'Macalister Calhoon, Knight Hospitaler, 1487-1522'. Our family records have very little about him except that he never married and had no children that we are aware of.

Last month, I employed a firm to clean the armor of my ancestors and to make any restoration that might be required. Falgrove, the super, reported to me that Macalister's shoulder armor on the right side had a strange marking, apparently scratched into it by a sharp object. He really wanted to know if, in his restoration, he should polish it out of the armor. Here, see for yourself."

With that, Lord Calhoon removed the shoulder armor and passed it to Holmes, who was puffing hard on his pipe as if to send further stimulation to his brain. What a queer grin he had on his face. I had become accustomed to seeing it when he was confronted with a mystery.

"Interesting, Watson, interesting indeed. What do you make of this?", Holmes said, passing the ancient relic to me.

It looked like a large mushroom, with indications of water on three sides, and some markings on the mushroom that might indicate buildings or formations of some kind. There was a strange cross which was eight-sided and there were five small circles below the top of the mushroom with squares in the center of them. There was nothing else.

I related my findings to Lord Calhoon and Holmes. "I can see nothing more," said I. "What do you make of it, Holmes?"

"Watson, I am surprised at you in not knowing about the Knights Hospitalers, having just returned from your rounds of the hospital. The Hospitalers or Knights Hospitalers was an order founded after the formation of the Latin Kingdom of Jerusalem which was approved by Pope Paschal II in 1113, I believe, and again by Pope Eugene III some 40 years later. The brothers were sworn to poverty, obedience, and chastity and to assistance in the defense of Jerusalem. Their full name was 'The Sovereign Military Order of the Hospital of Saint John of Jerusalem'. Gerard, their first leader, was called Rector and later heads of the order were called Grand Masters. They were the protectors of a hospital built in Jerusalem before the first Crusade by Charlemagne, who was one of the foremost Holy Roman Emperors. Of necessity, the order became a military one, and the armed knights were of noble birth. They formed a community under the Rule of St. Augustine, first devoting themselves to the care of pilgrims and Crusaders and later, when the Order left the Holy Land with the failure of the Crusades, became the Knights of Rhodes.

After the Knights Templars was abolished in 1312, the Hospitalers took over most of the property of the Order. The Knights of Rhodes became rich and powerful. The Knights of Rhodes built a fortress at Rhodes, and fortified an ancient castle in the Bay of Bodrum which is in Turkey, naming it Petronion in honor of St. Peter, sometimes called the Castle of St. Peter.

In the year 1522, Sultan Suleiman I attacked the Knights of Rhodes. The Ottoman Turks had developed a cannon capable of knocking down the castle's walls. Rhodes and Bodrum were attacked and, shortly after a desperate resistance, the knights sailed away from Rhodes and Bodrum under a truce. It is said that Suleiman granted their withdrawal as a tribute to their brave fighting spirit. For 17 years, the Order resided where they could in Sicily. The Order, under a grant of Charles V of Spain, landed at Valletta on the isle of Malta on October 26th, 1539. Later, the Order changed its name to Knights of Saint John of Malta.

The cross etched in the armor, which we now call the Maltese Cross, was their emblem. It is an eight-sided cross with unicorns adjacent to each other facing outward and lions, also adjacent, facing outward. Macalister did not embellish the cross with the animals, but it was not necessary. The cross is unmistakable. The date of Macalister's death, which was the date of the fall of Rhodes and Bodrum, tells us that he was at one of those two cities. The scratchings in his armor depict a map and, in all probability, refers to one of those fortresses."

"Holmes, which Saint John does this order refer to?" , said I, showing my interest.

"Watson, Saint John the Baptist, of course. More than this we cannot be sure of at this time. Since 1888, we have the Order of Saint John, which is now a nondenominational Christian order devoted to the relief of human suffering. Its full name is The Most Venerable Order of the Hospital of St. John of Jerusalem. Membership in the Order is an honor granted with the approval of the Queen of England. Its headquarters are right here in London and so, I suspect, are all of the records concerning the Knights of Rhodes."

"Mr. Holmes, what do you think that this map may show? Falgrove thought that it may be a treasure map. He seemed exceedingly interested in knowing what I was going to do with it."

"Lord Calhoon, we know that it was an important map and that if we knew more about the circumstances, it might tell us something. At this point, suffice it to say that it was very important to Macalister and that he kept it on his body unto his death. I would like to know more about this Falgrove and his interest."

"Mr. Holmes, Falgrove was in charge of the job of cleaning, restoring and repairing the armor in our castle. We employed the firm of McCleve and Handlen, Armorers of Edinburough. They come well recommended. Falgrove had two helpers. He is a man of medium height, thin, rather dark complected and speaks with a foreign inflection, I believe eastern. Probably a man in his middle forties. Pleasant enough chap...very intent, penetrating, large, coal-black eyes. He asked me directly, looking deeply into my soul, if I thought that it was a treasure map. I told him that it was balderdash, but I would have it examined. He really seemed a little reluctant to turn it over to me, which I thought was strange. He then returned to his duties and we had no further conversation. I made an appointment with you and here I am."

"Did you note anything unusual on your way to visit me?", queried Holmes in response.

"Coming here from the train station, I felt that another cab was following ours...but dismissed it as absurdity when it continued straight away when we turned off the street."

"What street did you turn on to?"

"Why, Mr. Holmes, it was on Baker Street, just a few blocks from your flat."

"Lord Calhoon, what is it precisely that you wish me to do?", queried Holmes, dismissing the subject. Holmes expression had become hardened, exhibiting conscious concern.

"I would like you to determine what this map is and what it means. The family is prepared to pay a reasonable retainer and before extending beyond that amount of services, I would ask that you advise me. Would 500 pounds be satisfactory?"

"Very generous, Lord Calhoon, that will do nicely. This will be a research problem extraordinaire...one quite to my liking...stimulating indeed. I will begin today and will phone you when I have something to report. I ask that you mention my involvement in this matter to no one until we see what develops. The results will be given to you in person. I would also suggest that you discontinue your armor restoration at least for the next few weeks. Please let me know of any strange happenings at Calhoon Castle. It is a convenient time for me, as I am between cases. Do you have any questions?"

"No, Mr. Holmes, I do not. I will take my leave and return on the afternoon train to Scotland. I am pleased that you have taken the case. I wish you good luck."

With that, Lord Calhoon gave Holmes an envelope, donned his coat and hat and departed to a waiting carriage. Holmes quickly finished his tea and summoned a cabby. His manner was concentrative and non-communicative. Introspective indeed.

He picked up a case in which he kept his note paper and removed a sheet of white paper. He took a pencil from the desk and placed the sheet over the etching rubbing the pencil vigorously over the paper. The map appeared on the sheet of paper. He returned the copied map to his case and was out the door. I had no idea of what it was that he intended to find. However, the mysterious map etched inside Macalister Calhoon's shoulder armor was intriguing, indeed.

I returned to Baker Street a little later than usual from my office practice, just in time to find Holmes alighting from a cab. He was exhilarated and pleasant. We entered Mrs. Hudson's establishment together and went to our rooms. I asked Holmes what he had learned and he admonished me, "After dinner Watson, after dinner."

We took up our usual positions in front of the burning fire and Holmes said, "I have been to the offices of the Order of St. John. They really could not tell me much about the Order before it was established here in London, as all of the records of the Knights of Malta were kept and protected by the Order in Malta. I should say that it was the Military Knights of Justice who took charge of these archives and they are maintained there today and available for inspection for a fee. They are written in English, French, Italian and Spanish. We will need to go to Malta, Watson."

"How long will we be gone, Holmes?"

"We should allow ourselves probably 45 days. I feel that our investigation will lead us on another trip. Lord Calhoon should accompany us."

"I can arrange that, with my new assistant getting along well with the patients."

"I will contact Lord Calhoon and set up a meeting. We should be able to leave within a few days."

MALTA

We arrived at Valletta, Malta, after 6 days of travel. We had trained to Plymouth and went by a new smaller ship, carrying only 100 passengers, supplies and mail to the British Colony. The most remarkable event on our trip was the speed of the ship, Turbinia II. This had a completely new type of marine engine designed by Charles Parsons called the steam turbine which more than doubled the usual speed of the steamships. Remarkable, indeed. The most baffling surprise was Lord Calhoon seeing Falgrove and another gentleman on deck. Holmes concluded that it was not a coincidence. Falgrove was traveling with us to find out where the map's peninsula was located. There was no doubt among the three of us that Falgrove had made a copy of the map as Holmes had done.

Holmes had continued to speculate what we might find and told us in detail about what he had found after dinner on our last evening on the ship. The story began with a glass of brandy which magically refilled itself as we progressed.

"I also spent a lot of time at the library in London before we left. Do you gentlemen know what the Seven Wonders of the World were during Greek and Roman times?"

"Well," said I, taken by surprise as a listener of an interesting subject, "I think that the pyramids of Egypt would be considered one...and the Hanging Gardens of Babylon another."

Lord Calhoon chimed in, "The Great Wall of China should fit."

"No, Lord Calhoon, the Seven Wonders included only the known world of the Greek and Roman times, which excluded

China. My friends, I hate to see you struggle. They do include the Pyramids of Egypt, built at Giza during the 4th Dynasty between 2600 and 2544 BC which are the oldest of the seven wonders and the only ones remaining intact today.

The Hanging Gardens of Babylon, thought to have been built by King Nebuchadnezzar II about 600 BC which were a mountainlike series of planted terraces. It is believed that he built this in his desert kingdom to make his wife more at home as she came from Media in northern Persia with more moisture. We will probably never know the real reason.

The 40-foot Statute of Zeus (5th century BC) by the Greek sculptor Phidias was the central feature of the Temple of Zeus at Olympia, Greece. This is where the first Olympic Games were held. The warring city states of Greece stopped fighting for the games and competed against each other, only to resume their fighting after returning home. Like the saying, 'Honor among thieves'.

The Temple of Artemis at Ehesus in Greece (356 BC), which combined great size with elaborate ornamentation, was destroyed by the Goths in 162 AD.

The Mausoleum of Halicarnassus (353 BC) was a monumental marble tomb, decorated by the leading sculptors of the age, for King Mausolus of Caria in Asia Minor. Only fragments remain, but I will tell you more about that later.

The Colossus of Rhodes was a 100 foot bronze statute of the Greek sun god Helios, erected about 280 BC to guard the entrance to the harbor at Rhodes. It was destroyed about fifty-five years later.

And the final one was the Pharos of Alexandria (280 BC), located on an island in the harbor of Alexandria, Egypt. It was a famous ancient lighthouse standing more than 440 foot tall. It was destroyed in the 14th century."

I was surprised that I did not know more of them, but could not understand how these Seven Wonders of the World had any relationship to the scratchings in the shoulder armor. "Holmes, how in the world can these Seven Wonders have anything to do with this mystery?"

"My dear Watson, of course they do...or at least, I believe one does. The Knights of Rhodes occupied two fortifications: one at Rhodes and another at Bodrum. I was able to find information on both at the Library in London, and concluded that the only fortification that would fit the description in Macalister's armor was that of Bodrum. Bodrum was formally known as Halicarnassus which King Mausolus of Caria ruled from. It flourished from 376 to 356 BC. Actually, the fortifications were located on two sites which contained the 5th and 6th Wonders of the World.

I found that the British Museum has about all that is left of this great Mausoleum, except for the stones used in building Petronion. The story of how the museum came by this treasure indicates that in November 1856, however armed with an imperial edict from the Turkish Sultan permitting excavation and backed by the cannon of H.M.S. Gorgon anchored in the bay, HM Action Counsel at Rhodes, Charles Thomas Newton, late of the British Museum, started digging for the ancient mausoleum. I should point out that the Mausoleum was demolished intentionally, quarried away at the turn of the 16th century. The soft green lava stone of the building's core was directly reused as building blocks for the castle. The fine exterior marble was broken up, hauled away, and mostly burnt and rendered into lime to make fine mortar. In the following centuries, though this brutal activity left a considerable mound of chipping lying all over the ground, the very site of the Mausoleum was forgotten and so was the location of the ancient city of Halicarnassus. The Turkish inhabitants called their town, a pretty little fishing port, Bodrum.

For years prior to the fall of Petronion in 1522, the Knights of Rhodes, as they were then called, systematically removed this stone to build up the fortification of the castle, putting the stone directly into the walls, which remain to this day. I suspect that in 1522, when Sultan Suleiman was preparing to attack Rhodes and Petronion with his new cannon, the Grand Master must have been frantic to build up his fortifications."

"Holmes," said Watson, "I have thought a great deal about the Seven Wonders of the World and I am troubled...why not six or eight?"

"The list of the Seven Wonders of the World was originally compiled around the second century BC. The first reference to the idea is found in History of Herodotus, written in the 5th century BC. Decades later, Greek historians wrote about the greatest monuments at the time, and since the Greeks never traveled to India, China or America before that time, their list included only the wonders of their own known world, which were the lands near the eastern Mediterranean Sea.

In the sixth century BC, Pythagoras, hypothesized that the number seven belonged to sacred things. It fits into philosophy and mysticism. Seven was considered a number of completeness because it combined the perfect numbers three (triangle) and four (square).

Many applications of the number seven are found in the Bible and New Testament. In the story of creation, the seventh day is sacred, which led to the seven days of the week. There were the Seven Wise Men of Greece, the Seven Sages of Rome, the Seven Sleepers of Ephesus, the Seven Champions of Christendom, the Seven Hills of the Holy City of Rome, the seven sacraments and the seven deadly sins. The Pleiades of Greek myth were seven, and Shakespeare distinguished seven ages of man. There are innumerable examples throughout time, extending across the seven seas."

"Holmes, you never cease to amaze me. I do not know how you can store and access so much knowledge."

"Lord Calhoon, the answers that we are seeking should be in the records at the National Library in the Valletta town center. This was once the library of the Order. This building was constructed in the late 18th century to house the collection amassed by the knights, and the Archives of the Order, which includes documents dating back to the 11th century. The Archives are located in the basement of the building. I believe that we will find that the Knights of Malta are in control of the Archives."

"Tell me, Mr. Holmes, what has happened to the Knights of Malta?"

"The Order came here to Malta in 1539 bringing with them their Archives, their sacred icon containing one of the hands of St. John the Baptist and a silver processional cross, now located at the Cathedral of Mdina in Malta. The three islands, Malta, Gozo and Comino, were given by Charles V, Holy Roman Emperor, upon the condition that the Order would pay one falcon a year for this grant. This was the famous 'Maltese Falcon'.

Suleiman the Magnificent in 1565 attacked Malta but abandoned it four months later. In 1798, Napoleon attacked Malta and demanded that the Order leave. After 268 years, the Knights of Malta left with their private property. When asked if they could take the relic of the hand of John the Baptist, Bonaparte contemptuously replied: 'They may keep the dead hand, but the ring on the finger looks better on mine.' Then he slipped off the bejeweled ring from the relic and placed it on his finger.

The Order was dispersed all over Europe. The Langue of England was revived in 1827 and opted to admit Protestants into its ranks. It called itself the 'Venerable Langue'. Strangely enough, the new Venerable Lange continued to function as if it were still an integral part of the Sovereign and Catholic Order of Malta. Independent orders were established in England, Germany, Sweden, Holland and also in the United States and Canada. Most were bogy organizations with no connection to the real Order of St. John, except in name and dress.

Nothing of this affected the Sovereign Military Order of Malta which continues with the strict selection of its members. There was also established the new principle of sovereignty without territorial possessions, except those of the Malta Palace which was established as the Order's seat in 1834 and the Villa on the Aventine, also in Rome. The Order continues hospitaler work and this soon led to the restoration of its old dignity. In 1879 the Grandmaster was made a Prince of the church and as such is entitled to all sovereign honors. The Order could send and receive diplomatic envoys. The Sovereign and Military Order of Malta came back on its feet and is healthy today. Their old vows of chastity, obedience, and poverty have been greatly modified."

"Mr. Holmes, such fascinating history! I have enjoyed the whole intrigue of this mystery. Do you have any idea why Falgrove has followed us here?"

"There can be only one reason, Lord Calhoon: to reach the treasure, if any there be, before us, or if we reach it first, then, to take it from us."

"What makes him think that we have a treasure here?"

"Elementary, Lord Calhoon. Falgrove has a copy of Macalaster's map. He knew that you were going to have it examined. It was he who followed you in the cab at our first visit. When you turned on Baker Street it would tell him that it was likely that you were coming to see me. He probably doubled back and checked where the cabby stopped. The map bore the eight-sided cross of the Knights of Malta. You then bought tickets to Malta, hence there is certainly something that you are trying to find that you must think is very valuable, hence you must think there is a treasure here. Why shouldn't he?"

"Certainly," said I, "and maybe we will all be fooled."

"In any event, gentlemen, we shall certainly keep our eyes on those two," cautioned Holmes.

We arrived at our hotel late in the day. It was located close to the Towne Centre of Valletta and our Library. The accommodations were pleasant and our rooms were close to one another. After dinner, we went to bed early and were glad to be on a steady deck.

At breakfast, Holmes advised us that he would be researching at the Library and that we should enjoy Valletta and it was a beautiful day. We would plan to meet at dinner. He said that it would be good to split our followers up as they would pose a less danger.

Lord Calhoon and I enjoyed a walking tour of the Town Centre of Valletta. We saw the massive fortification at Fort St. Elmo, the National War Museum and the Grand Master's Palace and Armoury. The Grand Master's Armoury was impressive indeed with all of the knights armor displayed including most of the Grand Master's pictures and weapons. Falgrove was always there, but at a distance. When we entered a site, he would remain outside and away from the entrance. His clumsy surveillance was almost comical, except for his sinister, penetrating glances. A huge bronze statue of Queen Victoria in all of her robes, crown and scepter guarded the entrance to the National Library where Holmes was researching. We did not enter, but moved on slowly, enjoying the beautiful island and quaint shops.

The three of us came together for dinner and after dinner we met in a private salon to discuss the matters that had transpired that day.

"Watson, I have had an interesting day. The Curator of the Archives, l'Isle Adam, a Knight of Malta, aided me in ferreting out the facts which I needed. Interesting that he is a distant relative of l'Isle Adam, who led the Knights to Malta and was their first Grandmaster here. Same name and truly an honorable one. He was most inquisitive as to my purpose and when I introduced myself, in response to his inquiry, he said, 'Mr Holmes, I am familiar with your work. What mystery brings you to my Archives?'

I explained that my client was trying to get information about one of his ancestors who was a Knight of Rhodes and died in the fight against Suleiman. He immediately led me to the records of the last days of Rhodes and Bodrum. I have spent the day sorting out the events that occurred. Remember, Watson, that these records contain notes and entries in French, Italian, Spanish and English. The most important records were in English. I confirmed that Macalister was at the fortified castle at the Bay of Bodrum. The Order named it Petronion in honor of St. Peter. The two squares on the map in the fort were churches, one for the Greek and one for the Latin rite. He was killed on the last days before the fighting ended. Each knight was assigned a portion of the castle to defend. Macalister and his entourage had been assigned a frontal station on the only access way to the castle. Petronion had water on three sides with only one way to approach the castle on land. He was served by two squires and two man servants and had employed five mercenaries to defend his assigned turret. Watson, you cannot imagine the quality of those 400-year-old records. I found that two days before Macalister's death, his entire personal entourage, excluding his mercenaries, were murdered. They suspected Sultan Suleiman's warriors, testing the strength of the fortress. This map is of Petronion. It would seem to me that something is hidden in the front walls behind the five round stones with a square in the center of each.

Watson, I did learn that the Castle garrison consisted of around 150 knights of various Western European nationalities, each one of which had built its own tower for eating and accommodation, and had its own section of the castle wall to guard and hold. Accompanied by their squires and servants and by many mercenaries, the garrison made up a sizable community on the edge of a hostile continent. Relations with the Turkish town were generally difficult. Sometimes the two communities were openly at war, and the Knights had to take care behind their battlements to dodge the casual arrows of archers of the town. Then the Knights would terrorize the townsfolk with destructive armored forays and with ferocious packs of dogs that were released by day and gathered in at night for feeding by blasts from the garrison trumpeters. Usually, though, a wary peace prevailed. During the peace, the Knights bought their water, food and firewood from the merchants of the town, sometimes ransomed the occasional Christian slaves and conducted a brisk trade in local carpets."

"Holmes, I thought that the Knights Hospitalers were sworn to work for the succor and protection of poor Christian pilgrims, not attack the townspeople with vicious dogs. There is nothing

Christian about that Order as you describe it. Disgusting, I say, disgusting!'"

"Watson, they had been driven out of Jerusalem and the crusades had ended. The embattled Knights had built their fortress in the Bay of Bodrum in the first quarter of the 15th century. A German Knight by the name of Schegelholt first planned the outpost to command a narrow straight and complement another on the opposing isle of Kos. These fighting monks were being pushed ever further from the holy places that they were sworn to protect and hold, and were fighting to retain a toehold on the eastern seaboard. During the 15th century, as Constantinople fell and Turkish armies reached even deeper into Europe, the Castle of St. Peter, the Knight's last Asian Outpost, was continuously and somewhat frantically enlarged.

Lord Calhoon and Watson, it will be my pleasure to share with you my findings. I believe that we have found the treasure of Mausolus and Artemisia of Caria."

"Mausolus and Artemisia? Never heard of them. Who were they, Holmes?"

"Mausolus was the King of Caria. He succeeded his father as satrap in ~~337~~ *373 BC*, which acknowledged him as an independent prince who did as he pleased while acknowledging the Persian king as his master. Artemisia was his sister and wife, which was the custom of Carian rulers. He was a warlike and ambitious man, descended from the shepherd folk of the Carian hills. He spoke Greek, behaved like a Greek, and wished his simple, rugged people would follow the Greek ways. He inherited a small kingdom covering most of Caria which was in Turkey and some of the adjoining districts. Mausolus extended his control over most of southwestern Asia Minor. Shrewdly, he saw that the Greek way of life had much to offer, so he forced his people to come out of their little mountain towns and live like Greeks, along the coast.

Mausolus founded new cities of Greek design and encouraged the growth of

Greek democratic ideas. Much of his energy went into the development of his capital city, Halicarnassus. There he erected a large brick and marble palace for himself and his queen, Artemisia. A shrine of Apollo, a handsome waterfront boulevard, and a mighty wall were among his other gifts to his city.

But the finest of all the new buildings was the one that Queen Artemisia caused to be constructed as the tomb and monument of her husband Mausolus after his death in 353 BC. Gentlemen, I saw a reconstructed statue of him at the British Museum and he was quite a handsome and dashing man. Her grief for the dead king was intense: it is said that she drank some of his ground-up, cremated ashes mixed with wine. She resolved to honor him by giving him the most splendid tomb the world had ever seen. The site chosen was a hilltop overlooking the city, where the tomb would be visible from all Halicarnassus.

She sent messengers to Greece, seeking the most gifted artists of the age: architects, sculptors, bronze-workers, painters, craftsmen of every sort. She did not care about the expense but demanded the best work and the best workmen and she got them. Scopas, Bryaxis, Timotheus, Leochares all contributed to this work, and on top was a four-horse marble chariot which Pytheos made.

Artemisia followed Mausolus in death by about two years. The artists did not abandon the incomplete work as they saw it as a monument to their individual glory and skill. This magnificent tomb, having escaped the fury of the barbarians and Alexander the Great, remained standing for a space of 2,247 years, only to be destroyed by an earthquake. The mass of marble and statues were discovered and ravaged to repair the Castle of St. Peter by the Knights of Rhodes, who immediately after this were driven completely out of Asia by the Turks. There is a model depicting what they think it looked like at the British Museum. Pliny, Natural History, xxxvi, 30-1, gives us some description of the mausoleum, which I will read from my notes if you please."

"Of course, Holmes. We certainly would like to know what this wonder of the world looked like."

"The length of the north and south sides is sixty-three feet, the length of the front and back is less, the whole perimeter being four hundred and forty feet. Its height is forty feet and it is surrounded by thirty-six columns. People called the sur-rounding colonnade 'pteron' (Greek for a wing). Above the pteron there is a pyramid of

a height equal to the lower structure, and in twenty-four steps it tapers to a point. At the top there is a four-horse marble chariot. Including the addition on top, the whole work is one hundred and forty feet high.

Watson, the chariot is being driven by a man and woman, believed by some to be Mausolus and Artemisia. The Mausoleum had at least 100 full, life-like sculptures. Fine, powerful marble portraits of large, personable, natural people strolling amongst the columns standing row upon row. It depicted a new way of seeing humankind."

"Holmes, is it from this tomb that we get the word mausoleum?", queried Watson.

"Good deduction, Watson. Yes, it is. It is the indurable ancestor of thousands of tombs, the inheritors of its very name who called them after the old monument of Mausolus. Quite a tribute.

I have some more background which I will need to pass on to you. Are you up to it, my colleagues?"

"Yes, Holmes. Let me have it."

Lord Calhoon nodded affirmatively.

Some of the more whimsical knights used a few of the Mausoleum's reliefs as elements of decoration on the fortress walls at Petronion. For several hundred years, Mausolus' battle frieze of Amazons and Greeks served to stir the blood of sentries standing at the castle gate. On one of the towers, which was called the English tower, English coats of arms were embellished with some of the fine Greek Mausoleum lions, an extraordinary mix of style and culture, and of course an extraordinary heraldic symmetry, too. Over the centuries, these sculptures in the grand old castle became well known to travelers. In the 1840s, Lord Stratford de Redcliffe asked the sultan's permission to remove them to England. An imperial firman was subsequently written and 13 damaged and eroded slabs were rescued from their perilous and obscure situation in the castle wall in Bodrum and brought to England. No record was made as to where they were removed from the castle. It was the arrival of those blocks at the British Museum that stirred Charles Thomas Newton. He was an assistant in the Museum's Antiquities Department with a good eye for classical sculpture. The Bodrum reliefs, which had been taken from buildings in the town, were Hellenistic in style and were generally believed to have come from the Mausoleum. Newton had traced similar pieces of relief in Genoa and Rhodes and thought there must be more of them.

Newton secured a government grant to secure the Mausoleum sculptures for the British Museum. He was provided a ship for his work at Bodrum. In November 1856, however, armed with an imperial firman from the Turkish sultan permitting excavation and backed by the cannon of HMS Gorgon anchored in the bay, Newton, the HM Acting Counsul at Rhodes, started digging for the ancient Mausoleum.

In the summer of 1857, Newton had 218 crates of sculpture loaded on the ship and set sail for the naval dockyard at Woolwich. The sculpture was badly damaged, but did contain the remains of the fifth wonder of the world. The Mausoleum Room was added to the British Museum in 1882 and that is where the better restored statuary is displayed and the rest is stored in the back rooms. Newton became head of a newly founded department at the British Museum and was knighted after a long career as the elder figure of British Hellensic studies.

Watson, getting to the bottom line, all that remains of the Mausoleum is in London at the museum, or in the castle walls at Bodrum. I have gone through all of the displays at the British Museum and the drawings made of all of the pieces and I cannot find the symbols shown on our map, which are the five circles, each with a square in it. My conclusion therefore is that they are in the wall at Petronion yet today and were probably placed in the wall of the castle by Macalister and his personal staff in the area where they billeted."

"Holmes, what do you think that means?"

"Watson, it means that something has been placed there in the wall. I believe that it is the treasure from the tomb of Mausollos and Artemisia."

"What makes you think that it is the treasure of Mausollos and Artemisia?", asked I.

"Gentlemen, I am sorry to have to give you another long story but in order for you to follow my deduction, it is essential. I found at the library a work referred to as 'The Melancholy Chronical' made some 50 years after the stonemasons finally arrived at the enclosure of the Mausoleum, 'steps of white marble...in the middle of a level field' by the Lyonnais Claude Guichard, one of the many citizens of that city who had served in St. Peter's Castle."

With that Holmes handed me a two-page handwritten document, which he had asked me to read aloud. I set it out for you, my reader, to digest. "In the year 1522, when Sultan Suleiman was preparing to attack Rhodes, the Grand Master, knowing the importance of the Castle of St Peter, and being aware that the Turks would seize it easily at the first assault, sent some Knights to repair the fortress and make all due preparations to resist the enemy. Among the number of those sent was the Commandeur de la Tourette Lyonnaise, a Lyonnais Knight, who was afterwards present at the taking of Rhodes, and came to France, where he related what I am now about to narrate to M. d'Alechamps, a person sufficiently known by his learned writings, and whose name I mention here only for the purpose of publishing my authority for so singular a story.

When these Knights had arrived at Mesy [the Knights' name for Bodrum], they at once commenced fortifying the castle and looking about for stones wherewith to make lime found no more suitable or more easily got at than some steps of white marble, raised in the form of a terrace in the middle of a level field near the port, which had formerly been the great square of Halicarnassus. They therefore pulled down and took away these marble steps, and, finding the stone good, proceeded, after having destroyed the little masonry remaining above ground, to dig lower down, in the hope of finding more.

In this they had great success, for in a short time they saw that the deeper they went, the more the structure was enlarged, supplying them not only with stone for making lime, but also for building. After four or five days, having laid bare a great space, one afternoon, they saw an opening as into a cellar. Taking a candle, they let themselves down through this opening, and found that it led into a fine large square apartment, ornamented all round with columns of marble, with their bases, capitals, architrave, frieze, and cornices, engraved and sculptured in half-relief. The space between the columns was lined with slabs and bands of marbles of different colours, ornamented with mouldings and sculptures, in harmony with the rest of the work, and inserted in the white ground of the wall, where the battle-scenes were represented sculptured in relief.

Having at first admired these works, and entertained their fancy with the singularity of the sculpture, they pulled it to pieces, and broke up the whole of it, applying it to the same purpose as the rest.

Beyond this apartment, they found a very low doorway, which led into another apartment, serving as an antechamber, where was a sepulchre, with decorated column tops and a tympanum of white marble, very beautiful, and of marvellous lustre. For want of time, they did not open this sepulchre, the retreat having already sounded. The day after, when they returned, they found the tomb opened, and the earth all round strewn with fragments of cloth of gold, and spangles of the same metal, which made them suppose that the pirates, who hovered along this coast, having some inkling of what had been discovered, had visited the place during the night, and had removed the lid of the sepulchre. It is supposed that they discovered in it much treasure."

"Then, Holmes, there really was a treasure? But how, by thunder did it get in the old walls at Petronion?"

"If you will indulge me a moment for a recap of what occurred according to Guichard's account. The accounts have already confirmed that the Knights had already found other tombs in earlier years and treasures, too, and it is indeed surprising, if not incredible, that, when they happened upon the largest tomb of all in Bodrum, they did not quickly plunder it despite the castle trumpeters having sounded the retreat. Here, after all, was a treasure lying within arm's reach and all that was required to take it was the opening of a sarcophagus and perhaps some other boxes, too; a work of minutes. This part of the story that tells us that it was the Turks, the 'pirates' as Commandeur de la Tourette Lyonnaise calls them, and not the Knights that plundered the tomb, has the effect of keeping the names of the treasure's holders a secret. Such stories were common enough in this period and gave rise to the legends of the Knights' great wealth.

I have spent hours going through the exceptionally detailed records of the Knights of Rhodes. The finding of the tomb had been in a report of the commander of the party working at the site. The day after it was found. Guess who the commander was, Watson?"

"Macalister?", said I.

"Right, Watson, Macalister. The other interesting thing is that all of his personal staff were killed within a few days after this discovery. His mercenaries had been left at the fort to guard the castle when this discovery was made. What do you make of that?"

"Jolly bad luck, Holmes, that's what I make of it."

"Bad luck indeed, Watson. What appears clear to me is that Macalster returned to the site with his personal staff as soon as he got back to the castle and removed the treasure."

Lord Calhoon with his face writhed in disbelief entered the conversation.

"I just can't believe this story. I'm a little embarrassed for my relative and, I guess, for myself. I know that I have been so quiet during this report, but your explanation is so thorough, Mr. Holmes, that all I could do was try to absorb all of that data. I just can't believe it!"

"Lord Calhoon, we have arrived here by deduction. It is not a fact as yet. The only way we will know is to make a visit to Bodrum and remove those stones in the fortress walls. You can believe it or not but the investigation will confirm what it is that you finally believe."

"What do you think that the treasure consisted of Holmes?", Watson enthusiastically inquired.

"A knight's sword, shield and armor. Jewelry. Crowns for both and probably a scepter or two. As Mausolus was a vain man and, after all, Artimisia was his royal sister, there should be all kinds of possessions."

"How in the world would Macalister get all that treasure into the wall at Patronion?", inquired the non-believer Lord Calhoon.

"He could not get it into the walls in the form that it was in. You can only reach one conclusion. In the blacksmith's shop in Macalister's turret, all of these treasures were dismembered and smelted into bars of metal and the antiquities obliterated forever."

"Pray tell me, Holmes, how in Heaven's name do you reach such a conclusion?"

"Elementary, my dear Watson, elementary indeed. He did not want the Order of Rhodes to get the treasure. If they knew of it, the Grand Master would want a large share. If the mercenaries employed by the knights learned of it, his life would probably be taken and the treasure stolen. No, the only way that he could ever hope to remove it, was to render it into its baseness. The larger pieces would not fit into such a small space anyway. I feel certain that the jewels were removed and the metal smelted into some size that could be easily handled and stored. On top of that, the castle was under a sort of seige and facing an imminent attack from Sultan Suleiman and his superior forces. He could not leave it lying around and had no assurance that he would not be captured or killed."

"And you believe that, after his four personal servants helped him transport the treasure, smelt it, and move the metal to its hiding place in the wall, he killed them all in order to protect the secret?"

"Excellent Watson, excellent! You've got it!"

"What a dastardly deed! The non-believer Lord Calhoon was suddenly becoming a believer. I just can't believe that one of my flesh and blood would have done that. We will just have to go to Bodrum and determine the facts for ourselves."

"Splendid," retorted Holmes, " splendid indeed, and as we say, Watson, the game is now afoot."

At that moment, there was a knock on the door and one of the reservation clerks handed Holmes a card. "There is a gentleman to see you, Mr. Holmes."

The card advised us of our caller, "l'Isle Adam, Curator of the archives of the Knights of Malta."

"Please usher him in," matter-of-factly responded Holmes, as if he expected him.

"Good to see you again, Mr. Holmes," said the handsome, impeccably dressed, tall, dark-haired man standing in the doorway. I hoped to meet your client whose ancestor was a fallen brother of the Order."

Holmes made the introductions and invited Mr. Adam to join us which he did. Mr. Adam began by informing us that the Order was alive and well although it had been a hard struggle for it after leaving Malta. Most of the knights were French, and those who did not pose a threat to Napoleon were allowed to stay on and they had continued with the Order even though the Malta Palace was located in Rome and was occupied by the Grand Master of the Order. He stated pointedly to Lord Calhoon that any treasure confiscated by a knight of the order while on duty was to be shared with the Order equally and that if this investigation sought a treasure of any kind, the Order would want to share equally with the heir of the knight.

It was at this point that Holmes asked Adam to leave the room so that we might have a discussion, which he agreed to do. Homes then recapped the situation and problems. "We will need transportation from Malta to Bodrum and back again. A fast vessel. We will need a stone mason, probably a member of the Order. We will need influence in Bodrum to avoid any problems. We will need to send Falgrove and his friend on a false goose chase, probably to Sicily. We will need protection. If they could furnish us this and allow us our expenses for coming here, we could agree to split anything that we found of value, over and above our expenses, but with no assurances." Lord Calhoon was quick to agree.

This offer was presented to Adam. He asked Lord Calhoon to estimate the expenses. He inquired as to the nature of the treasure. Holmes conservatively estimated what we might find but only as speculation. Holmes told of the source of our information and our conclusion.

Adam explained that the Order which had been the Knights of Rhodes when it occupied Bodrum had been greatly feared and hated by the Townspeople, but the Order was nonetheless respected and had, since they were forced out, been on good terms with the people there. He felt that they could secure whatever support that they needed without any questions. The Order had a fast ship and plenty of stone masons. He would see that Falgrove and his companion would not interfere with the expedition. He would guarantee our safety. We all shook hands and agreed to meet at 10:00 A.M. the following morning for our trip to Bodrum and our treasure. Adam said that we would have several knights here to prevent Falgrove and associate from following us or knowing where we were going. Adam and several other Knights would attend in addition to the crew and stone masons.

Adam left and Holmes had a smile of a hungry hunter following a fat bird. "I hope that you are pleased, gentlemen. Adam has helped us with a dangerous mission. Half a loaf is better than none at all. I don't like the thought of a Turkish prison or paying off Turkish officials. I will sleep well tonight and hope that you both do, too."

We met Adam and his associate at 10:00 and were whisked away to the small ship. It, too, was a steam turbine. Falgrove and associate had been arrested by the Malta Police and taken away to the station. One does not ask under what charge, as this one does not care.

Two days later, in the late afternoon, we entered the sleepy fishing village of Bodrum and saw the Castle of St. Peter outlining itself on the sky. Excitement filled the air. Adam checked in with the Mayor or head man for the city and got permission to remove some of the wall of Petronion, under the old edict from the Turkish sultan permitting excavation. Adam gathered the stone masons, two guards and our party, and led us to Petronion.

Petronion sat magnificently as a tall fortified castle, with water on three sides and a narrow strip of land leading to its gate. As our party approached the castle from the front, we could see the five circles of stone, side by side, with a square in the center, as if to house an axle. It was located on the second story rampart and covered an area I would judge about 20 feet long. No one occupied the castle and people were allowed to roam at will. We quickly entered the castle and went to the second floor and began to examine the stone wheels.

Adam had understood our theory, but Holmes had not given him the location and sign.

"There!", directed Holmes to Adam, who immediately dispatched the stone masons to complete the work. As the first of the five wheels was removed, it was obvious that there was a chamber behind it, and so it was for the other four. It was a chamber about twenty feet long, three feet wide and two feet deep. The old and hastily applied plaster came off easily. Inside were wrapped bars of gold and silver, probably four or five pounds each. When removed, we found that we had 62 bars, 41 gold and 21 silver. Just as Holmes had deduced, it was reduced to its base metal. There were four large bags of jewelry. The stones were lovely and large, reflecting the lights of the torches' dancing light on the walls. There were all types of precious stones and some that I did not recognize. Gold jewelry and engravings. There was also a bag of ashes, wrapped in golden cloth, which contained the names of Mausolus and Artemisia on the outside. They were together in death. Quite a love story, I thought.

Adam's men moved quickly to restore the wheels and transport our treasure, which it truly was, to our ship. Adam was pleased at what we had found.

"Well, Mr. Holmes, you are truly remarkable. How in the world did you do it?"

"I do believe it, Mr. Holmes," gleefully chattered Lord Calhoon, as he moved the jewelry through his finger, "I do believe it."

Our first course of business once on board and under way, was to complete an inventory. The gold and silver was an easy matter and was divided equally after setting aside enough to cover Lord Calhoon's expenses. Adam told Lord Calhoon that he should have the ashes of the loving monarchs and that perhaps they should be with the remaining ruins of the mausoleum in London. The jewelry and stones were divided by Adam taking first choice, then Lord Calhoon, alternating, until all was divided up.

We learned that Falgrove and friend had been deported to Italy. I really wonder if they ever got back to England. Our trip back was uneventful and very pleasant. Lord Calhoon, who was very pleased and enriched, had given Holmes for his part two bars of gold, two bars of silver and three pieces of the jewelry and some stones. I might add that Holmes, which was his nature, shared his "treasure" with me. They estimated that our one half of it was worth over one million pounds.

It had been an exciting and profitable adventure for us both. I was very glad to get back to my practice and my quiet life on Baker Street.